"All I'm after is a little honesty.

"I drove back because, crazy as it may seem after all this time, I think you still feel some of those old Fourth-of-July sparks just like I seem to—"

"I don't. I don't feel a single spark, Walker."

She watched him move closer. She started to protest, but it was too late. His lips were touching hers and she found herself wishing that he'd wrap his arms around her.... Instead, he drew back. "I just needed to know, Chelsea," he said softly.

She forgot all about her plans to work him round to her corner, to make him see it was to his advantage to let her continue her research on his property. Walker had too many plans of his own. "We're not starting anything again here, Walker."

"Too late, Chelsea. We've already started. Anyway, you can tell me all about the Battle of Corbet over dinner."

A spark of hope glimmered. "Does that mean you might change your mind?"

Walker grinned seductively. "No, it means I love it when you talk history to me."

ABOUT THE AUTHOR

Elise Title's first venture into American Romance
was *Till the End of Time*, the Vietnam War book
in our A Century of American Romance series. In
Nearly Paradise she's taken a lighter look at
American life and love. Like the characters in
Nearly Paradise, Elise Title and her family live in
a small town in New England.

Books by Elise Title

Don't miss any of our special offers. Write to us at the
following address for information on our newest releases.

Harlequin Reader Service
P.O. Box 1397, Buffalo, NY 14240
Canadian address: P.O. Box 603,
Fort Erie, Ont. L2A 5X3

**ELISE
TITLE**

NEARLY
PARADISE

Harlequin Books

TORONTO • NEW YORK • LONDON
AMSTERDAM • PARIS • SYDNEY • HAMBURG
STOCKHOLM • ATHENS • TOKYO • MILAN

To Helen
Ever closer

Published July 1991

ISBN 0-373-16397-5

NEARLY PARADISE

Chapter One

It was one of those glorious sun-dappled afternoons, gentle glittering rays of light falling over the meadows and woods. A palette richer than artists' paints covered the land, the sky a soft, even spread of pale blue. As Walker Jordan headed through the woods down to the brook on his newly purchased property he had a hard time believing this was real, that this was truly his home now. The beauty and tranquillity of it was nearly overwhelming. He took in greedy swallows of fresh country air—his air, he thought. He'd come home.

Walker smiled. He knew he was overromanticizing a bit. Maybe more than a bit. Corbet, Vermont, wasn't actually home. He'd spent exactly two summers here in his teens. His folks had rented a little cottage on Lake Worley and he'd had himself a ball swimming, boating, hiking...and falling in love for the first time.

And now he was falling in love again. Not with a cute young local girl this time, but with Corbet itself. With the tranquillity, the beauty, the warmth of the spring sun, the sense of peace that seemed to envelop him like a cozy, down-home patchwork quilt. Being here in this bucolic setting was such a glorious change from his pressure-packed, fast-track L.A. life. Walker had played legal hardball for a long time. Now the only ball he wanted to play was softball on a local Corbet team.

His feet crunched on the bed of yellowish pine needles as he moved deeper into the woods. He could hear the soft ripple of the brook now. Damned if his heart didn't outright sing at the sound. He laughed aloud.

Nearing the brook, Walker caught sight of a brilliant red cardinal swooping across the branches of the pines. He slowed his pace and followed the bird's flight, thinking how glorious nature was, how happy and carefree he felt—young again, alive with new ideas, filled with renewed energy. The whole world was at his feet.

And then he took his next step, his gaze still on the cardinal, only to discover, suddenly, there was absolutely nothing at his feet. With a shocked gasp, he went sprawling forward, landing facedown in a shallow pit the size and shape of a grave. A grave replete with a body. Still warm. Right under him. Indeed, still moving.

It was a toss-up who screamed louder.

"You're suffocating me. Get your hands off me. Are you mad?"

The "corpse" was alive and kicking. Walker pushed himself up, wincing as he struggled to his feet in the narrow pit. He'd bent his wrist back in the fall and it throbbed. But he instantly forgot the pain as he found himself staring down at the best looking "corpse" he'd ever laid eyes on.

"Don't just stand there. Help me up." The "corpse" had a sexy, throaty voice.

"Sorry," Walker said, shaken. It took him another moment to pull himself together enough to stretch out his hand.

Her grip was firm, but she, too, winced as she rose.

"Are you okay?" he asked.

She nodded, absently rubbing at some dirt on her chin. Walker inspected her as she brushed herself off. She was of medium height, somewhere around five feet, five inches tall, with chestnut hair, fine bone structure, not quite lavender but not quite blue eyes, a mouth at once delicate and determined, and a slender athletic body, clad in tight-fitting dungarees and over-size work shirt.

He held his injured wrist absently, noticing that she wasn't putting all her weight on her right foot.

"Ankle?"

"Shin."

He knelt down. "Let me have a look."

"It's all right."

She put some more weight on her foot and Walker straightened up. He smiled wryly. "Don't tell me you're Corbet's local grave digger?"

She gave him a calculating look, sitting down on the edge of the pit. "Don't tell me you don't remember me, flatlander?"

"Flatlander?" Walker sat down, too, a reminiscent smile on his face. It had been a long time since he'd been called a flatlander. More than fifteen years. When he'd spent those two summers up here in Corbet, he'd often been teased about being a flatlander by the Corbet kids he'd gotten friendly with. Anyone who came from anywhere else on the map, especially New York where most of the summer visitors came from, were labeled flatlanders. One local in particular used to rib him all the time about being a flatlander. One cute, shy young girl by the name of Chelsea Clark. But surely this fiery, self-assured, beautiful woman couldn't be...

Her gotcha smile told him she could.

He'd brilliantly argued landmark cases before some of the toughest juries in L.A., but, "My oh my" was all he could manage to say.

She smiled. "You've changed a little yourself, flatlander."

"Hey wait, how long does a guy have to live in Corbet to get rid of that moniker?"

Chelsea's smile winked out. "You've got to be born and bred here, Walker Jordan. And even then you've got to marry yourself a local gal, have yourself a couple of babies that are gonna take over the family business—"

"Okay, okay, I get the picture. I guess I'm stuck with flatlander for life." He switched the subject. "So, how have I changed?"

In truth, Chelsea had to admit he hadn't really changed all that much. Sixteen years had only added character and maturity to a still ruggedly attractive face. His thick dark brown hair had a more professional cut now, but it still had a way of curling a little over the collar of his shirt. And just like those long ago summers, he was still tan, thanks to the California sun. If anything about Walker was different, it was his eyes. They were sharper, shrewder, with a tinge of world-weariness in them. But they were still that unusual dusky gray shade. Chelsea kept all of those observations to herself.

Aloud, after what she knew had been an overly long pause, she said crisply, "You look older." Then a smile crept into her face. "Not bad."

Walker laughed. "You certainly know how to sweet-talk a guy, Chelsea."

Shifting her position, she observed him closely for a moment longer. "I can't believe you've actually bought this place, Walker."

"Hey, how did you find that out already? I just signed the papers about an hour ago."

Chelsea laughed. "Word travels fast in a small town. You better be prepared for that if you really plan to spend any serious time up here."

"If? Why, I'm planning to spend all my time here, Chelsea. You're looking at a year-round resident of Corbet, Vermont."

"Mr. L.A. Legal Eagle, lawyer to the rich and famous."

"I'm glad to see you've kept abreast of my career. I thought maybe you'd forgotten all about me."

"Forget about you, Walker Jordan?" There was an intentional and not altogether flattering coyness in her tone. "A rich, smart, handsome New York City boy spends a couple of fresh-air summers in New England and tells a cute little hick that she's just about the best thing to come along since the first Fourth of July. It was on July fourth that we first met, Walker. And those were your exact words, if memory doesn't fail me."

"Memory doesn't fail you, Chelsea. You were very special."

"So special that once you went off to Yale University you forgot all about me?"

"I did write..."

"A few postcards. I still remember the first one. 'Wish you were here.' How original, Walker. How clever."

"Obviously that was why you didn't answer it. Or any of the other notes I sent you. They weren't all postcards, if I recall. I even phoned a couple of times, but you were always too busy to talk."

"What did you want to talk about, Walker? The scandal that according to you was going to just...blow over. Or did you feel sorry for me and want to cheer me up with your glib advice?"

"Don't talk nonsense, Chelsea. What happened between your mom and dad had nothing to do with you and me. Why should the kids bear the sins of the parents? I certainly hope you never bought into that."

"Well, at least you didn't keep at it for very long, Walker. I guess Yale was everything you hoped it would be."

"Yale was great," he said, angry at himself for sounding defensive. "I met some wonderful people—"

"Girls, you mean."

Walker sighed. "Yeah. I did meet someone else. Don't tell me you sat around pining for me? You never even sent me an unoriginal postcard. Or are you going to blame that on the big scandal?"

Chelsea winced. Walker didn't know the half of what had happened to her after that summer. He'd left for Yale before the real tragedy had struck the Clark family. All he knew was that Chelsea's mother, having discovered that her father was having an affair with her best friend, had gone berserk and made a scene outside the church one Sunday morning in front of the whole town. But Walker didn't know what had happened after that. His parents had given up summers in Corbet for retirement in Florida. And Walker hadn't stayed in touch with anyone but her.

And, then or now, Chelsea had no intention of sharing that particular piece of history with him.

Walker didn't know exactly what was going through Chelsea's mind, but her face bore the strained look of a runner who'd just heard the gunshot signaling the start of the race. He caught hold of her hand before she could climb out of the shallow pit and take flight.

"If it makes you feel any better, the girl dumped me a few months later. Anyway, that was...what?... fourteen, fifteen years ago."

"Sixteen, but who's counting."

Walker smiled. "I'm sorry now I wasn't more persistent. Maybe I can make it up to you."

Chelsea studied him thoughtfully, forcing memories of old wounds to a back burner. "Maybe you can at that."

Walker's smile fairly radiated with anticipation. "What do you have in mind?"

"You see, Walker, I'm head of the Corbet Historical Society and I'm a professor of history at the community college. My specialty is the history of New England...principally this area...Corbet and the surrounding towns. It's quite a fascinating region. I always was a history buff. Even back in high school. You probably don't remember."

She didn't give him a chance to respond. She was on a roll. "Anyway, I've been researching this particular spot for a good ten years, Walker." She paused for a moment to clarify. "The Fremont property."

"Soon to be called the Jordan property," Walker broke in.

Chelsea gave his comment a dismissive smile and continued. "The thing is, Walker, I'm convinced this very property we're standing on has enormous historical significance. I tried desperately to get the place declared an historic landmark. But the Vermont Historic Commission insists on physical proof to justify a landmark designation. I would have bought the place myself if I'd been able to get my hands on enough money.''

Chelsea paused to study Walker's response, but he was poker-faced. He was a hotshot lawyer. What did she expect? She fixed an earnest look on her face. ''Anyway, it was way over my budget. But as long as the property remained on the market, I didn't think it was doing anyone…any harm…'' She caught Walker staring at the pit. ''I always refill them when I'm done. You'd never even know. And…anyway, you told Ned Hunt that you were heading straight back to L.A.''

''Just to settle up my affairs.''

Chelsea gave him an impatient shrug. ''Walker, I am certain a previously undocumented, pivotal, Revolutionary War battle—a battle that may well have been a deciding factor in our actually winning the war for independence—was fought on this very property. I've found certain documents, letters, diaries. Enough for me to know that if I keep digging—''

''You want to go on digging pits all over my property? Forget it.''

Chelsea tried a new tack. ''If I can prove my theory right, I could put Corbet on the map, and make a name for myself in my profession, Walker. It would mean a chance at research grants, the opportunity to teach at a top university, travel…''

''So, it's fame and glamour you want. Small-town girl makes good. Prestige, professional accolades—''

''What's wrong with that?'' Chelsea retorted. ''You have it, don't you?''

"And I'm more than willing to give it all up for this. Peace, tranquillity, a place to become rejuvenated."

"Well, a little digging won't stop your rejuvenation," Chelsea argued persistently.

She stuck her hand into the pocket of her snug jeans and pulled out a small Ziploc bag. Inside the plastic pouch was a jagged fragment of metal. "See this?"

Walker took it from her hand and examined it through the plastic. "It looks like a piece of an old tool. A spade maybe."

Chelsea took it from him and slipped it carefully back into her pocket. "Maybe. Or maybe it's a broken fragment of a musket."

"A musket?" He studied the pit Chelsea had dug. "You found it there?"

She nodded. "I've found a few other fragments on the banks of this brook." She leaned a little closer, giving Walker a conspiratorial look. "I believe, Walker, that George Washington, himself, had a direct hand in a battle fought right here on the Fremont estate and he very likely slept in the master bedroom of your house."

"Washington slept here?" He laughed.

"I'm serious. Don't you see . . ."

Walker cut the laugh short. He saw that she was very serious, indeed. An uneasy feeling was building inside of him.

"Oh, I see, all right. I see that a discovery like the one you're talking about could turn my little piece of paradise into a three-ring circus."

"You're exaggerating—"

"Forget it, Chelsea. This property, Corbet itself, is unique. A true throwback to the way life used to be in this country. Simple, charming, friendly, warm. No hassles, no dirty dealing, no star treatment, no—'' he paused ''—no way am I going to help to change that. I want this. I need this. For my soul. For my sanity. Corbet is my haven, my own private paradise. And I intend to keep it just the way it is, sweetheart.''

"Don't call me sweetheart, Walker," Chelsea said acerbically. "It's awfully out of place up here in the sticks. Folks around these parts don't take too kindly to flip endearments.''

"I wasn't flipping it at folks," Walker said tightly, his anger building, his sense of peace and tranquillity quickly evaporating. "I was flipping it at you.''

Chelsea eyed him narrowly.

"Okay, okay," he relented with a hint of a smile. "No *sweethearts*, no *babes*, no *darlings*. You caught me red-handed. There, do you feel better?''

"No, I don't feel better, damn it. Why are you being so stubborn, Walker?''

"I'm not being stubborn, you're being unreasonable. This is my property. I have a right—''

"Walker, think of it this way. In six months, probably less, you'll be bored silly with Corbet and be ready to move back to the West Coast. If my theory proves right, this property of yours could be worth ten times—''

"I'm not selling, Chelsea. I'm not leaving.''

"What was wrong with the Elgin property Ned showed you? It was in much better shape.''

"What did Ned Hunt do? Phone you as soon as I left the Realtor's office? What is he? A relative?''

"A good friend.''

"Well, your good friend tried his best. He never even mentioned the Fremont property was on the market. Someone else in the realty office suggested it, and Hunt reluctantly took me here. And even then he did his best to talk me out of buying it."

"The point is, Walker, the Elgin place is a much better investment."

"The Elgin place didn't sing to me."

Chelsea studied him carefully. "Walker, are you on drugs or something?"

Walker laughed heartily. "Don't you hear it, Chelsea? Listen to those birds chirping, listen to the wind whistling through the trees..." There was a twinkle in his eyes. "And talking about trees, I seem to recall one particular tree on this property where a pretty young local gal and a self-centered kid from New York carved their names inside a heart."

"Damn it, Walker, you're not going to look me in the eye and tell me you picked this place because of some silly old memories."

Walker grinned. "You still can blush, Chelsea. I always did get turned on by that blush."

Chelsea sneered. "I am not blushing. I'm just a little sunburned, that's all. What with digging..."

"Well, too much sun isn't healthy."

"Damn it, Walker, you're still as self-centered and stubborn as you used to be. I was a fool to think you'd ever understand."

"I don't think there's anything self-centered about yearning for roots."

Chelsea gave a harsh laugh. "These aren't your roots, Walker Jordan. Your roots are on Park Avenue in New York. Your roots are bankers, politicians. Your roots are the Mayflower. If anyone wants to claim roots here in Corbet, I'd say I have as good a claim as there is. And I'm not standing here bragging about it, believe me. I'd just as soon forget some of my roots, Walker.''

"Chelsea, I'm sorry about what you went through..."

"Don't, Walker. I didn't want your pity sixteen years ago. And I don't want it now." She hated him for bringing back old memories—a long-ago summer love that had gotten tangled up with summer sorrow, summer tragedy.

She heard Walker sigh and saw him open his mouth to say something else, another try at pity, Chelsea guessed, but she wanted to get off the topic. So she shot him a glare. "What's the real story, Walker? What would make a hotshot legal eagle with so much fame and fortune give it all up for the tweeting of birds, the whistling of the wind? A love affair gone sour? A case you finally didn't win? A brush with the law? What are you running away from, Walker?"

"You've got it all wrong," Walker said with a soft smile.

Despite all her efforts, his smile doused some of her fiery anger.

"I didn't move up here to lick any wounds, Chelsea. I'm just dropping out of the rat race." He tested his injured wrist—still a little sore, but not as painful. Probably just a sprain. He climbed out of the pit, then turned back to give Chelsea a hand.

She let him help her up, then she said sharply, "That's too trite, Walker. Surely you can do better than that."

He shrugged. "Look, a few days ago, I woke up and out of the clear blue I asked myself if I was happy. I mean, there I was in my king-size bed in my very sumptuous penthouse in one of the best sections of

L.A. asking myself all of a sudden if I was happy. And you know the answer I gave myself, Chelsea?"

"You have it all, Walker. Success, money, prestige, a chance to do anything you want, go anywhere you want."

"My answer was no, Chelsea. I wasn't happy. I felt empty, alone..." He hesitated, turning away from her steady gaze. "Afraid."

"Afraid?" Her voice had a little catch to it.

Chelsea spontaneously reached out her hand and touched Walker's shoulder. He looked at her again and Chelsea found herself thinking of the young man who had so dominated her dreams and private thoughts for more years than she cared to admit. Dreams and thoughts filled in equal measure with longing, pain and harsh resentment.

Walker was surprised at how aware he was of her casual touch. His mouth curved into an uneven smile. "They were dumb, thoughtless postcards. I should have done better." His voice was low and husky, and he wondered if she had the faintest idea of the kind of impact she was having on him.

"Forget it, Walker. It's history."

"But I thought history was your thing."

"Only some areas. Like this property, for instance."

Walker's face brightened. "I've got a deal for you."

For a minute Chelsea thought he might change his mind about letting her pursue her excavations.

"How about helping me restore the old place, Chelsea? You're the history expert on the area. Together we could make the house an historical showplace, bring it back to all its original glory. It would be a great project. And…we'd get a chance to get to know each other again. What do you say?''

''Walker, this is crazy. You won't half begin before you get bored. This is just some kind of half-baked whim on your part. I mean people don't wake up in their penthouse apartments, decide they're not happy and give up successful, lucrative careers and all the perks that go with them for a broken-down house with a few acres—''

''Eighty-five acres, to be exact. A little kingdom all my own.''

''Okay, Your Majesty, and just what are you going to do with your kingdom?''

He gave her a sly, provocative smile which Chelsea deliberately did not respond to. ''I can stop and smell the flowers here without getting a citation for walking on the grass.'' The smile turned into a grin. ''Of course, I'll have to plant the flowers first. I'm gonna plant me a meadow full of wildflowers, sweetheart. Oops, sorry, bad habit.''

''Smell the flowers? Come off it, sweetheart,'' Chelsea mimicked. ''No one talks like that anymore. And you certainly never waxed poetic sixteen years ago.''

He laughed. ''I had more pressing thoughts than poetry on my mind then, Chelsea.''

Chelsea couldn't help noticing he still had a great laugh. It had deepened over the years, giving it a richer, even more appealing, quality.

''When are you planning to actually move in here?''

He started to answer, but then gave her a shrewd look. ''You want to know how much more time you'll have to dig around before I get back.''

"No, it was just...idle curiosity." But even she could hear the lack of conviction in her voice.

"The digging's over, Chelsea," he said firmly. "I have no intention of showing up back here to discover bus loads of tourists and eager-beaver scholars trampling over my pristine homestead, because during my absence you dug up tangible proof of a big-time Revolutionary War battle."

Chelsea started to argue, but Walker glanced at his watch. "I've got to get going. I'm driving back to New York. I'm catching a plane out of Kennedy...." He turned and started through the woods. Chelsea limped a little as she tried to keep up with him.

"You can think about it, Walker. Where's your sense of history, your curiosity, your...your heart?"

Walker quickened his pace. "I lost my heart in L.A., Chelsea. Don't you get the point. I came here to find it again." He stopped short. Chelsea almost stumbled into him. He shot her a backward glance, a glance mixed with irritation and disquieting temptation. "And you aren't helping any."

Chelsea was thrown by the remark, not sure how to interpret it. "Aren't you overreacting a little?"

He turned his face from hers and started walking again, faster than before.

Chelsea picked up her pace to keep up, but it caused a sharp pain to her shin. She let out a little cry.

Walker looked back again and stopped. "Want to let me see the damage?"

She gave him an awkward smile. "These jeans are too tight to roll up. My shin hit a rock when you fell on me before. It's nothing serious. I probably just bruised the bone. Go on ahead. I'll just limp on home and lick my wounds."

Walker returned her smile tentatively, then said, "Let me help." He came over and bent down. "Hey, there's blood seeping through the denim. I better have a look."

"Forget it. I'd rather lick my wounds in private, thanks."

He looked up at her with a rueful smile. "Sixteen years hasn't altered your stubborn streak, Chelsea."

As he tried to ease the jeans up a bit to have a look at the damage Chelsea flinched.

"If you take 'em off," he said, pulling a newly purchased red and blue bandanna from his back pocket, "we can use this for a bandage."

"Wait. Do you have a pocketknife? I can cut the jeans."

"Sorry, no pocketknife. But aren't you being just a bit adolescent about this, Chelsea?"

She couldn't bear to ignore the challenge in his tone, though she hated to admit he was right. Her hand went to the snap at her waistband. "Turn around."

He gave her a little salute and did as she ordered.

"Ow...ouch...damn. Ow...okay. Give me the bandanna. I'll...do it."

The corners of Walker's mouth curved into a smile as he turned around but, after catching Chelsea's "watch yourself" gaze, he tried his best to focus his attention on the nasty gash on her shin and not the shapely leg that went along with it.

"Doesn't look good," he said solicitously. "We better wash it off back at the brook. The water isn't on up at the house yet."

Chelsea tugged her work shirt down, but no amount of tugging would get the material much past the very top of her thighs.

Despite the fact that she looked as volatile as a grenade with the pin pulled, Walker stood and lifted her in his arms.

"I can walk," she protested, disconcertingly aware of his warm breath rustling her hair.

He hoisted her up a little higher. Chelsea's arms moved around his neck. It just seemed the natural thing to do. To her mounting dismay, it reminded her of all the things that had come so naturally to her when she was with him sixteen years ago.

They were in sight of the brook before either of them spoke again. Walker started with a question.

"So, is there someone special in your life these days? A steady guy? A . . . husband? A few kids to leave the family business to?"

Walker's questions didn't penetrate immediately. Chelsea was distracted by being held so close in his arms. "No," she said finally, and then, after a moment's hesitation, "What about you?"

"No. No wife. No...sweetheart, in the literal sense." He smiled as he set her down on the bank of the brook. Then he slipped off his docksiders, rolled up the cuffs of his trousers, and waded into the brook to soak one end of the bandanna.

A few moments later he knelt down beside her and very carefully began ministering to the gash on her shin.

His touch was very gentle, and while there was nothing seductive about it, it provoked some erotic fantasies in Chelsea's mind. To get her mind off them, she started talking. "So what are you going to do here, Walker? Besides smell flowers."

"I can ski, ice-skate on Lake Worley. You used to tell me how great a place it was to skate, remember?"

"I don't skate much anymore," she said sullenly.

But her glum mood in no way dampened Walker's excitement about starting his new life. "And there's renovating the house. Now that I've learned George Washington himself might have actually slept in it—"

"And after you finish the house?"

"I'm considering opening a small law practice in town. I was chatting with your Realtor friend, Hunt, and he mentioned that Corbet's only lawyer is planning to retire pretty soon. I could fill a necessary gap."

"You honestly think a law practice in a town with a population of three thousand is going to be stimulating enough for a man who handled million-dollar cases for over ten years in one of the most cosmopolitan cities in the world?"

"Population, three thousand and one now, Chelsea. Besides, I came here to Corbet to live the simple life."

There was a moment's hesitation. "Nothing is ever that simple, Walker."

Walker lifted his gaze back to her face and smiled. "Maybe not."

Chelsea found that smile as enticing as it was unnerving. For a few minutes, while they'd been talking, she'd managed to forget that she was sitting half naked with the man who'd broken her heart at a time when she was at her most vulnerable. She'd spent a long time suppressing that vulnerability and, until Walker showed up again, she'd been very successful.

She pulled her gaze away first and concentrated on watching him wrap her wound with his bandanna.

"Good job," she said as he finished, pulling her leg away and grabbing for her jeans. "Thanks."

"That's all right," Walker said, watching her struggle back into them. "I was sort of responsible."

"You really should look where you're walking." Tugging gingerly, she somehow managed to get the narrow jean leg over her wrapped shin.

"Then again, you really shouldn't have been digging holes the size of graves on someone else's property."

"It just became your property this morning." Chelsea felt more in control now that she was once again fully dressed. She got to her feet, wincing as she put pressure on her injured leg.

"It still hurts, huh?" he asked sympathetically.

Chelsea wasn't receptive to his concern. "I have to tell you, Walker, when Ned phoned to say it was you who'd bought the property, I actually felt, well if anyone had to buy it, I was glad it was you." Realizing that Walker might misinterpret the remark as flirtation, she hastily added, "I was sure I could get your cooperation. I thought you'd be thrilled to discover the piece of property you'd bought might end up being a valuable historic landmark. I still can't believe you would actually stand in the way—"

"Look, I don't want to fight a second battle on this site, Chelsea. Can't we declare a truce?"

Frustrated, Chelsea merely threw up her hands, turned and started off.

Walker watched her hobble up the path. "Where did you leave your car?"

"I rode my bike over." She kept on walking, trying to ignore the pain.

A few long strides and Walker caught up to her. "You can't ride with that bum leg. I'll give you a lift home."

Before she knew what was happening he was once again scooping her up in his arms.

"I didn't think you meant that literally, Walker."

"I know." He drew her closer. Much to her consternation some things hadn't changed, even in sixteen years. He still had a way about him, Walker Jordan, a way that she found uncomfortably appealing.

Carrying her with remarkable ease, he followed a path that led round the side of his house. He paused for a moment to look at the weathered-clapboard, two-story colonial. Sadly enough, it really was on its last legs. But not for long, he vowed. He had great plans. "Seventeen seventy-two, your friend Hunt said. And you really believe Washington slept here? It makes you think, doesn't it?"

Chelsea was buoyed by Walker's musings. Her features brightened. Maybe she could spark his interest in history after all, get him to change his mind. "Yes. In fact, you might drop in at the Historical Society some time when you get back and I'll show you the research I've been doing on the original Fremont who built this house. He was a Green Mountain Boy."

"A Green Mountain Boy?"

Chelsea had certainly never delivered a history lesson in the arms of a man before—a man who could still make her pulse race—but she gave it her best shot. "It was the Green Mountain Boys who fought all the Revolutionary War skirmishes up here in Vermont and New Hampshire. Not ten miles from Corbet is a fort in a town called East Hoseck where the Green Mountain Boys stored their ammunition, cannon and mortar." Her voice held excitement, enthusiasm and anticipation.

"How'd our boys do?"

"Well, Burgoyne—he was a top British general—wrote in his journal that the Green Mountain Boys of Vermont were the most active and rebellious military force he and his men had come across. You see, unlike Valley Forge, where soldiers had trekked far from home to fight, and so supplies had dwindled and facilities were poor at best, the Green Mountain Boys all lived in this area. Literally thousands of them could be called up in no time at all. They'd cart supplies from home for a skirmish, then turn around and go back that night, ready to tend their farms the next morning. They were a rugged, self-sufficient, fiercely independent group."

Walker smiled. "Well now, I feel a kind of kinship with those boys already. I knew this was the place for me."

"They were also fiercely loyal and patriotic," she added, a little edge in her voice.

"Hey, I can't sing the 'Star Spangled Banner' through without a tear coming to my eye."

"Seriously, Walker, doesn't this all fascinate you . . . just a little?"

His hold on her tightened, his eyes trailing her vibrant, lovely face. "Oh, but I am fascinated, Chelsea. More than a little."

After they were both settled in his rental car, he gave Chelsea a bright smile. "I am glad we ran into each other again. I hope once I'm settled here—in a couple of weeks—you'll drop over for a glass of wine, some dinner. We can discuss the restoration. You're welcome anytime, Chelsea. As long as you leave your shovel home."

Chelsea gave him a cold stare, her finely etched nostrils flaring. "I wouldn't hold my breath . . . flatlander."

Chapter Two

Chelsea was so worked up from her encounter with Walker Jordan that she didn't notice Ned Hunt sitting on her porch, at first. When she did, she merely shook her head in exasperation.

"Oh, that man is impossible," she muttered climbing the porch steps. "Walking his land like he was king of the manor. His untouchable land. Walker Jordan is the most unreasonable—"

"So you two ran into each other, then."

"It's okay, Ned. The best Realtor in the world wouldn't have swayed that man from buying the Fremont place. Why, didn't you know it had his name written all over it? And I wouldn't be surprised if he told you all about how we'd once carved our names in some damn tree down by the brook. As if I was supposed to think that had some influence on him. Well, I'm not a sixteen-year-old starry-eyed, love-struck—"

"No, he didn't mention a tree." Ned got up from the porch rocker.

"Paradise. His little piece of paradise. That's what he called it. And do you know what he plans to do up here, Ned?"

"What's the matter with you, Chelsea?"

Chelsea's exasperation spread to her old friend. "How can you ask me that, Ned?"

Ned wore a bemused expression. But before he could utter a word, Chelsea was off again.

"Oh, he gave me some cock-and-bull story about setting down roots. But that's plain...nonsense. I'll lay odds he won't last two months. Told him as much. But right now he's all starry-eyed and love struck." Hastily she added, "With his paradise, his kingdom of tranquillity. But I know what's really going to happen—" Chelsea gave Ned a hard stare "—and you know, too."

"I do?"

"As soon as he's restored the house, he'll unload it for triple his investment, walk away with a hefty profit, and some flatlander from Manhattan will have himself a quaint little weekend retreat. In the meantime Walker's bound and determined not to let me dig one inch of his precious land," she spat out vituperatively.

"I see that boy can still steam you up," Ned said, his smile revealing some well-crafted bridgework.

"Oh, I would have loved to take a sock at him. Kick him in the shin—"

"But he got you first?"

Only then did Chelsea realize she was still limping. In her agitation she'd forgotten all about her injured leg.

"Oh, this." She could feel her face heat up as she looked down at her leg. "I...scraped my shin. Walker was generous enough to wrap it up for me in a brand-new bandanna," she added sarcastically. "Which I plan to replace first thing tomorrow. I don't want to be beholden to that man for anything. Not even a dumb bandanna."

"Sit down here and let me have a look, girl," Ned said paternally, taking her arm and gently urging her onto a porch rocker.

"It's fine," Chelsea muttered. "Walker washed it off and . . . everything."

Ned went down on one knee to inspect the damage. "How'd he ever get at it?" He glanced at Chelsea only to see her face was bright red. "Oh. . ." Ned muttered, not quite able to suppress his smile.

Chelsea scowled at him as she sprang up from the rocker. "Oh Ned, stop acting so . . . adolescent." She spun around and did her best not to hobble as she strode into the house.

Ned sauntered in after her.

"Still a pretty good-looking fellow isn't he? Didn't remember me, but I was the one who was the agent for the property his folks rented over on Lake Worley when he was a boy. And then there were those times I ran into the two of you around town. You made a nice-looking couple. Quite a charmer, that Walker."

"He's lost his charm," Chelsea lied.

Ned grinned. "Seems to me he charmed the pants right off you, Chelsea Clark."

"Oh, for heaven's sake, Ned. He did nothing of the sort and you know it. If you must know, I was digging in a pit, he wasn't looking where he was going and he fell right on top of me. My shin was bleeding and. . . It was no big deal."

Ned raised a salt-and-pepper eyebrow, his green eyes twinkling. "Who said it was?"

"Walker hasn't changed a bit," she persisted. "He's as egocentric as ever." She limped across the living room toward her bedroom. "I need to put on a different pair of pants," she muttered.

Ned ambled into the kitchen and helped himself to a cold glass of water from the sink while Chelsea changed. He smiled to himself. He'd figured from the minute Walker Jordan signed the papers that when Chelsea and Walker met up again there'd be fireworks. Sixteen years back there'd been plenty fireworks between the two of them.

It'll do her good, having Walker back, Ned mused. Done her some good already, he decided. More sparkle in her eyes, more color in her cheeks, some of that fiery spirit of hers channeled finally into something other than her work. History. History was all well and good, thought Ned. History had its place. Wasn't he a volunteer himself over at the Historical Society? Had a lot of feelings, he did, for the history of Northern New England. Same as Chelsea. Well not as much feeling for it as Chelsea. Still, he felt it only right to support her efforts... within reason.

The way he saw it, though, the girl was too single-minded. Chelsea was missing out on a lot, burying her head in the sand half the time looking for muskets and the like, spending the rest of her time reading historic documents and daydreaming about fame and glory... and escape. Not that she'd use that word, *escape*.

Ned had always had a special fondness for Chelsea. Not only was he her godfather, over the years he'd proved more of a parent to her than her own father. Poor George. He'd always been a drinker, but after the scandal, and especially after the subsequent tragedy sixteen years back, he'd stayed drunk pretty much around the clock right up to the day he'd died nearly two years ago. Not that Ned had ever held the boozing against George. He hadn't drunk for the pleasure of it, after all. Just to numb his guilt, pain and sorrow.

Ned had to admire Chelsea. Through it all—the scandal, the tragedy of losing her mother, her father's drunkenness—she'd kept her head up high. She'd graduated high school with honors, won a scholarship to the University of Vermont, came back to Corbet to look after her dad, teach at the community college, get appointed head of the Historical Society. People in Corbet had a special fondness and admiration for Chelsea Clark, and as far as most folks were concerned the old scandal and tragedy that had befallen her family was long forgotten.

Chelsea acted as if she'd put it all behind her. But Ned knew different. He knew that Chelsea, deep down, still bore invisible but painful scars that kept her from allowing herself to get seriously involved. She always had plenty of excuses but Ned knew the real reason. Chelsea avoided intimacy because she was scared. She'd seen love turn to betrayal, to shame, to tragedy, and she was scared that history would repeat itself, plain and simple.

Chelsea walked into the kitchen. She had donned a fresh pair of looser-fitting jeans and scrubbed her hands and face. Ned inspected her with fatherly interest...and pride. Yes, he thought, she was a natural beauty all right. Didn't need any fancy cosmetics to prove it, either. He leaned casually against a counter.

"So Walker fell on you, you said." He spoke in a teasing drawl.

Chelsea crossed the kitchen, opened the fridge and grabbed a Tupperware container full of potato salad and a plate of cold roast chicken, leftovers from last night's dinner. She pulled open a drawer and took out a tablespoon.

"Want some?" she asked, flipping the plastic lid off the potato salad.

"No thanks." Ned smiled. Whenever Chelsea got worked up, her appetite seemed to know no bounds. He watched her attack the potato salad straight out of the container, then pick up a meaty chicken leg and go at it with vigor.

After cleaning off the chicken leg and downing several more spoonfuls of potato, she gave Ned a sassy grin. "He not only fell on me, I think he was actually feeling some old sparks."

"Just Walker?"

"Now don't go getting any ideas, Ned Hunt. Walker Jordan broke my heart once. He's not getting close enough this time to even leave a smudge."

She grabbed another chicken leg, absently studying it.

"I admit Walker still looks pretty good and, okay, he's not in bad shape." She thought about how easily he'd carried her over meadow and dale without a huff or a puff. "Probably belongs to a posh health spa in Beverly Hills. Whatever will he do for exercise here in sleepy old Corbet?"

"There are other ways to get exercise, girl."

"Ned!'

Ned proffered an innocent smile. Chelsea didn't buy it for one minute.

"There is going to be no hanky-panky between me and Walker Jordan, Ned. My only interest in the man is figuring out some way to imbue him with a proper sense of historic responsibility."

"I think if you put your mind to it, Chelsea, you'll inspire him."

Chelsea gave Ned a sharp look. "I'd think you'd be the last one pushing me back into Walker Jordan's arms. I was nothing more to him than a summer fling."

"You were both kids then."

"That was his excuse, too."

"You know what I think, Chelsea? I think you never got over him."

Chelsea dumped the untouched chicken leg into the potato salad. "That's complete nonsense. I think you've been out in the sun too long, Ned. You should wear a hat."

"Now, I know I've been on your case not to snub the local boys who are always beating a path to your door."

"No one's beat a path in...ages," Chelsea protested.

"But maybe a gal like you does need a man with a little more sophistication, a man who's seen something of the world. Someone—"

"Someone like Walker? No, Ned. He's the last person I need. He's standing in the way of my ticket out of Corbet, my chance to really make something of myself." She plucked the chicken leg out of the potato salad and took a bite. "Not that I'm giving up on trying to convince Walker. He did invite me over for dinner sometime. He said he wants me to help him restore the old Fremont house. I was too angry at him for stopping my digging to agree."

Chelsea finished chewing. "Maybe I overreacted a little."

"I guess it's possible." Ned cast her a quirky smile.

Chelsea grinned. "Okay, I was a little worked up. But he was so unreasonable about my not digging on the property. He claims he's afraid if I did discover anything important it would turn his paradise into a three-ring circus."

"Well now, he has got a point there, Chelsea."

"Nonsense. That's a complete exaggeration. Okay, there'd probably be a small increase in the local tourist trade. And it would be a draw for historians of the period. But that doesn't add up to a three-ring circus."

"Depends," Ned persisted. "You prove there really was an important Revolutionary War skirmish here and that Washington himself took part in it, well, there are those who'd want to cash in on a discovery like that, milk it for all it's worth."

This was clearly not a discussion Chelsea wanted to be having. She munched on the chicken leg and finished up the potato salad.

"Thinking about it now, I realize I was naive to expect Walker to blithely jump at the notion of my digging up his property. He hasn't even settled in yet. Next time I see him, I'm going to try a whole new approach."

Ned grinned. "That's a thought."

Chelsea raised an eyebrow. "I'll be pleasant, charming, I won't lose my cool. Let's face it. I pushed him into a corner, and he came out fighting. He's stubborn. He was stubborn at eighteen. Well, so was I. So am I."

"See, you two do still have something in common."

She looked sharply over at Ned, having almost forgotten he was still there. "We have nothing in common, Ned. He wants to spend his days smelling flowers. He's lost all his drive and ambition. And, worst of all, he has no sense of historic perspective.''

Ned glanced out the kitchen window. ''Well, it seems like you'll have a chance to try that new approach of yours sooner than you expected.''

''Huh?''

''That looks like Jordan's car coming back up the road.'' He went closer to the window. ''Pulling up your driveway now.'' He glanced back at Chelsea. ''Yup. That's him.'' He gave a wry smile as he watched Chelsea leap nervously off the counter, knocking the empty potato salad container to the linoleum floor.

Her brow creased. ''He said he was going straight to New York to catch a plane to L.A. What's he doing back here?''

They both heard the sharp rap on her front door. Chelsea hesitated. She shot Ned a nervous look.

''Go on,'' Ned ordered. ''Ask him yourself why he's here.''

Chelsea's lips compressed. She took a steadying breath. ''Maybe he's had a change of heart. Maybe he came back to tell me I could dig on the property after all.''

There was a louder series of raps. Ned had to literally give Chelsea a shove to get her moving.

She was halfway to the front door when it opened and Walker's head popped in. He didn't spot her immediately. ''Hi. Anyone home?'' When he caught sight of Chelsea he quickly apologized. ''Oh, sorry. I knocked several times before opening the door.''

Chelsea came to a stop. ''Yes, I know.''

He smiled amiably, leaning one broad shoulder against the doorjamb. ''I see people still don't lock their doors around here, do they?''

Chelsea shrugged. "I don't even own a key."

"I like that."

Chelsea didn't respond immediately. She was thinking about her vow to be pleasant, winning, maybe even charm Walker into changing his mind about her digging.

"Anyway," Walker said nonchalantly, "I thought no one was home. I suppose I could have left your bike unlocked out here on the porch, but I wasn't sure and I didn't want to be responsible for it getting stolen."

Chelsea peeked her head out the door to see her bike leaning against the porch railing.

"You didn't have to go back for it. I could have—"

"How's your shin feeling?" He glanced down. "I see you changed your jeans."

Chelsea laughed softly. "Too bad I wasn't wearing these earlier." She lifted the loose leg of the jeans easily up over her shin. "Ned had himself quite a chuckle over my...predicament...caused by those tight jeans. He was here when I hobbled in."

"I hope he didn't get the wrong idea," Walker said with a teasing smile.

Chelsea didn't tell Walker that Ned's fondest dream would be that his wrong idea was right.

"Ned thought you kicked me in the shin. Didn't you, Ned?" she called out in the direction of the kitchen.

When she got no response, she called out louder to Ned. Still no response. "That's funny." She swung round and went to see what had happened to the older man. A moment later she returned to find Walker in her living room, giving it a thoughtful appraisal.

Chelsea clasped her hands awkwardly together. "Ned's gone. He went out the back way. That's not like him. He loves to shoot the breeze."

"Maybe he had another piece of property to sell," Walker said, smiling at her. "Place still looks nice. But different. Your doing?"

"Yes. After my father died—" there was a little catch in her voice "—I did it over."

"I'm sorry. I didn't know he'd passed away."

"Two years ago." She met his gaze evenly. "Liver disease."

Walker merely nodded. He knew Chelsea's dad had a drinking problem. Sixteen years ago, when he and Chelsea were going together, it hadn't seemed all that bad. Once or twice when he'd brought her home, he couldn't help but notice that Chelsea's dad was none too steady on his feet. Nor had his after-shave masked the boozy scent about him.

Walker now wondered if Chelsea's father's drinking had gotten worse after the scandal. He remembered trying to comfort Chelsea at the time by telling her that sort of thing happened among his parents' set in Manhattan all the time and it would blow over fast. Maybe he'd been wrong.

He'd already gotten the message that Chelsea had no interest in discussing the past so, instead, he merely gazed approvingly around the cozy living room.

"I like what you've done," he said softly, then walked over to examine a watercolor landscape over the brick hearth. "Local artist?"

"Mine."

He turned to her with a look of surprise. "You've got a lot of talent."

Chelsea accepted the praise with an awkward shrug. Then Walker moved over to one of a matched pair of built-in bookcases on either side of the fireplace. "So you like mysteries now," he observed, running his index finger along some of the book bindings.

"No, they were my mom's," she said succinctly.

"Right," he said with a lazy smile, "you're strictly American history."

She bridled. "I like history in the broadest sense. American history just happens to be my specialty."

He turned, giving her a brief glance and fixing his concentration on the wide pine floor. "The Fremont living room has similar flooring. How old is this house?"

"Seventeen ninety-four."

He grinned. "No chance Washington slept here?"

Chelsea stiffened, but she silently vowed not to get into a continuing battle with Walker Jordan. "No chance," she said quietly.

He gave her a lingering look, then he turned his attention back to the brick hearth. "Is it the original fireplace?"

"Yes."

"It looks like you did some restoration work here yourself."

"A little."

Walker nodded.

Chelsea found his presence increasingly unsettling. "Well, thanks for bringing the bike back. I hope you won't be late now...getting to New York. I could have gotten the bike tomorrow."

"The bike wasn't the only reason I came back," Walker said with deliberate slowness.

Chelsea's eyes brightened with anticipation. "You've changed your mind?"

His expression was quizzical.

"About letting me dig on your property?"

He smiled. "Don't you ever think of anything else, Chelsea Clark?"

"What else, then?" she asked hoarsely, her nervousness multiplying as his seductive smile deepened.

For a moment he remained standing where he was, head cocked to one side observing her thoughtfully, thoroughly. Then he began walking slowly toward her, his dusky gray eyes unwavering on her face.

Chelsea was held mesmerized by his gaze. She told herself he was only playing with her, provoking her. He was probably used to women falling all over him. Well, she hadn't fallen over him this time, it was the other way around. He'd fallen over her. And as far as she was concerned he could just pick himself up, brush himself off and be on his way.

Instinctively she stepped back as he drew near. "We aren't teenagers anymore, Walker."

"That's exactly what I was thinking, Chelsea. I was thinking it all the way back here."

"Listen to me, Walker Jordan. At sixteen I may have found your big-city looks and smooth style irresistible. And maybe your women friends in L.A. still do. You've gotten better at it, I'll admit that much. But I'm not sixteen anymore, Walker. And I'm no longer affected by that glib charm of yours, or your seductive smiles..."

"I don't feel at all glib at the moment, Chelsea. I left glib back in L.A. I'm tired of glib just like I'm tired of the rat race. Truly, Chelsea, all I'm after is a little honesty. I drove back because, crazy as it may seem after all this time, I think you still feel some of those old Fourth-of-July sparks just like I seem to—"

"I don't. I don't feel a single spark, Walker." She watched him move closer to her, and she tried desperately to will herself to move back. But some invisible force seemed to be holding her frozen. She started to protest, but it was too late. His lips were already touching hers.

Walker kissed her with deliberation, his palms pressed to her heated cheeks. Chelsea kept her own hands glued to her sides. She was afraid to let them alight anywhere on Walker, afraid he would feel their trembling, afraid he would know how weak he made her feel.

The pressure on her mouth increased and she responded, completely unaware that her hands had moved until she felt her fingers twined in his soft hair. She found herself wishing his hands would leave her face, that he'd wrap his arms around her, pull her fiercely against him...

Instead, he drew back before she wanted the kiss to end. When she looked up into his eyes, she saw that he was well aware of her desire to continue.

He was still cupping her face with his hands. "I just needed to know, Chelsea," he said softly, his thumb moving lightly across her mouth, his fingers spread on her face with a touch that was at once sensual and protective.

Breath caught in Chelsea's throat, freed only after he released her face and stepped away. The air inside her lungs came out in a whoosh.

"You shouldn't have done that, Walker. It wasn't called for." Chelsea crossed her arms over her chest, hoping to hide how hard her nipples had become with that kiss.

"It's been calling to me ever since I saw you again...along with the tweeting of the birds, the whistling of the wind..."

"And you claim not to be glib anymore," she accused.

Walker laughed as he ambled across the room to the front door. When he got there he turned back to Chelsea with a contrite boyish expression that was very disarming. "Well," he said in a low, husky voice, "I suppose a little of that big-city glibness is still clinging to me." He reached for the doorknob and opened the door. "Tell you what. I promise to have eradicated all sign of it by the time I get back from the Coast and we have our first dinner together."

She forgot all about her plans to play it cool, work him round to her corner, make him see it was to his advantage to let her continue her research on his property. All those plans went out the window as she realized Walker had too many plans of his own. "I'm not having dinner with..."

He was already out the door, crossing the porch.

Chelsea hurried to the open door. "Walker, forget it."

"See you in about two weeks, Chelsea," he called back.

"We're not starting anything again here, Walker."

He kept going, cutting across the lawn to his rental car.

"Do you hear me, Walker?"

He stopped and turned back to her. "Too late, Chelsea. We've already started again. Anyway, you can tell me all about the Battle of Corbet over dinner."

A spark of hope glimmered. She knew where he was coming from, but he didn't know how persuasive she could be, given the chance. "Does that mean you might change your mind?" she called out.

Walker slid behind the wheel of his car, stuck his head out the window and grinned seductively. "No. It means I love it when you talk history to me."

Chapter Three

Corbet's Historical Society shared space with the water department, the office of the town manager, Owen Fowler, and that of the tax collector, Jared Porter. They were all housed in a two-story brick building circa 1846 that stood on the south edge of the pocket village green.

Chelsea's office was in the back of the building in what had originally been a secret room where slaves had been hidden during the days of the underground railroad. Just outside the room was a plaque Chelsea had commissioned commemorating the life of Rowland Ashton, who had not only owned the house and hidden runaway slaves, but had also gone off to do battle for the North in the Civil War.

This sunny morning, a week after her encounter with Walker Jordan, Chelsea was sitting in her office poring over copies of the Fremont papers that had been donated to the Historical Society. Beside her was a box of chocolate-covered doughnuts, a thermos of coffee and an empty mug. She was just biting into her second doughnut when the town manager's clerk, Lucy Bedell, popped her head in.

"Someone's looking for you," announced Lucy, a short, plump woman on the far side of sixty, with clever brown eyes and a cloud of red hair liberally highlighted with gray.

"Who?" Chelsea asked, taking a bite of the doughnut and looking up.

"Stranger." Lucy gave Chelsea a sly smile. "Handsome fellow. You might want to wipe those chocolate smudges off your top lip before I bring him along." Lucy dug a clean tissue out of her pocket and brought it over. "He's got a bouquet of wildflowers. Keeps sniffing them."

The last bite of the doughnut hit Chelsea's stomach like a rock. She pressed her arm into her middle hoping the pressure would soothe it. It didn't.

"No..." Chelsea murmured.

Lucy looked at her askance, the tissue still extended in her hand. "You don't want to wipe off your face?"

"No. I...was just— What's he doing back here so soon?" she mumbled more to herself than to Lucy as she absently took the tissue and rubbed at her mouth with it.

"So it is him." The clerk's big brown eyes sparkled. "That old summer beau of yours from when you were in high school, the one who just bought the Fremont property. I hear the two of you had a run-in over there about a week back."

Chelsea shook her head. It didn't take long for word to spread. "What did Ned Hunt tell you?"

"Oh, I heard about you and Walker Jordan from Dot Prescott. Of course, Dot sides with the Jordan fellah about you not poking around his property. She never was keen on your proving there was a big battle in Corbet. She's convinced it would bring in hordes of tourists, and worse, flatlanders buying up property, forcing us townfolk out. I reminded Dot that Walker Jordan was a flatlander himself. So if she's worried about getting stripped bare..."

Chelsea looked up sharply at Lucy. Surely Ned wouldn't have mentioned anything about her brief "strip." No. The clerk was merely going on about Chelsea's project, and how Corbet deserved its place in the history books.

"Well, don't worry, Lucy. I don't intend to give up something I've been working on for so long. Especially now that I feel I'm really close to nailing it down."

Lucy's eyes sparkled. "It could be the fellah still has a bit of a crush on you, Chelsea. I always say that a woman can get farther with honey—"

"Really, Lucy. That isn't my style at all. You should know that."

Lucy did know, all right. Chelsea, for all her beauty, never used her looks or any other feminine wiles to get what she wanted. No, it wasn't Chelsea's style. Nor was it common to see such heightened coloring in the historian's cheeks, not to mention the look of anticipation in her lavender-blue eyes. Well, well, well, thought Lucy.

"Should I bring him along?"

Chelsea tried and failed to appear nonchalant. "I suppose I ought to see what he wants. Although I bet I know."

Lucy raised a brow. "Yes, I guess the flowers are a giveaway."

Chelsea gave Lucy a severe look. "Walker Jordan is a man who only gives something when he wants something in return." She saw the clerk's brows raise even higher and quickly went on to add, "He wants me to help him restore the old Fremont house."

"Oh, so he plans to fix it up and sell it?" quizzed Lucy. "See. I'm right. Another flatlander buying up property, renovating it, then selling it for a whopping profit to some other flatlander looking for a little summer place."

Even though Lucy was voicing Chelsea's earlier sentiments exactly, Chelsea felt inexplicably annoyed. "Walker says he plans to settle here, Lucy. He's going to open a law practice in town. He thinks Corbet is paradise."

"Chelsea's right, Lucy," came a male voice from the doorway. "I plan to plant perennials in my garden, raise a family here, hopefully live to see my grandchildren digging for buried treasure down by the brook." Walker grinned in Chelsea's direction.

"I was just about to come fetch you, Mr. Jordan," Lucy muttered, her face flushed with embarrassment. She quickly walked past Walker and made a hasty retreat.

"Hi," Walker said as he ambled into Chelsea's office, perched himself on the corner of her desk, plunked the bouquet of flowers in her empty coffee mug, and reached across for a doughnut. "So, did you miss me while I was gone?" He didn't straighten back up. His face was inches from Chelsea's.

She wanted to pull back, but decided that would merely clue Walker into her discomfort at having him so close. She'd made dozens of vows this past week to put Walker Jordan out of her mind. It disturbed her greatly that, after their one brief—albeit intense—encounter a week ago, he'd made such an impact on her life. He infuriated her, excited her, intrigued her. Their relationship had been a lot less complicated when they were teenagers.

"You weren't due back for another week," she said, forcing herself to meet his close, steady gaze. Today his eyes were darker than dusk, almost a Nile blue.

He took a bite of his doughnut, chewed, then smiled. "So, you've been keeping track."

She pulled back then. She couldn't help it. He will not affect me, she vowed. "What do you want, Walker?"

"You invited me to drop in, remember?" He took another bite of doughnut.

"Well . . . this isn't a good time. I have a lot of work to do here this morning. And I have a class at one over at the college."

"When does your class end?" he asked after finishing off the doughnut.

Chelsea hesitated. "Two fifteen. But then I have to—"

"I'll pick you up." He grinned. "In my car, I mean."

"No, you can't. I've got errands to do. Then I'll probably come back here to finish up some work."

He glanced down at the paper she'd been studying before he arrived. "What's this?"

"It's a letter from Josiah Fremont to Chittendon."

"Chittendon?"

"The governor of Vermont in the early eighteen hundreds. Josiah was the grandson of Harmon Fremont."

"The Green Mountain Boy who built my house."

Chelsea couldn't help the flash of irritation. "Yes, your house."

"Look," Walker said, leaning in close again. The scent of his lemony after-shave, mingled with the scent of wildflowers, proved very distracting for Chelsea. "I only came by today to see if we couldn't start fresh. We both got a little...overheated during our first reunion."

"I thought you were going to quit being glib, Walker. Why do you want to start fresh, anyway?"

"Why can't we just be neighborly, Chelsea?"

"You know very well why not," she retorted.

"Right. I forgot. You're bound and determined to dig for fool's gold."

"The only fool here is you, Walker."

"Fame and fortune isn't what it's cracked up to be, Chelsea. Take it from the horse's mouth."

"Don't you have your equine ends mixed up, Walker?" Chelsea snapped.

Walker grinned, leaning closer, but this time Chelsea was having none of that.

Walker let out a sharp gasp of surprise as lukewarm black coffee spilled from Chelsea's tipped thermos and poured down the front of his pale gray linen slacks.

"Damn, you did that on purpose, Chelsea," Walker exclaimed, astonished.

"Why, it was an accident, Walker. We both know how accidents can happen when you don't watch where you're going."

Walker grabbed some tissues from a box on the desk and began blotting the spill, to no avail.

"Gee, Walker, maybe you have a change in your car. Don't let me keep you."

"I dropped my suitcases off at home before I came here."

"Then I guess you'd better get back home and change."

Walker looked down at the damage, then slowly raised his eyes back to Chelsea. "Rather embarrassing." His lower lip quirked.

Chelsea scowled. The stain was in a rather embarrassing spot.

"Where's the men's room?" he asked.

Chelsea's lips compressed. If he walked out of her office and Lucy caught sight of that stain, heaven only knew what rumors would be flying around Corbet within the hour.

"Take your pants off, Walker."

"I beg your pardon."

Chelsea folded her arms across her chest. "There's already gossip about us spreading around town. You can't walk out of here...like that. I've got a sink in my supply closet. If we get some cold water on the stain and let it dry..."

"So, you want me to remove my trousers. Tit for tat?"

"For heaven's sake, Walker, now who's being adolescent."

Walker stood up, not bothering to ask Chelsea to turn around, and made an irritating production of removing his trousers. "I guess this makes us even," he said handing them over to Chelsea who was busy staring down at the floor.

Chelsea abruptly spun around, but found herself smiling as she crossed her office to her supply closet. "Really, Walker, if every time we have an encounter one of us ends up having to undress..." She stopped short, keeping her back to him. "Well, it'll get... awkward."

Walker laughed. "You didn't think it was so... awkward... sixteen years ago."

Chelsea walked into the supply closet, switched on the light and turned on the tap in the sink. "Honestly, you act as if we had some wild, torrid affair when we were teenagers. Okay, we did a little experimenting... just a little. I'm not ashamed... it was perfectly natural... innocent..." She'd raised her voice, thinking that Walker had stayed put in her office but when she turned to glance at him he was standing at the doorway to the supply closet, casually leaning against the doorjamb, wearing a blue rugby shirt and very skimpy gray bikini-style undershorts.

Chelsea couldn't stop herself from taking one quick look at his body. When her eyes reached his he gave her a conspiratorial wink.

Chelsea jerked away and busied herself again attending to Walker's stained trousers. He came up behind her to watch her at the task. The supply closet was actually quite roomy, but at the moment it felt confining. Not usually bothered by tight spaces, Chelsea was suddenly beset with an attack of claustrophobia. Or was it Walkerphobia?

"Did you really want to get rid of me so bad...?" His voice was low, insinuating, provocative. He was so close his warm breath ruffled her hair.

Chelsea cast him a rueful look. "No. It was... an accident. Walker, it isn't summer, and I'm not sixteen years old. And if you're looking to be neighborly, you're going about it all wrong."

He stepped back, much to Chelsea's relief. "You're right," he mused. "I guess it's going to take me a little time to get acclimated to country life. I'm not really on the make, Chelsea. If anything, I came here to Corbet to find myself before I go looking for anyone else. I suppose it was just seeing you again, after all these years...seeing you look even better than I'd remembered..."

"Come on, Walker. You haven't spent much time remembering me."

Walker leaned against the wall. "You're wrong. I have some very fond memories," he admitted. "I remember those carefree, happy summer days. I remember our excitement over the littlest discoveries, our openness, our belief that anything was possible."

Chelsea remembered, too. But, unlike Walker, those happy memories were tied up with too many sorrowful ones for her to want to linger over them now. They overlapped and tangled.

"What did happen between your mom and dad after I left?" Walker asked softly. So softly, tears filled Chelsea's eyes.

"My mom committed suicide, Walker. I guess it was about a week after you started at Yale." She slowly turned around to face Walker.

Walker stared at her, dumbstruck. "I...can't believe it. That's awful."

"You see, Walker, a man having an affair with a neighbor's wife, his wife's best friend to boot, is not a casual everyday sort of event around these parts, not like it is on Park Avenue. My mother was devastated. And she...she went over the edge. She felt like everyone in town was laughing behind her back, whispering about her. It wasn't all paranoia. They did stare. I'm sure they did whisper. But they felt sorry for her, too. And my dad...well, he was so ashamed.... He begged her to forgive him. He swore he'd never cheat on her again, never even look at another woman. I think she believed him. I don't think she swallowed all those pills to punish him. I think she just couldn't handle the shame and humiliation.''

''Maybe it was an accidental overdose, Chelsea. Maybe she was so distraught she didn't realize...''

Chelsea gave him a weary look. ''It was no accident, Walker. My dad took it hard, real hard. Mom may not have meant to punish him but he punished himself for fourteen years...punished himself to death.''

''With booze.''

''Yeah,'' she said in a low voice. ''His drinking got even worse after my mom...died. I used to get a call two, three times a week to come pick him up at the local bar because he was too drunk to drive home. Ned helped out a lot. I don't know what I would have done without him. Then, about four years ago, dad got sick, really sick and ended up in the hospital. The doctor told him he had to swear off booze or he'd be dead in six months.''

''He couldn't quit?'' Walker asked softly.

''He tried. He tried real hard. Stayed on the wagon for almost a year.''

Chelsea was so lost in the past that for a moment she forgot she was having this emotionally wrenching conversation with a half-naked man. When she remembered she blushed and looked away.

''Chelsea, I'm so sorry. I had no idea.'' He shook his head. ''I never dreamed...I really was a heel not to have been more sensitive. When you didn't answer my letters and you refused to return my calls, I should have realized you were hurting.'' He reached out and took her hand but she pulled it away sharply. She didn't want his pity. She was sorry she'd gone on as she had.

She turned around, blinking back tears while she attended to the stain in his trousers again.

"Hey, take it easy," he said in a light, teasing tone, closer to her now. "You don't want to remove the material along with the stain."

Chelsea quickly turned off the taps. "There, that should do it." She strode out of the supply closet with the trousers and went over to the open office window to inspect them more closely in the bright light.

"Yes, it looks like all of the stain came out, thank goodness."

She hadn't gotten all the words out of her mouth when the door of her office opened.

"Oh..." the young woman at the door gasped, staring first at Chelsea who was holding up Walker's slacks to the light, and then at Walker standing in his undershorts at the doorway to the supply closet.

"Phyllis..." Chelsea gasped in response, her eyes wide as she stared at the college student. It was a toss-up which of the two looked more mortified. Even Walker seemed a bit...awkward.

"Coffee stain," he muttered.

"Yes...coffee...an accident," Chelsea stammered, displaying the large wet spot running down the front of Walker's pants. "I had to...wash it off...the coffee stain."

Walker discreetly, if belatedly, stepped back into the supply closet. Chelsea sighed, realizing that any further explanations would only make matters worse.

Phyllis stood rooted to the spot, red as a beet and speechless.

Chelsea pulled herself together. "Did you want to see me for a particular reason, Phyllis?" she asked in her most professorial voice.

"Uh...yes. Oh, but...if this is a...bad time...Miss Clark...I mean..."

"I know what you mean, Phyllis. Now will be fine. What is it?"

"It's just...I didn't want to get marked down...for turning in...my term paper late. And you'd said...if I could bring it over...before class today...you wouldn't mark me late."

She fumbled for the report in her backpack. "Oh, Miss Clark...I should have...knocked. I always... knock. I was just...I guess I wasn't thinking."

"Sometimes not thinking too much is just as well, if you know what I mean, Phyllis," Chelsea said, taking the term paper from the girl's hand.

"Yes, Miss Clark."

"I'll see you in class at one then."

"Yes, Miss Clark." Phyllis backed up, colliding with Lucy at the open door as she rushed out.

It was the prospect of even greater humiliation and embarrassment that made Chelsea fling Walker's trousers under her desk before Lucy, like Phyllis, caught her red-handed. Walker's head had popped out just as she was chucking his trousers, though he'd ducked back as soon as Lucy entered the office. Chelsea prayed he'd stay put until the clerk exited.

"Oh, did Mr. Jordan leave?" Lucy asked, looking around.

"Yes," Chelsea said in an overly loud voice, causing the clerk to give her an odd look.

"Funny, I didn't see him go," Lucy mused.

Chelsea hurried over to the door. "If you don't mind, Lucy, it's been just one interruption after another this morning. I really must get to my work."

"I just stopped by to see if you had anything to mail this morning. I'm on my way to the post office."

"No, nothing. Thanks," Chelsea said, edging the door closed as she spoke.

Walker waited until the door clicked shut before stepping out.

"You're right. This is getting pretty awkward," he said with a broad grin. "Now what?"

Before Chelsea could respond, he raised a hand. "No, don't tell me. Let me guess. You want me to put on my damp, and now very likely dirty, trousers, climb out your window and sneak back to my car."

"You're a good guesser, Walker," she said, fishing his pants out from under the desk.

They both smiled. He took his pants from her and began putting them on.

"Okay. Here's another guess. Phyllis isn't likely to keep quiet about this," Walker murmured.

"It doesn't matter." At that moment Chelsea actually believed it. Why get bent out of shape because of some steamy town gossip about her and Walker? Let tongues wag. She had more important things to concern herself with. Anyway, wasn't this a perfect example of why she wanted out of small-town life?

"Walker, let's have dinner tonight."

Her invitation clearly surprised him. He'd been certain after this little episode Chelsea Clark would never again want to set eyes on him.

He finished fastening his trousers and studied her cautiously. "How come?"

"You don't want to have dinner with me?"

"Sure, I want to. I also want to know why you want to."

She met his gaze evenly, an easier task now that he was once again fully dressed. "Well, for one thing, I owe you. I did spill that coffee on you on purpose. And I am responsible for you having to make a less than graceful exit. Besides—" she hesitated, eyes sparkling "—I'd like to give you that history lesson," she said frankly.

Walker smiled. "About Harmon Fremont?"

"Yes."

"You think if I become fascinated with the old fellow I might change my mind about letting you dig up my property?"

"I'd like to think you'd at least keep an open mind, Walker. That's all."

He stared at her assessingly for several moments. Finally he said, "Fair enough."

"You mean that?"

"I always try to mean what I say, Chelsea. So I should add that I doubt you'll change my mind. But I won't rule it out."

Chelsea smiled. "Fair enough, Walker."

He eyed the window. "Believe it or not, this is the first time I've ever had to make this kind of an exit."

Chelsea smiled, watching him open the window. "I don't believe it."

Walker had already swung his legs out the window when he turned back to Chelsea.

"I dreamed about that smile of yours, Chelsea, when I was back in L.A. On more than one occasion."

Chelsea stopped smiling. "Just dinner, Walker."

"And the history lesson," he answered, his eyes dancing with humor.

"I THINK I'm overdressed." Walker gave his red and blue paisley tie a tug as he scanned the dozen or so casually dressed diners at the Stony Brook Restaurant, the "best" eatery in town. "I forgot Corbet was strictly casual."

Chelsea smiled. "You look very nice, all dressed up."

"You mean you prefer me overdressed to underdressed?"

She laughed. "Let's just say it's a change."

"The night isn't over yet."

Much to Walker's delight, she laughed again. He was fascinated by the grown-up Chelsea Clark. She had depth, honesty, beauty and brains. And she was delightfully unpredictable.

"You look very nice yourself," he said softly.

She'd taken pains with her appearance tonight. Not something she usually bothered about. Actually, right after her last class that afternoon, she'd run into Ivy's, an expensive and fashionable boutique on Main Street that was run by a couple of flatlanders from New York City, and purchased the ensemble she was now wearing. She'd spied the red V-neck cotton-knit top in the window. Red was her best color. While she was trying it on, Ivy had talked her into a costly but beautifully cut pair of creamy white, pleated cotton slacks to complement it.

Chelsea recognized the petite, attractive young waitress who arrived at the table to take their order as one of her students, in the same class as Phyllis Marshall.

Walker was glancing down at the menu as he asked, "So, what's the specialty of the house?"

"The specialty is chicken à la Stony. It's a spicy variation on fried chicken," the waitress explained, her eyes positively riveted on Walker who was now looking up at her. "Or if you want traditional, our pot roast can't be beat." She gave him a "chicken, pot roast or me" kind of smile.

Walker smiled back. "I feel adventurous tonight. Let's go with the spicy chicken."

It took a couple more moments for the waitress to pry her eyes away from Walker. When she finally turned her attention to Chelsea, the girl smiled awkwardly. "What would you like, Professor Clark?"

Chelsea gave the girl a cool stare. "The pot roast, Maureen."

Walker smiled tenderly at Chelsea as Maureen beat a hasty retreat. "A friend of Phyllis's no doubt. I have made your life tough, haven't I?"

Chelsea wondered if he realized yet how tough.

"You really can't let rumors get to you in a small town, or you'll go crazy," is what she said aloud.

His look made her aware of an edge in her voice that even she hadn't realized was there.

"Is that why you want out?" he asked.

She hesitated. "Corbet has its good points and its bad. I'm ready for something more, that's all."

"What did that hunk of metal you showed me turn out to be? A piece of a musket?"

She smiled wryly. "It was what you thought. A fragment of an old farm tool."

"Sorry."

"The man who accused me of digging for fool's gold? No you're not."

He looked across at her. "I know it doesn't make any sense—and it doesn't change anything—but I

Nearly Paradise

really am sorry. I guess it's got to do with imagining how your face would light up if that scrap of metal had been a musket. Even though it would have turned my world upside down."

"You're already turning my world upside down," Chelsea blurted out.

Walker leaned forward and reached out for Chelsea's hand. "Now for that I'm not sorry," he said in a low, sexy voice.

Chelsea held his gaze for a long moment and then let her eyes drop. "Walker."

"Yes?"

"Your tie's in your glass of water."

He looked down. Then he laughed as he looked up to meet her gaze again. "Well, I guess I'd better take it off."

Chapter Four

Chelsea glanced at her lecture notes and munched absently on a tuna fish sandwich while her longtime friend and colleague, Julie Martin, finished grading the last of her students' world history term papers.

"Done," Julie said with a sigh of relief as she circled a big, fat *C* at the top of the final paper. She gave Chelsea a perky smile. "Now, I can spend the weekend getting down to serious business. Like whether Zach and I go to the Bahamas or Martinique for our honeymoon."

"Didn't you go to the Bahamas...?" Chelsea stopped herself, but not in time. Julie's perky smile winked out.

"Roger and I went to Jamaica for our honeymoon," Julie said in a hurt voice.

"I'm sorry." Chelsea gave her friend a winsome smile. "I think Martinique sounds incredibly romantic."

But Julie, a tall, gangly woman with puckish red hair and freckles, was not going to let Chelsea off the hook that easily. She frowned, only the creases at the corners of her eyes showing that she was over thirty. "You have a lousy attitude when it comes to marriage, Chelsea Clark. I mean, I should be the cynical one here. I'm the one who's been through it before. But here I am, bright, confident and optimistic that Zach and I are going to live happily ever after.''

''I said I was sorry. I thought you and Roger had spent your honeymoon in the Bahamas. And I was only thinking that it might be wise to...start the second one off differently.''

''The second one. Honestly, Chelsea, you say second as if you're assuming there'll be a third, a fourth.'' Julie grinned. ''I could try to match Helen Ortman's record. What's Helen on? Her fifth?''

''I stopped counting after Bill Laird. I think he was number three.''

Julie grinned. ''Speaking of Bill.'' She leaned forward, ''How's our flatlander, Walker Jordan, doing?''

Chelsea gave Julie a bemused look. ''There must be a connection there somewhere, I suppose. Let's see. Bill and Walker both have dark brown hair. Although Bill's missing most of his. Maybe it's something more basic, like both men happen to live right here in Corbet.''

''Okay, okay, so I'm dying to know what gives with Walker and you. I still remember this starry-eyed young thing who couldn't stop talking about the most handsome, most charming, sexiest, best built, most brilliant...''

''Why does everyone in this town think my whole life revolves around one innocuous, teenage, summer romance with some flatlander I haven't seen or heard from for years?'' Chelsea snapped. ''Walker Jordan pops up again out of nowhere and the whole town is buzzing.''

Julie grinned. "Is it only rumor that Walker was in your office in the middle of the morning...not quite fully clothed? There's a story going around..."

Chelsea knew she'd been overly optimistic to think her student would remain mum. "Didn't you know? I usually entertain my half-clothed men friends at my office in the middle of the night. I just couldn't fit Walker into my busy schedule."

"Be facetious all you want, Chelsea. Rumor or not, you don't fool me one bit. I know you too well."

Chelsea dumped the other half of her tuna fish sandwich back into its plastic bag. She no longer had any appetite. "Everyone in this town knows me too well. That's one of the reasons I want out."

"You don't need a major historic find to get out, Chelsea. If you've really had it with Corbet—"

"You don't understand."

Julie smiled. "I thought you just accused me and everyone else in Corbet of understanding too well." Julie gave Chelsea serious study. "I don't know about the rest of the town, but I think I do understand. I may not be overly ambitious myself, and I may put more stock in having a husband and a bunch of kids than making a name for myself, but I do know how driven you are, Chelsea. Why, you've been bound and determined to make a name for yourself ever since—" Julie faltered "—ever since you were a kid," she finished lamely.

Chelsea knew precisely what Julie meant to say. Ever since the scandal and her mother's suicide. Usually when her own personal past was brought up, Chelsea could feel her whole body stiffen up. Not today, though. Maybe she was just too preoccupied.

"I really thought Walker, of all people, would understand. Don't you remember, Julie, how fired-up he used to get when he talked about becoming a big-time lawyer?"

"Oh, I remember. He was going to be the most successful corporate attorney in the country." Julie laughed. "Walker never was the modest sort. Then again, he did do precisely what he set out to do."

"Funny, I always figured he'd settle in New York," Chelsea mused. "I wonder what made him move out to L.A."

"*Cherchez la femme,*" Julie said, her brown eyes sparkling.

"What does that mean?"

"Find the woman."

"I didn't mean the translation, Julie," Chelsea said wryly.

Julie laughed again. "What's happened to your sense of humor? I thought that was funny."

"What woman?"

"You mean, which woman?"

Chelsea knew Julie was getting a great deal of pleasure from egging her on. "Okay, so I'm curious," she relented. "I'm sure there've been plenty of women in Walker's life in the past sixteen years. I just didn't know...there was any one particular woman."

"That's because you keep your nose buried in moldy old documents instead of the society pages of the *Times.*"

"So, give me a news update," Chelsea said acerbically.

"Well, it's old news now. But once upon a time, about nine years ago, Walker Jordan's name was linked with Vanessa Harper's." When she saw no reaction from Chelsea, Julie emphasized, "*The* Vanessa Harper."

Chelsea still drew a blank. "An actress?" she guessed, not being up on that particular topic. There was only one movie theater in Corbet—in what had at one time been a granary. Of course, twenty miles away was a six-cinema complex, but most of the time, having that many choices usually left Chelsea opting to stay home.

"No," Julie announced. "Harper isn't an actress. She's got the looks, though. And the magnetism. But she's a very flashy, very wiley attorney who handled some of the biggest names in Hollywood. She and Walker met at some society bash in Manhattan, they got to know each other real well, and when Harper went back to Hollywood, she had a big fat diamond ring on her finger and Walker in tow."

"An engagement ring?" Chelsea stared at Julie. "Walker got married?"

Julie shook her head. "The engagement was broken off."

"Who broke it?" And then, before Julie could answer, Chelsea answered her own question. "It must have been Harper who broke it off," Chelsea decided. "Walker's too stubborn to ever change his mind about anything."

"Actually," Julie reflected, "I'm not sure about who broke it off."

"Don't tell me. Your subscription to the *Times* ran out?"

Julie smiled. "No. Roger and I were honeymooning in Jamaica at the time." Her smile faded. "I did read about the trial when I got back, though."

"What trial? You never told me—"

"I wasn't living in Corbet then, remember? Roger and I were in Florida. Boy, was that move a mistake. Then again, name one thing that involved Roger Godfrey that wasn't a mistake."

"What was the trial about?" Chelsea broke in before Julie went off on one of her favorite tangents.

"Vanessa Harper was brought up on charges of embezzlement."

"Embezzlement?"

"And guess who defended her?"

"Walker?"

"Her ex-fiancé is how the papers referred to him, if I recall."

"And?" Chelsea prodded.

Julie grinned. "And, he got her off, of course. If I ever need a good lawyer..."

"I wonder if she did it," Chelsea mused.

"You could always ask Walker."

Chelsea frowned. "Right now, I wouldn't ask Walker Jordan for the time of day."

"Oh? No give on letting you excavate on his property."

"I've never met anyone so stubborn."

"I thought maybe that cozy candlelit dinner you two had over at the Stony Brook the other night might have swayed him."

Chelsea sighed. "The Stony Brook has no candles and you know it. I suppose everyone in town not only knows that we had dinner together, but what we ate, for heaven's sake."

"You had the pot roast." Julie laughed at the amazed expression on Chelsea's face and relented. "You always have the pot roast."

Chelsea did crack a smile.

Julie gathered up her graded papers and rose. "And I bet Walker had the chicken à la Stony," she added with a wink, before heading across the faculty lunchroom to the door.

"What did Maureen do? Post our order on the town bulletin board?"

Julie laughed and looked back over her shoulder at Chelsea. "Just a good guess. He seems the type to like things that are spicy. Oh, and another thing, there was a connection between Bill Laird and *your* Walker Jordan. Walker's hired Bill's company to do his landscaping."

Julie headed out the door as Chelsea muttered. "He is not *my* Walker."

EVEN BEFORE HE ARRIVED, Bill Laird's partner, seventy-two-year-old Harry Newell, was less than enthusiastic about spending the morning listening to a flatlander's "high-fallutin' ideas" about landscaping the old Fremont place. First glance at Walker Jordan, with his crisp, white pullover shirt and perfectly creased khaki trousers, and Harry was downright grumpy.

Walker was surprised to find himself intimidated by the old gent in his worn overalls and faded work shirt, whose face looked as if it had been retreaded. Walker told himself to relax. He blamed his uneasiness on Chelsea, who had intimated that, whether they were for or against her digging, folks in Corbet weren't likely to welcome him with open arms.

Harry Newell's arms were folded across his chest and he was giving the north field an expressionless survey.

"So, tell me, Mr. Newell," Walker began, hoping to break the ice, "have you lived in Corbet all your life?"

Harry Newell took his time turning his attention from the field to Walker. Even when he finally had his gaze square on Walker's face he took his time answering. Then, without moving so much as a muscle in his ancient, craggy face, he replied, "Not yet."

It took a moment for Walker to get the joke. If it was a joke. There was no way of knowing from old man Newell's expression. Walker decided, the hell with it, and grinned. Maybe he should try out an old New England joke on Newell to break the ice a little more. He'd found a whole book of them on a shelf in his bedroom.

"There was this tourist stopped by my place this morning," Walker said in a light, conversational tone as Harry Newell returned to his survey of the field.

Walker, too, looked off at the field. "He asked me if this was the way to Jericho."

Old man Newell just kept on staring out across the grass, but Walker sensed he'd gotten his attention.

"Dunno, I said. So he says, where does it go? Dunno, I said."

Newell dug his hands into his pockets and Walker followed suit.

"You don't know much, do you? he says."

Newell turned to Walker.

Straight-faced, Walker tossed the punch line. "Nope, I says. But I ain't lost."

Harry Newell didn't crack a smile, but he did scratch his nose and eye Walker like he was doing a second sizing up. Walker, a pro at sizing people up himself, knew he'd scored a point with the old guy.

"You paid top dollar for this property, but you'll get full value if you mean to carry out the plans you talked over with Billy," Newell said laconically.

"Oh, I mean to, all right," Walker said emphatically, chalking up a second point for himself. "I want to return this whole property, the house and the land, back to the way it was in the late seventeen hundreds. There are some old floor plans over at the Historical Society..." Walker noticed a faint change in Harry's expression at the mention of his visit to the Historical Society. Chelsea had been convinced her student would keep quiet about his trouser fiasco in her office a few days back, for fear of winding up with an *F* on her term paper, but Walker wasn't so sure some gossip hadn't leaked.

Walker kept his expression blank and went on. "Bill Laird said you were the man to help me with the land itself. I've been doing some research, and I believe this area up here used to be a vegetable garden, and then beyond that were the corn and wheat fields."

Walker may have moved on but Harry didn't move so quickly. "Hear you want Chelsea to help restore the house. Got real feelings for this property, she does. Course she wanted to buy it herself, but not too many locals have that kind of money to burn. Probably told ya about George Washington. That's somethin', isn't it?"

Walker was caught off guard by Harry's sudden loquaciousness. "Uh...yes. If it's true."

Harry raised a brow, and Walker got nervous that he'd just blown everything.

"Chelsea told me she wasn't certain about Washington," Walker added hurriedly. "Course, she's still doing her research. And if she ends up convinced Washington slept here, you can count on my being convinced, Mr. Newell."

Harry Newell cracked a smile for the first time. "I think the whole thing's a bunch of hooey myself."

IT WAS AN UNCOMMONLY hot day for early May as Chelsea toiled in the vegetable garden on the Fremont property, working the plowed and harrowed ground with hoe and rake, lining up the rows, dropping in the seeds, covering and patting them down. She felt as if sweat was dripping from every pore of her body. The oversize work shirt and the thick denim overalls she wore to disguise herself were not helping matters any. Even the wide-brimmed hat, not worn solely to keep the sun from beating down on her head, wasn't helping much.

Most of the men in the crew were working in T-shirts and shorts or cutoffs. A couple were bare-chested, including Walker Jordan himself. Chelsea hadn't bargained on Walker joining in with the crew. She'd figured he would merely pop around every now and then to check on their work and she could make herself scarce when he appeared. Now, all she could do was try to keep as big a distance from him as possible.

"Damn, but it's hot," Cal Grimes, who was working the next row to Chelsea's, muttered, as he stripped off his T-shirt. Catching him glance her way, she pulled the brim of her hat lower.

"Hey you, Chet, is it?"

Chelsea did a quick nod.

"Why ya all covered up? You must be boilin' in that getup."

"Allergic to sun," Chelsea muttered, making her husky voice even huskier.

"Oh man, what a drag. I'm ready to strip down naked myself."

Chelsea said a quick, silent prayer that he wouldn't. But her prayer wasn't answered.

Not that her co-worker stripped down right then and there. No, that happened about an hour later, when Walker called a break and suggested everyone get naked and jump into the creek to cool off. His offer was greeted with loud whoops of approval. It didn't take another minute before the men were all trying to beat each other to the creek. All except the one worker from out of town who went by the name of Chet.

"Hey," Walker called out to her just when she was thinking she'd successfully ducked off without attracting any notice. "What's your problem? Can't swim?"

She kept her back to Walker as she heard Cal Grimes calling out about her sun allergy. Chelsea squeezed her eyes shut, hoping that explanation would satisfy Walker.

Didn't she know by now that Walker Jordan wasn't easily satisfied?

She could hear his footsteps approaching, and she started to take off.

"Hey, wait up," her new boss commanded. Chelsea froze.

He was right behind her. "I know a spot further up where the brook's completely shaded by oaks. Come on, I'll show you."

Chelsea shook her head.

"What's the matter? Can't you swim?"

Chelsea shrugged.

"Look, I intend to get another three hours of work out of you after this break. You need to cool off if you want to give me your best. And you do want to give me your best, don't you?"

Chelsea gave a weak nod.

"Come on. I'll show you the way."

Chelsea waited for him to turn before she did, then she followed at a fair distance, keeping her head bowed so that every time Walker glanced back, all he could see was the top of her straw hat.

"You from around these parts?" Walker asked.

The hat shook.

"You been doing this kind of work long?"

The hat nodded.

"Just around the bend here. See, I told you," Walker said, "nice and shady."

From beneath the brim of her hat, Chelsea saw Walker's T-shirt hit the ground. She did a quick turn and started for the woods.

"Hey, where you going now?" Walker called out.

She heard a splash as Walker dove into the water.

"Gotta...you know...take care of business," she called back huskily, feeling her already heated face get even hotter.

She headed for the woods, having no intention of returning. At least not today. She'd get Bill to give Walker some excuse about Chet being sick....

Before she'd gotten five feet from the creek a wet hand gripped her shoulder, forcing her to stop short.

"I...uh...don't feel too good," Chelsea muttered, attempting a step forward only to find Walker's grip tighten on her shoulder, forcing her to remain.

Before she could come up with another excuse, Walker plucked off her hat, tossing it to the ground, releasing her damp hair to tumble down around her shoulders. She turned to find Walker grinning broadly.

"You knew it was me the whole time, didn't you, Walker Jordan?" she said between clenched teeth.

"You just thought you'd humiliate me for your own amusement."

"I'd say this was another one of those awkward situations, *Chet*."

His grin disappeared and he eyed her narrowly. "This was a pretty sneaky maneuver, Chelsea."

"And a pretty dumb one," she muttered. Further up the creek she could hear the other workers having a grand time skinny-dipping. She was grateful, at least, that Walker had kept on his shorts. Still, his bare chest, tanned, well-muscled and glistening from his dip in the creek was definitely distracting.

"Somehow, I can't picture Harry Newell falling for your impersonation."

"I talked his partner, Bill Laird, into it," she admitted.

"I guess you could talk a guy into *almost* anything, Chelsea." He sighed.

"You aren't going to let this business drop, are you?" There was a distinct edge of frustration in Walker's voice.

"No," she said firmly. "It's too important."

"To the town of Corbet."

"To me," she admitted. "Mostly, it's too important to me."

"Because you feel you've got to prove something to the people in this town? That's a big part of it, isn't it, Chelsea?"

"Maybe out in L.A. it's glamorous to be a woman with a past. Not here in Corbet. Sure, all the whispering eventually dies down, but people always remember, Walker. You can see it in their eyes."

"It wasn't your past, Chelsea. You just got caught in the terrible cross fire your parents set off."

"Let's not start that again."

"Okay, let's not start anything again, Chelsea."

"Fine. That's fine with me, Walker."

"Well, did you find what you were looking for?"

"No."

"I guess you were disappointed we started with the garden instead of the corn fields closer to the creek."

"Look, Walker, I don't see what you've got to gripe about. I did my job, the same as everyone else."

"I suppose you know that if you did take anything from property that didn't belong to you that would be theft. You could be arrested, tried..."

She gave him a hard, cold look. "And would you defend a thief, Walker? Or do you only defend ex-lovers who are embezzlers?"

Walker glared at her, but he finally decided that the past was the past, and that no good could come of digging around in it. "As of now, Chet, you're fired."

"Damn it, Walker, you have no grounds for firing me. I'm doing the same job as everyone else. And if I do *accidently* dig anything up..."

"No, on second thought..." Walker said meditatively and then stopped.

For the briefest moment Chelsea thought he might relent. She should have known better. The next moment, she found herself being scooped up once again into Walker's arms. But this time he wasn't nearly as gentle about it.

Her protest sailed through the air as Walker pitched her unceremoniously into the center of the brook.

She came up, spewing water, cursing and ready for a fight.

Walker grinned at her from the bank. "Now, you're fired," he said.

"The hell I'm fired. I quit," she shouted back. Then she struggled to shore in her drenched clothes, eager to get home where she could get them off.

Chapter Five

"Of course, Jim and I usually go down to Concord, Massachusetts, for the July fourth festivities. The kids love the way the townsfolk dress up like Minute Men and British soldiers and reenact the famous Revolutionary War battle," Norma Lund, Corbet's third-grade teacher and newest Historical Society member, said. "And it's so educational."

Chelsea had been counting on Norma to help run the society's annual house and garden tour for the Fourth. But, she had to admit her project seemed dull in comparison to the excitement of a recreation of a famous military battle and all the hoopla that went along with it.

"Crass commercialism," Graham Sawyer, original owner of Sawyer General Store, muttered. Sawyer, long retired, spent his days tending a garden behind the general store now run by his two sons. Sawyer was a crusty old gent with a heart of gold. Unfortunately for Chelsea, he was also a dyed-in-the-wool conservative when it came to any changes in the town.

A couple of months ago, when Chelsea had suggested that the members of the Historical Society chip in and purchase the old Fremont Property and move the Historical Society's offices out there, Graham Sawyer drummed up enough opposition to the idea to kill its chances. He knew, as did everyone else in Corbet, that once Chelsea had permanent access to the Fremont property she wouldn't quit until she'd found proof for her theory about the Revolutionary War battle at Corbet. The very idea that Corbet might turn into another Concord made Graham Sawyer and his cronies shiver in alarm.

"If you want my opinion, Chelsea," declared Nan Prescott Green, "another house and garden tour seems rather...dull."

"What did you say? Bull?" Nan's older sister, Dot Prescott exclaimed.

"Dull. I said dull," Nan shouted. "Will you turn on your hearing aid for once," she said, exasperated.

"I hear you perfectly well, thank you," Dot said archly. "And I see nothing dull about our annual house and garden tours."

"We do it every year," Nan argued. "Wouldn't it be fun to have a big parade...?"

"They have a parade over in Clarendon. Anyone here wants a parade all they need to do is drive ten minutes."

"I don't see why we can't have our own parade," Nan persisted.

"I'll tell you why. They're noisy, more bother than they're worth, they clog up the streets, and afterward there's rubbish strewn everywhere from the crowds," Dot retorted. Then narrowing her eyes at her younger sister she added, "And don't say bull."

Chelsea smiled faintly. She could always count on one of the Prescott sisters' support. Just as she could always be certain of the other's opposition, whatever the issue. The two sisters' disagreements had little to do with the issue at hand. They simply disagreed with each other as a matter of principle. Despite their bickering, they were close as two peas in a pod. When Nan, the younger Prescott sister, married forty-seven years ago, she and her husband, Vern, moved up to Rutland, but after two months of "city" life, Nan had insisted on returning to Corbet. They purchased the Godfrey house right next door to the house that had been home to the Prescotts for four generations, and the two sisters hadn't been more than a house apart since that day. They also hadn't stopped bickering since that day.

"I'd be more than happy to offer my home and garden once again for your tour," Dot offered with one last snicker in her sister's direction.

"Thanks," Chelsea said, darkening the check mark she'd already made next to Dot's name on her list.

"I must say," Isabelle Alpert said, "that I was rather distressed last year by how many visitors paid no attention at all to the marked paths around my garden. I think we should definitely limit the number of tickets we sell."

Besides being on the board of the Historical Society, Isabelle Alpert was the head of the Corbet Natural Resources Council, a local environmental protection agency. She was especially concerned with the preservation of rare wildflowers and wildlife. Needless to say, she had been one of the first to join forces with Graham Sawyer when Chelsea wanted to get her hands on the Fremont property and dig it up.

"Tell me, Chelsea," Alice Wilson, the pretty blond loan officer at the Upper Valley Bank, spoke up. "Is the Fremont estate on your list? I must say that Walker Jordan's new flower gardens are really something."

Chelsea swallowed a smart-ass reply. Ever since Walker had dumped her into the creek and fired her from his landscaping crew, she'd refused to have anything to do with him, his house or his gardens.

"Yes, his gardens are wonderful," Isabelle agreed enthusiastically, a distinct glint lighting up the thirty-four-year-old divorcee's blue eyes.

Isabelle, normally distrustful of "city slickers" whom she felt had a total disregard and disrespect for nature, was nevertheless charmed by Walker's enthusiastic restoration plans, and by his solemn pledge to see to it that the valuable wildflowers on his property were protected and nurtured by his landscaping crew— now minus one hand. Much to Isabelle's delight, as well as enriching her romantic fantasies, Walker had even joined her preservation group. When it came to turning on the charm, Walker had few equals.

"Oh, have you seen Walker's new beds, too?" There was a pouty quality to Alice Wilson's voice as she cast Isabelle a jealous glance.

"Visiting a man's bed?" Dot Prescott, who wore her hearing aid but refused to turn it on because, as she'd say with perfect logic, it wore the batteries down, gave both Isabelle and Alice sharp, disapproving looks.

"Not his bed," Nan snickered beside her sister, "his beds."

"Yup, from the rumors I hear about the fellow, he needs more than one bed," Graham Sawyer said with a laugh.

"What rumors?" Norma Lund asked eagerly. When it came to passing on rumors, she was right up there with the best of them.

"Well, he comes from Hollywood." Graham stretched it out so it sounded more like Haaaa Leeee Woooood.

"He does not come from Hollywood. He comes from an altogether different part of Los Angeles," Chelsea corrected.

All eyes turned to Chelsea and she could feel her cheeks heat up. "It's not the same thing," she finished lamely.

"I was only ribbing," Graham said with a little wink in Chelsea's direction. "So, is your old friend opening his house and gardens for your tour?"

"He isn't my old friend, Graham. And, no, he isn't on my list."

"Well, of course, his house won't be in any condition to show," Isabelle pointed out. "He'll be in the midst of the restoration all summer, but his gardens. You simply must have him on the list for the garden tour, Chelsea. I'm certain I can count on Walker to see to it that people don't stray from the walking paths. Why, he's almost as fanatic about protecting his property from damage as I am."

Tell me about it, Chelsea thought grumpily.

"I'm heading out to Walker's place after we finish up here," Alice said with a guileless smile. "Why don't I ask him if he'd be agreeable to showing his gardens?"

Chelsea surreptitiously checked her watch. It was already nine o'clock. Awfully late at night for a neighborly call. And far too dark to admire Walker's *flower* beds!

CHELSEA WATCHED Alice Wilson hurry out of the meeting at the Historical Society for what she'd clearly hinted was an assignation with the newest and most eligible bachelor in town, Walker Jordan. Walker's offhanded remark to Lucy Bedell, the town manager's clerk, weeks earlier about looking to settle down, find himself a wife and have a bunch of kids, had quickly filtered through the town. Within days—no, probably hours—most of the marriageable women in Corbet were figuring out a strategy for getting acquainted with Walker.

Alice Wilson had an advantage, having been the loan officer who'd approved his mortgage. Since then, she'd found endless reasons for getting in touch with Walker or needing to confer with him in person.

Not that Alice had the only advantage. Isabelle Alpert, one of Alice's notorious rivals when it came to courting eligible bachelors in town, had been the one to track down the original Fremont estate house plans in the Historical Society's files for Walker. And she'd made it clear on numerous occasions, that she'd be more than happy to assist him in any way she could, with the restoration of the house or with anything else he might need help with.

Contrary to Chelsea's predictions, Walker's reception in Corbet, at least among the eligible female segment of the population, had been very warm, indeed.

Isabelle stood beside Chelsea outside the town offices as Alice zipped out of the parking lot in her Toyota.

"I'm surprised she didn't burn rubber," Isabelle muttered snidely.

"Maybe Walker's taking out a second mortgage or something to finance the restoration." Chelsea was embarrassed by how naive her remark sounded even as she said it.

True to form, Isabelle laughed dryly. "You know him better than anyone else in Corbet, Chelsea. Do you honestly think Alice Wilson stands a chance with an urbane man like Walker Jordan?"

"A chance?"

Chelsea echoed the words so low, Isabelle heard them as a statement rather than a question.

"Oh, I suppose even a man like Walker might be taken in initially by Alice's simperingly seductive style," Isabelle conceded. "But can it last?"

This time Chelsea was saved from having to make any response at all. Isabelle was warming to her topic.

"If Walker is looking for a long-term relationship—a wife—he's not going to settle for someone like Alice. At the very most, Alice will be a diversion," Isabelle persisted. "Not that I know him all that well yet, but it's obvious just talking with Walker that for anything lasting he needs a woman who's sharp, independent, intensely committed to the environment, to saving our planet..."

"Our planet?" Chelsea gave Isabelle an incredulous look. "I don't think Walker is thinking much beyond Corbet. At the moment, anyway."

"We have to crawl before we can walk, Chelsea. Walker understands our preservation council's philosophy perfectly. By preserving the land in our own small town, we are crawling—"

Chelsea couldn't help laughing. "You definitely don't know Walker all that well, Isabelle, or you'd know he never crawls. *Tromps,* is more like it."

Isabelle laughed back. "But I bet when he tromps, he does it gracefully. I wonder how he dances. I bet he doesn't step on his partner's toes, does he, Chelsea?"

"We haven't danced together in years, Isabelle."

Isabelle gave Chelsea's shoulder a little squeeze. "But he was a great dancer even then, I bet. And I'm sure he's gotten even better with age."

"I wouldn't know."

"Well, I'll test him out at the July fourth dance over at the Norton Farm," Isabelle said, "and give you an update. Assuming you won't be taking him out for a test run yourself," she added slyly before heading for her car.

CHELSEA WAS SURPRISED when she returned home from the Historical Society to find Walker sitting on her front porch, chatting amiably with Ned Hunt.

Chelsea couldn't resist an inward smile at the thought of Alice Wilson coming up empty-handed. Nor could she completely ignore the little rush of arousal she felt at seeing Walker there. Not that she was about to give Walker Jordan even the slightest hint of it. Anyway, being aroused was a strictly physical response, she told herself firmly. Purely Pavlovian. Not, of course, that she was actually salivating!

As Chelsea climbed the steps of the porch, she deliberately avoided any extended eye contact with Walker. Walker, on the other hand, clearly used to confronting hostile witnesses on the witness stand, studied Chelsea quite openly and unabashedly. He immediately recognized the squared shoulders, the stern set of the facial features, the defensive stance. When Chelsea made up her mind to be unapproachable, she was quite effective. That hadn't changed about her, either.

"You missed a rousing meeting, Ned," Chelsea said, injecting a false cheeriness in her voice. She gave Walker the briefest and coolest of nods.

"Sorry about the meeting. Had to show a couple the Bellows' place," Ned said laconically. "Came up from New Jersey and only had this evening to give the property a final check," he explained, offering no explanation, however, as to what he and Walker Jordan were doing conversing on her porch at this late hour.

"Then we had to go back to the office and sign the purchase and sale agreement," Ned went on with his explanation.

"Uh-oh. Two more flatlanders added to Corbet's roster," Walker murmured drolly.

Chelsea merely cast Walker a wry glance, then turned her attentions back to Ned. "We've pretty much finalized our July fourth plans."

"Oh right, a house and garden tour, isn't it?" Walker broke in.

"Yep, Chelsea organizes one each year on July fourth—"

"I'm sure either Alice Wilson or Isabelle Alpert has told Walker all about our annual July fourth tour," Chelsea said, cutting him off.

Walker gave Chelsea an amused look. "Both of them, as a matter of fact."

"You oughtta show your gardens, Walker," Ned said. "Surprised neither of those ladies signed you up yet."

Chelsea's mouth tightened. "I believe Walker's gardens did come up as a possibility during the meeting tonight."

"I'd love to offer my gardens," Walker said, his tone fairly brimming over with generosity. Chelsea looked ready to punch him.

Ned only contributed to Chelsea's irritability by chuckling, rising abruptly and announcing that he'd be sashaying along.

Chelsea's irritability, however, quickly gave way to anxiety as Ned started down the porch steps. Being alone with Walker had proved too unsettling for her on too many occasions since his return. Frustration, anger and arousal coupled with sweet, naive memories kept her constantly off balance around the man. The effect was dizzying and distressing.

"What's your hurry, Ned?" she called out, embarrassed by the note of panic that had crept into her voice, despite her best efforts.

"It's getting late. And I'm getting old," Ned called back with a laugh. "Anyway, I was just passing by when I saw Walker rocking away all by his lonesome up on your porch. I was just baby-sittin' him until you got home."

"Thanks, Ned," Walker said with a cheery wave. He, too, rose, but instead of following his "baby-sitter" down the steps he followed Chelsea to her front door.

"It's late, Walker," she said churlishly, opening the door.

"And if it were early?" Walker queried, his flat hand keeping her front door pressed open even as she stepped inside the house, clearly determined to shut the door in his face.

"It would still be late," she retorted coolly.

He stretched out his free hand. For a moment Chelsea thought he was going to grab hold of her. Instead he flicked his fingers a fraction of an inch above her shoulder.

Chelsea gave him a bewildered look. "What was that all about?"

"I was just wondering if that chip on your shoulder ever budged."

"Very funny, Walker."

"I didn't mean to be funny, Chelsea."

"I know."

Their eyes met and held. Chelsea sensed that Walker was seeing not only her recent anger and frustration at him, but all of the bitterness and resentment she'd carried for years, most of which had nothing to do with him. It disturbed her that Walker had this way of making her feel so vulnerable. She prided herself on giving everyone around her the illusion that she was above old hurts. Only the people closest to her, Ned Hunt and her girlhood friend, Julie Martin, knew that she was a woman who could not easily forget or forgive. Or let go.

"I brought you a peace offering," he said, breaking the tense silence.

Chelsea gave him a wary look. "Don't tell me. An olive branch."

"I haven't planted my olive grove yet," Walker said. His smile was full of charm; sexy, tempting. So was the scent of his lemony after-shave, and the seductive way a single lock of his dark hair fell in a curve across his forehead. Chelsea could feel her wariness slipping like a loose gear. But she couldn't quite shift into neutral.

"Didn't you have a date tonight, Walker? Or do you think the women of Corbet are so desperate you can treat them—"

"Whoa," Walker cut her off. "Where did that come from?"

"Poor Alice is probably—"

"Poor Alice who? Is probably what?"

"Poor Alice Wilson, that's who. So, you did forget."

"I happen to have a memory like an elephant, Chelsea. When I make a date, I remember it. And I keep it. If I say I'm going to call, I call. If I promise to write, I write. Even if I don't always do the greatest job of it."

Chelsea couldn't help wondering how it was that every time she made an offensive move against Walker, he always managed to put her on the defensive.

Walker studied her and sighed. "Look, I really didn't come over here to hash up the past, Chelsea. Actually I'm trying my damnedest to put the past behind me, start over..."

"That's exactly what I'm trying to do, too, Walker. Start over, move on."

He studied her for a long moment. "Could we begin by moving on into the house? It isn't really all that late, Chelsea."

"Weren't you the guy who used to complain that the biggest drag about Corbet was that we pulled the sidewalks up at 10:00 p.m.?"

Walker made great ceremony out of studying his watch. "It's only nine fifty-five."

"What about Alice Wilson?" Chelsea persisted.

"Poor Alice Wilson?"

"You didn't know she was coming out to see you tonight?"

He shook his head, his smile becoming a broad grin.

After a moment's hesitation, Chelsea stepped aside and let him enter her house. Okay, so his grin was even more winning than his smile.

He walked into the living room. Chelsea followed him in and switched on the light. Like last time, Walker did a survey of the room. Only this time he didn't comment on the books, or the fireplace, or the floorboards. Instead he said, "I have some fond memories of this room."

Chelsea couldn't help smiling. "I don't think you ever saw this room in the light, Walker."

He turned to her, still grinning. "That's why the memories are so fond." He sat down on the flowered chintz-covered sofa.

Chelsea crossed the room and started opening the windows. "It's warm in here."

Actually it was cool enough for Walker to be comfortable in his light linen jacket. "I remember it being much warmer," he teased.

She heard him chuckle and turned to face him. "I thought we were moving on, starting fresh."

"First, one piece of history..."

"Walker—" she started to protest.

"Not our history. I'm talking about my peace offering." He patted the cushion beside him. "Something I found up in the attic that I thought might interest you."

Chelsea hesitated. History? Something he found in the Fremont attic? This time she felt a rush, not of arousal, but of anticipation. It increased as Walker carefully pulled out an envelope from his inside jacket pocket.

"What...is it?"

"Come and have a look for yourself," Walker said, enticing her by raising the envelope in the air.

Chelsea came over to the sofa and sat down beside him. With mock ceremony, he handed her the envelope.

Gingerly, nervously, she opened it. The envelope itself was quite new, one of those functional white business-size varieties. But the sheet of stationery inside the envelope was neither new or functional. It was a very old folded piece of parchment paper—a letter.

"I found it stuck to the bottom of an old, empty trunk," Walker said, watching Chelsea unfold the paper with utmost care and study the faded, flowery script.

"It looks very old," Walker pointed out. "I thought you'd be interested . . . even though it's got nothing to do with any Revolutionary War battles as far as I can tell. Actually it's kind of hard to make most of the words out."

"It's a . . . love letter," Chelsea said, her breath catching.

"Yes." He watched her face as she studied the letter closely. There was heightened color in her cheeks. He felt a rush of pleasure. And then, almost immediately, his mouth went dry and he wondered whether it was really *peace* he'd come to offer Chelsea.

Chelsea looked over at Walker. Her face was glowing with excitement. "It's from Abigail Fremont. She was Harmon Fremont's daughter."

Walker smiled. "Our Green Mountain Boy."

"Oh Walker, this is incredible. Do you realize how incredible it is?"

Walker looked down at the heading of the letter, which along with the signature, was the most legible. "Don't tell me. 'My dearest and most beloved' is none other than George Washington himself. Maybe they fell in love while Washington was sleeping in the Fremont house."

Chelsea laughed. "Oh Walker, not Washington. Henry Cotton. And Abigail didn't fall in love with him in Corbet. She fell in love with him in England, while she was in finishing school as a girl.''

Walker had still not gotten around to reading any of the books on local history he'd taken out of the library. The name Henry Cotton didn't ring a bell.

"Abigail Fremont and Henry Cotton were star-crossed lovers. Everyone in Corbet knows the story.'' Chelsea said, seeing Walker's blank look. As she spoke she rose from the sofa, carefully carrying the letter to her desk where she secured it within a specially treated plastic folder.

"Not everyone,'' Walker pointed out.

Chelsea stared down at the letter. "Oh, Walker, this really is a wonderful find.''

"As good as a musket?'' The teasing remark was a mistake. He knew it from the way Chelsea's shoulders stiffened and her jaw locked. He quickly changed the topic. "So tell me the story of our star-crossed lovers.''

Chelsea hesitated, then finally relented. After all, Walker had brought her the letter. "Well, a lot of the story is more myth than fact at this point. We do have some documents, however, verifying that Harmon's daughter, Abigail, did become officially engaged to British army officer, Henry Cotton.''

Walker raised an eyebrow. "Scandalous,'' he said wryly.

"Oh, there was scandal all right. And even two hundred odd years ago, this town thrived on scandal, rumor, gossip,'' Chelsea said, her voice dropping a notch.

"Because the daughter of a Green Mountain Boy got engaged to a British soldier?'' Walker asked softly, tugging her thoughts away from the more recent scandal.

"No," she said with a small smile. "They got engaged before the war broke out. After the war for independence started, Harmon Fremont wasted no time in seeing to it that his daughter's engagement to Cotton was broken off. A couple of the letters we've acquired, that Harmon wrote to his sister confirmed as much."

Chelsea looked back down at the letter and again her face lit up. "And now we have this document, the first in Abigail's own hand. She must have written this heartfelt note to Henry shortly after her father called off the wedding."

She leaned closer to the letter, examining it through the clear plastic. "Listen to this. 'I pray mightily that our days of affliction will soon have an end.' And then later, near the end—" Chelsea paused, squinting to make out the faded words "—'I long for the time when I may see thy dear face again.'"

"Do you think papa Fremont found the letter and confiscated it?" Walker wondered.

"That would explain what it was doing up in the Fremont attic."

"So, what was the scandal about?" he asked, his curiosity piqued.

"The rest of the story is mostly myth, Walker," Chelsea cautioned, "but supposedly Henry was part of Burgoyne's regiment. Burgoyne was in command of the British Army in Canada. Anyway, the story goes that Henry went AWOL and snuck down to Corbet for an assignation with Abigail. According to the story, the two of them were...um..."

"Caught in the act?"

"By a neighbor."

Walker tsked.

"That's right. Make light of it, Walker. But how do you think the town must have treated poor Abigail after she was caught...cavorting with the enemy? She must have been taunted, shunned, treated like an outcast. People probably passed her in the street and looked right through her. Even her own father—" Chelsea stopped abruptly, aware that she was getting worked up.

Walker crossed the room and stood in front of Chelsea. "What were you going to say?" he murmured tenderly. "That he probably drowned his shame in booze just like your—"

"Shut up, Walker."

Walker saw the lines of pain pinch Chelsea's face. Instinctively he reached out for her.

"No, don't," she protested. "You don't have the vaguest idea what it's like to be laughed at, pointed at, whispered about, pitied..."

"Don't I? You think you're the only one who has ever endured ridicule? You think that only happens in small towns? Well, let me tell you something, sweetheart, there are plenty enough small minds in big towns, too. Small, jealous, ugly minds."

Chelsea was brought up short by Walker's outburst. This was the first time she'd ever heard so much raw emotion in his voice. Where, she wondered, had all that come from? A bad case of *cherchez la femme?*

Walker was a bit shaken by his outburst himself. And here he'd been patting himself on the back about having successfully put his own past history behind him.

Chapter Six

A storm was brewing. The pine trees spit like surf in the gusts of wind. Walker could feel the old house rumble. His old house. He smiled to himself, finding the rumbling, creaking sounds oddly comforting, a welcome relief from the clanking and banging of electric saws, hammers and drills that had gone on all week. How wonderful that it was Sunday.

Funny, he'd always hated Sunday in the past, feeling that this supposed day of rest held him trapped in a kind of limbo. Oh, not that it was ever really a day of rest for him in the literal sense. There had always been plenty of work to do—reviewing briefs, studying corporate updates, negotiating deals out on the golf course.

But that was all behind him now. His old life. Old games. The wheeling and dealing, clinging to that competitive edge, the restlessness, the tension, the fear of ridicule. He had become an expert at deception while living in L.A., hiding brilliantly behind a sardonic, lighthearted, almost careless air of self-confidence. He'd always firmly believed it was too great a survival tool to tamper with. Now, a young

woman more like him than she would probably ever
know, had shaken that belief.

Last night, at Chelsea's place, Walker had come
close to losing his cool self-control. What was even
more unnerving, a part of him had been tempted to just
open up, talk about some of the demons in his past,
come to terms with them. While neither of them had
admitted it openly, Walker was discovering that both
he and Chelsea were being held captive by their pasts.

Walker shrugged off his glum thoughts. This was,
after all, Sunday in Corbet, not L.A. He had no briefs
to study, no business golf games, no obligatory ap-
pearances at tedious social functions, no need to don
a mask of deception. He was free, at one with nature
and with himself. His time was his own. And he was
not about to ruin the day by dwelling on the past.

Grabbing up his windbreaker, Walker headed for the
front door. It had started to rain, but the real storm was
still edging over the hills. He figured it would be a while
in coming yet.

Walker spent some time each day playing "master of
all he surveyed," ambling over his property, but today
he had a particular destination in mind. He'd decided
to investigate the old barn that sat at the northeast edge
of his property in a field about a quarter of a mile from
his house.

When Ned Hunt had first shown Walker the Fremont estate that early April day, he'd pointed out that
the barn was even older than the house. And in far
worse shape.

"I never take clients inside. Too risky. Never know
when the whole darned thing's gonna collapse. The
front of it isn't too bad, but rot's got to the whole back

loft section where the hay used to be stored,'' Ned had said. ''And the roof leaks something awful.''

Walker, viewing the barn from a distance in the field, had shrugged off-handedly. ''Probably the best thing would be to have it torn down. Maybe I could use some of the barn board . . .''

''You can't tear it down,'' Ned had exclaimed.

''Why not? If I buy the property, that is?'' Walker had amended, not wanting the Realtor to think he was an easy mark. Which, of course, he was, knowing even then that he would take the place even if he couldn't bargain down the price.

Ned had grinned. He'd been in the business too long not to know when he had a solid bite. ''You can't tear the barn down even if you do buy it, Mr. Jordan. This here barn is a pre-Revolutionary War antique. And, unlike the house, it hasn't been tampered with. Meaning it's still in its pure state.''

''Its rotting pure state,'' Walker reminded the Realtor.

''True. And, like I say, one of these days it might collapse. Although, with a fair investment, and a very skilled restoration crew, maybe the collapse could be forestalled for another two hundred odd years. Of course, any restoration plans would have to be approved by a special town board—the same one that designated this here barn an historic landmark, it being one of the oldest standing structures here in Corbet.''

''What about the house?'' Walker had asked.

Ned had tsked. ''Pity about the house. After the last Fremont died in the nineteen thirties, the property stayed empty for about five years and fell into disrepair. Then, after the depression, a pair of sisters bought the place and opened a boarding school. This was a good twenty years before the town began actively trying to preserve and protect its historic landmarks. No reflection on the two sisters,'' Ned said with a twinkle in his eye. ''I almost married one of 'em. But they were more concerned with providing space for their girls than they were with maintaining the integrity of that fine pre-Revolutionary War home.''

''Meaning that rather functional addition off the rear of the house?'' Walker had asked.

''Now, talk about tearing something down...''

''So, I'd be free to do whatever I wanted with the house itself?'' Walker had checked.

''If you bought it,'' Ned had responded with a quick smile.

Walker had known from that moment on that what he wanted to do more than anything else was restore the Fremont house to its original pristine state. Make it worthy of a landmark designation.

As for the barn, in truth Walker had pretty much forgotten all about it. Until last night at Chelsea's place. For some inexplicable reason, after hearing Chelsea recount the story of Abigail Fremont and Henry Cotton, Walker had started thinking about the old barn. And not just thinking about it in general. He'd gotten it into his head that the barn was where Abigail and Henry, the two star-crossed Revolutionary War lovers, had met for their last romantic rendezvous. And where they'd been found out.

Walker smiled, remembering the faint rosy hue that had come to Chelsea's cheeks when she'd mentioned the lovers' exposure. He wondered if she'd remembered the time, sixteen summers back, when they'd been caught necking in the woods by a local lumberer. Chelsea had turned scarlet then with embarrassment and Walker had teased her until she'd pointed out his coloring had deepened a few shades, too.

Walker was about fifty yards from the barn when the storm hit. A real nor'easter, pouring across the landscape with stunning ferocity. Pushing aside Ned Hunt's warning about the integrity of the structure, he ran for cover into the barn. After withstanding two hundred odd years of storms, Walker figured the odds were in his favor that it would withstand one more.

Getting the barn door to slide open even a few inches was no easy feat, and by the time Walker squeezed through the narrow opening he was soaked to the skin. And the barn wasn't exactly the greatest shelter from the storm. There was water leaking through dozens of holes and gaps in the roof. Still, there were dry spots and despite the obvious decay and the dankness, Walker had the exhilarating sensation of stepping back in time.

For a few minutes, as he roamed around the barn, Walker found himself imagining the lovers' meeting—the British soldier and his young Colonial miss sneaking through the barn door, which no doubt opened more easily then, and climbing up the ladder, which was no longer there, to the hayloft to be out of sight—or so they'd thought.

Walker felt the urge to get a better look at the loft. Who knew? Maybe tucked away under an old board was some relic that would lend credence to his fantasy of a Revolutionary War lovers' assignation. Wouldn't Chelsea's face light up then, he thought, smiling to himself, not wanting to question why the idea of pleasing Chelsea gave him so much pleasure.

Walker gathered up three ancient-looking discarded crates, which he stacked and climbed. He flirted with disaster when the bottom crate started to collapse under his weight, but he managed to grab on to the ledge of the hayloft and haul himself the rest of the way up. It was comforting that little of his old athleticism had gone to ruin on the golf course. Could old Henry Cotton have done as well?

A faint scent of hay still clung to the rafters up there. Walker began aimlessly checking around the loft, idly looking in corners, feeling for loose hideaway floorboards, continuing to cast his imagination back in time to that fateful love scene. He even found himself giving the lovers, Abigail and Henry, faces. Only the faces weren't invented. They were quite familiar. His own face. And Chelsea's.

He was just thinking to himself that this was an excellent way to spend a Sunday, all right, when he heard a weird, crackling sound. At first he thought it was the sound of the storm itself. As he turned around, he realized that he was wrong. He saw the massive beam just as it came crashing down. The giant timber and Walker thudded to the floor of the loft in unison.

The ancient loft groaned and shook. Now that it was too late, Walker remembered Ned Hunt's remark about the hayloft being the most precarious section of the barn. It didn't seem to be collapsing, but Walker found little consolation in that fact as he realized that the enormous post was pinning his left calf and ankle.

Walker tried to assess the damage. He couldn't tell if anything was actually broken, but his ankle throbbed painfully. He struggled to a sitting position and tried to slip his leg out from under the post. The result was immense pain and no gain. Next, he concentrated his efforts on trying to lift the weighty hand-split oak timber high enough to allow him to pull his injured leg out.

No luck. He couldn't get any useful leverage. The post wouldn't budge. And that wasn't Walker's only problem. The stability of the loft area, now minus one crucial supporting post, had taken a distinct turn for the worse. The whole loft trembled with each gale. Suddenly it seemed likely the barn had met one storm too many.

Walker, already soaked from the rain, broke out into a cold sweat as he labored to free himself. But all his maneuvering proved fruitless and served only to make the pain in his ankle close to unbearable.

He lay back, trying to catch his breath and build up his strength. He prayed that his barn would remain a historic landmark and not collapse into a pile of rubble, at least until after he'd made his escape.

He took in deep, steadying breaths, ignoring the raindrops from the leaky roof falling in loud plops on and around him. He was lying there, reflecting ruefully on how just a short while earlier he'd been relishing his opportunity to be one with nature, in touch with the elements, when he heard a new sound amid the rumble and roar of wind and rain. A rustling sound inside the barn.

An animal, Walker guessed, seeking shelter from the storm. Little did the animal know.

When the sound was almost directly under him, Walker felt a shiver of panic. What if it was a mountain lion or a bear? With those two damn crates that were still stacked up and intact, an animal could easily make its way up to the loft. Walker swallowed hard. And what better way for it to pass the time of day during a raging storm than a nice meaty dinner!

He tried to calm his jagged nerves by telling himself it was probably just a jackrabbit or a field mouse. Then he heard the distinct creaking of the crates as some creature a lot heavier than a jackrabbit climbed on them. His breath caught as something covered in dark fur edged up over the loft platform.

Then, to his relief, he saw that it wasn't fur at all, but hair. Shiny, wet chestnut hair. A moment later two lavender eyes appeared.

"Walker?" Chelsea gasped, so surprised to find him sitting up there she almost lost her precarious balance atop the crates.

"Hi," he croaked, trying mightily not to appear as foolish as he felt.

"What are you doing up here?"

"Nothing much at the moment," he muttered, wincing in pain.

Chelsea, on tiptoe now, her eyes adjusting to the dim light, gasped as she saw the massive timber across his leg. "Walker... Oh, God, Walker."

Before Walker could say anything, her head disappeared.

"Chelsea? Chelsea, where'd you go?" he called out anxiously.

"It's okay, Walker. I've just got to get something. Hold on. Just hold on."

"Well, don't worry," he called back acerbically, "I couldn't go anywhere even if I wanted to."

It was probably less than five minutes later but it felt like hours to Walker before Chelsea popped back into view.

"How ya doing?" she asked gently.

"Better now," he said with a smile. Actually it wasn't just seeing her return that had improved his spirits. His ankle had started to go numb, and while he wasn't sure that was a good sign, it was a relief not to feel the throbbing pain.

He watched as a coil of rope landed on the loft floor. Throwing the rope up was no sweat. Getting Chelsea up to the loft was another matter altogether. Standing on her tiptoes on the crates she just barely came up eye-level with the floor. And there were no more crates in sight, or Walker would have used them to get up there himself.

"Chelsea, you better go get help."

"Grab on to one end of the rope Walker, and toss down the rest of it.

"Chelsea . . ."

"I just need a little lift, Walker. Or, can't you manage it?" she asked with concern.

"It's not that. I'm just not sure this loft can support the two of us."

"Worry about what is, Walker, not what if. Come on. Just a few inches and I can pull myself up the rest of the way."

Walker frowned, but tossed her one end of the rope and gripped the other end tightly. Compared to trying to lever that fallen timber, helping Chelsea up was like tugging a feather. Once he got her up waist-level, she was able, with athletic ease, to hoist herself up and over with no further help.

Nor did she waste any time in setting to work. After a quick assessment of the damage, she tied one end of the rope around the end of the fallen post and then, with a quick prayer, chose the sturdiest looking overhead beam and tossed the other end of the rope over it. Walker marveled at her quick, confident movements. She might have been used to rescuing foolish flatlanders every day after breakfast!

She deftly looped and tied the loose end of the rope around the post, noting with chagrin that the other end of her makeshift pulley wasn't long enough to reach Walker's hands. She'd have to manage the lifting herself. Shrugging the problem off she hurried over to Walker, kneeling down by his pinned leg.

Gingerly, she lifted the narrow cuff of his trouser to examine his ankle. It was badly swollen.

"Be gentle with me, darling," he quipped.

"Really, Walker, I thought you'd given up the glib routine." But when she saw the swollen blue-veined ankle which she feared was broken, she regretted her snappy rejoinder.

"How's it look?"

"Not . . . too bad," she lied, tucking the cuff of his chinos back over the worst of it, not wanting Walker to add more worries to his list.

Not that she didn't have plenty to worry about herself. The loft was trembling disturbingly. And getting that timber off Walker was going to be no mean feat. Then there was still the small matter of getting Walker down from the loft and out of the barn. . . .

Taking her own advice to stick to the worry at hand, she rose quickly and gave Walker a confident smile. "Okay, let's get this thing off you. Do you think you can pull your leg out of the way when I get 'er lifted a few inches?"

"I'll do my best," he quipped.

Chelsea winked. "Me too."

Reaching up, she grabbed the rope and tugged for all she was worth. Her first half dozen attempts failed miserably. The palms of her hands were soon red and sore and she had to stop to catch her breath. Pushing her long dark hair away from her face, she tried to dispel her anxiety by giving Walker a winning smile. "Next try."

Before her words were out, there was an explosive crack of thunder almost directly overhead. The whole barn quaked. Chelsea could feel her heart thumping.

"Chelsea..."

Her response was an involuntary scream as another rotting timber crashed down only a few inches behind her.

"Get out, Chelsea," Walker barked.

"No." She eyed him defiantly as she gripped the rope, twining it round her hand and wrist for more leverage.

"Go on, damn it. Get help..."

But they both knew the odds were that by the time she brought someone back with her, the barn would have collapsed on top of Walker. She couldn't leave him.

"Chelsea, damn it. Don't play hero."

"It's heroine, Walker. Now shut up and concentrate. Try pulling down on my belt while I pull down on the rope. One, two, three."

Using every ounce of strength they both could muster, they heaved. And heaved. Chelsea let her knees buckle to maximize the effect of Walker's strength. That made a difference. Their desperate tug-of-war rope pull finally made headway.

The timber started to lift. An inch. "Just...a drop...more," Walker gasped.

With grim determination, Chelsea tried for another inch.

"Al...most, baby. Almost." Walker's voice was a bare cracked whisper as new stabbing pains shot up his leg.

Chelsea's hands and wrists felt as if they were being rubbed raw now, and every muscle in her body cried out from the strain. The violent wind had blown open the weakly hinged hayloft door, allowing the gusty rain to rage in on them.

Biting back searing pain, Walker tugged furiously on Chelsea as he strained at the same time to reposition his body so he could turn his foot sideways and slide it out from under the timber.

Chelsea watched Walker's maneuvers anxiously as she kept pulling with all her might. She could feel panic rise up like bile in her throat, not sure how much longer she could maintain her grip.

There was another flash of lightning and crack of thunder. The sound of Chelsea's shallow breaths was lost somewhere in the pounding fury of the storm. Her eyes weren't fixed on Walker now, but the post, as if willing it to lift some more.

If her strength gave way now, the impact of the post hitting Walker's leg again would certainly smash it for good. And smash any hope of them getting out of there before the barn came tumbling down. It was unthinkable. Her iron will redoubled her strength. "Now," she screamed over the tempest.

Will, physical strength, sheer fortitude, whatever it was, the post lifted that one extra bit that enabled Walker to shift his throbbing leg free.

Chelsea was so intent on her task, she wasn't even aware Walker had freed himself until he cried out for her to let go of the rope. Fortunately, even in her relief, she was smart enough not to let go too fast, and risk that being the last straw—or timber as it were—that would break the camel's back, or in this case topple the barn.

Walker gazed at her with tender admiration and gratitude. "You're one hell of a heroine, Chelsea Clark."

Chelsea's whole body shuddered with released tension. "You played your part, Walker," she said, unwinding the rope from her sore, chafed palms and wrists.

Chelsea hurried over to the edge of the loft, trying to figure out the best way to help Walker down to the barn floor. It was going to be more than a little tricky for him to manage a secure drop to the top crate on one leg.

Walker crawled over beside her and looked down.

"I guess the worst that can happen is I break my other leg in the fall," he muttered, giving Chelsea a grim smile.

"You can't do that, Walker. The July fourth dance is less than eight weeks away. And every eligible woman in Corbet is fighting to sign your dance card. With one good leg, I'm sure you could manage to sweep them all off their feet, but you break both legs and—"

"What about you?"

"What about me?"

"Are you fighting to sign my dance card?"

Chelsea shifted away as Walker's face drew closer to hers. The platform creaked, reminding them both that this was no time for seductive banter.

"Maybe you should get down and go hunt for a ladder?" Walker said, again anxious to at least see her safely out of the barn.

"No time, Walker."

She started to make a move but when Walker grabbed her wrist Chelsea let out a sharp cry of pain.

She tried to pull her arm away before Walker got a close look at the damage to her wrists and hands, but she didn't quite manage it.

"It's nothing," she protested, seeing the sharp look of concern on Walker's features.

Gently Walker shook his head. Then softly he said, "Climb down, Chelsea."

"But..."

"Go ahead. I'll help lower you."

"Walker..."

"Shut up." But he said the words with infinite tenderness.

Flat on his belly, he held onto her arms above her bruised, skinned wrists as she swung over the edge.

"Okay," she said, once she'd gained secure footing on the crates.

"Okay." But he waited an extra moment to make sure her balance was steady before releasing her.

She looked anxiously up at him as she climbed off the crates to the dirt floor of the barn. "Now what?"

"Now, steady the crates. I'm coming down."

"Walker, are you sure about this?"

"I have a plan."

Another crack of thunder shook the loft. Walker frowned, listening anxiously for the crash of more timbers.

He crawled to the timber that had pinned his leg, grabbed hold of the rope and pulled it down from the cross beam. Crawling back to the edge of the loft, he tossed the rope down. Giving it a good tug to assure himself it was still well secured to the post, he slipped over the edge of the loft and slid down the rope.

Once his good leg touched the top crate, Chelsea grabbed on to him to steady him. Walker let go of the rope, and gripping Chelsea's shoulders for balance, got down to the ground.

Their arms slipped around each other as he reached the floor. Neither was quick to let go, until they heard the crackling sound of another beam giving way.

Hobbling, his arm around Chelsea for support, the two of them made it safely out of the barn. Once outside, oblivious of the drumming rain, thankful to be in the wide open spaces, they embraced again. Walker laced his fingers through her wet hair. The pain in his ankle had numbed again and the only sensation he felt was strictly pleasurable.

The cold, wet air rushed against Chelsea's body as Walker's lips found hers. She kissed him back with greedy relief.

When they finally drew apart, Walker glanced back at the barn. "Do you think it'll survive the storm?" he asked.

Chelsea needed a moment to steady herself before answering. "I hope so."

"If it comes down it'll be kind of like putting Humpty Dumpty together again."

"You mean . . . you'd have it restored anyway?"

He grinned. "It's an historic landmark, Chelsea."

She laughed, then pointed to a brass plaque over the barn door. "I nailed that up myself, eight years ago."

Walker squinted, wiping the rain from his face. The plaque read Fremont Barn—Built by Harmon Fremont, 1743.

Walker's arms were still around Chelsea. They felt good there.

They felt good to Chelsea, too. Too good. That was a serious concern for her. The last thing in the world she wanted was to fall under Walker Jordan's spell all over again. Especially now that he was determined to go native and put down his roots in Corbet. She had places to go, heights to reach, her mark to make in the history books. Corbet might be Walker's paradise, but as far as Chelsea was concerned Corbet had absolutely nothing to offer her but bad memories and the chains of small-town tradition.

"Your...ankle. We'd better..."

"Right," Walker agreed.

"I left my car on the Burgess Road and made my way across the field on foot. I didn't think you'd appreciate tire tracks digging into your good earth..."

"I'd appreciate it now," Walker said with a faint smile.

Before she left for the car Chelsea helped Walker to sit on the ground. Just as she was starting to straighten up, Walker's hand on her arm stopped her.

"Say, what were you doing out here at the barn, anyway?"

Chelsea grinned. "You want to have me fined for trespassing, Walker? A minute ago I was a hero."

"Heroine," he corrected with a grin. "And I meant to say, how did you manage to show up just when I needed you?"

An enigmatic glow lit Chelsea's face. "You have Abigail Fremont and Henry Cotton to thank for that, Walker." And then, without further explanation, she kissed Walker lightly on the lips and hurried off for her car.

Chapter Seven

"Good news," Walker said brightly to Chelsea as he hobbled out of Doc Saunders's office in Corbet's small, modern medical center. "We'll be able to dance the night away on the Fourth of July after all."

Chelsea, her own minor lacerations tended to earlier by the nurse practitioner, set aside the *Health Today* magazine she'd been thumbing through. Her eyes skipped up from Walker's bandaged ankle and brand-new wooden crutches to his face. "It isn't broken?"

Before responding, he checked the damage to her hands and wrists, relieved to see it wasn't too bad. Then he looked into her eyes and smiled. "Nope, just badly sprained and bruised. And he gave me a shot, so for now I feel no pain. Doc says I'll be able to do a jig by the time Independence Day rolls around." Swinging on his crutches, he came closer to Chelsea. "I was embarrassed to tell him I didn't know how to do the jig."

Chelsea grinned, relieved to know that Walker wasn't as badly injured as she'd feared. "Relax. No one does the jig at Corbet dances." As she spoke she touched his shoulder. It was a friendly, glad-you're-okay kind of touch. Or so she told herself.

"How about nice, slow fox-trots?" Walker's eyes danced. He was feeling high-spirited at the moment, despite his incapacity. It might, of course, have something to do with that shot of painkiller. Then again, it might have to do with how Chelsea's light, innocent touch stirred him, made him feel good, solid, connected.

Chelsea let her hand drop from his shoulder, embarrassed by the sense of intimacy it had suddenly taken on for her.

"Isabelle Alpert is the best dancer in Corbet. Foxtrot, disco...even the lambada," she said, slightly embarrassed by the prissy tone in her voice.

Walker only grinned, an intoxicating grin. "Ah, the lambada. Very hot, very sexy..." He swayed a little.

For a moment, Chelsea thought he was demonstrating a lambada dance step, then she realized he was actually having trouble with his balance. "Steady, Walker. I better get you home and put you to bed."

Walker's grin was downright cockeyed. "Now that sounds even better than doing the lambada with you."

"You're hopeless, Walker."

"That's the nicest thing you've ever said to me, sweetheart."

CHELSEA HADN'T BEEN inside the Fremont house—she still couldn't call it the Jordan house—since Walker had moved in.

The farmhouse was torn up at the moment, because of the renovation work that had gotten underway. Chelsea and Walker had to pick their way cautiously around the sawhorses, wood, tools and the like strewn around the rooms. Fortunately, there wasn't much in the way of furniture. Chelsea knew from Ellen Unger,

Corbet's leading antique dealer, that Walker planned to furnish the house with Revolutionary War period pieces to recreate the original style of decor. Ellen, another of Corbet's long-suffering divorcees, had eagerly taken on the assignment of looking for just the right antiques for Walker.

"My, you're an untidy man," Chelsea teased, as she guided Walker around a pine plank.

"I need a good woman..." Walker started, his speech fading off into a drug-induced slur.

"What you need is to get into bed." She saw his glazed eyes brighten for an instant. "Alone, Walker."

He frowned. "There's...a problem, sweetheart."

Chelsea grimaced. She was running out of patience with this "sweetheart" business. "What's the problem, Walker? You can't sleep alone?"

He chuckled. "I don't like to sleep alone. But the problem is...I can't remember where my bed is."

"It's usually in the bedroom."

"There are three bedrooms." He held up four fingers, and started to sway again because he'd let go of one of the crutches. "And only one bed," he added as Chelsea grabbed on to him to keep him from toppling over.

"Hold on to those crutches, Walker."

"Mmm. I'd rather hold on to you, Chelsea." He let the other crutch clatter to the floor and pulled Chelsea closer to him, dropping his head onto her shoulder. "You smell good, Chelsea."

Chelsea pulled her head back and smiled. "I smell wet and dank, Walker. Just like you."

He grinned lasciviously. "You're right, sweetheart. We better both get out of these wet, smelly clothes."

Chelsea drew back further, eyeing him suspiciously. "I'm not so sure Doc gave you enough painkiller, Walker."

"You don't want to get pneumonia, Chelsea. It's real chilly today. Spring's taken a detour. Just think, if you get sick, we'll both have to take to bed. The two of us."

"Okay, okay, Walker. First things first. You stay put, I'll find your bed, and then I'll come and direct you to it."

He still had a firm enough hold on her so that she couldn't bend to retrieve his crutches.

"Walker, cut me some slack," she protested.

Surprisingly he let her go almost instantly, nearly losing his balance in the process. Chelsea quickly grabbed his crutches and guided them under Walker's armpits. She eyed him baffled. His expression had turned suddenly cool and distant.

"What is it, Walker?"

He took a firmer hold of the crutch handles and quickly donned that cool, sardonic expression that had always been his trademark.

"Nothing, sweetheart," he said breezily. "Just that 'cut me some slack' is a common expression among my set out in L.A. It was funny hearing you say it."

There was something about the way Walker had reacted that made Chelsea doubt his words, and sparked her intuition.

"Is it something Vanessa Harper said?" she blurted out.

Walker gave her a funny look, withholding an immediate answer. Chelsea wondered if he would ever respond. Maybe the mention of his ex-fiancée still evoked too many troubled feelings. Chelsea half expected him to play up his drugged state again. Interesting how he could act tipsy from the painkiller one minute and be dead serious the next.

"Cut me some slack. Sailor types use it," he said finally. "Lots of sailor types in L.A." He paused. "Van was a sailor," he said finally, his voice sounded smoky and rough around the edges. "An expert sailor. But then, Van was expert at everything she did."

Chelsea, feeling uneasy and not sure what to say in response, muttered, "I went sailing once."

"Yeah," Walker murmured in an acerbic tone, "Van would try anything once."

Chelsea knew Walker wasn't only referring to sporting activities. She recalled what Julie had said the other day about Walker defending his ex-fiancée. Embezzlement. Had Van Harper tried that once, too? Had she been guilty? Had Walker defended her, knowing...? Ah, Chelsea thought morosely, what we do for love.

A little shiver ran down her spine. It wasn't solely a reaction to her wet clothes, although she probably was courting a first-class cold. And Walker, too. She looked around for him. He was making his way, not too successfully, across the room. As she got to him, he was just about to trip over a pile of floorboards.

"Easy does it, Walker," she cautioned, steering him clear of disaster.

He gave her a funny look. "That's why I came to Vermont, Chelsea. To take it easy." He gave her a slightly crooked grin. "How am I doing so far?"

"I suppose you could do worse, Walker." Chelsea laughed. "Although I'm not sure how."

Now his look was quite easy to read. "Let's go find that bed together."

They did find it, in the larger of the two spare bedrooms on the second floor, the master bedroom being in the same reconstructive disarray as most of the rooms downstairs.

When Chelsea started to enter the bedroom, Walker grabbed her.

"Shh. We don't want to disturb old George," he whispered.

"What?"

"George Washington sleeps here," Walker said, suppressing a drunken chuckle. "Believe me, I have it from an expert. An authority."

Chelsea scowled. "Very funny, Walker." She pointed to the bed. "There it is, sweetheart. Just tell old George to roll over and get yourself some sleep."

But Walker was blocking the doorway. "Chelsea..."

"I'm beginning to think you lied about that painkiller, Walker."

He quirked a half smile. "I've never lied to you, Chelsea."

She knew he was teasing her, but there was something so appealing and vulnerable in his smile. He seemed to have a smile to fit every occasion, this man. And they all worked so well for him.

"Walker, I'm wiped out. I've got to go home and get out of my wet clothes and crawl into my own bed. But first you've got to do the same."

"Now wouldn't it save time..."

"Walker," she threatened, "I could always kick you in your good ankle and then there'll be no lambada for you for a long time."

Walker grinned. "You're beautiful when you're angry, Chelsea." His grin edged into yet another kind of smile. "You were even more beautiful back there in the barn saving my life. You did save my life, Chelsea. You know what this means, don't you?"

"Please, Walker..."

"It means I'm beholden to you for life." He dropped his crutches.

"Walker, one more minute of this and I'm going to begin regretting I saved your life."

He started to sway again and reached out for Chelsea's shoulders to steady himself.

"Okay Walker," she relented, helping him over to the bed.

"There," she said, settling him down to a sitting position on top of the blanket. "You should be able to manage from here."

He caught hold of her arm. "That's the problem. I can't."

"Walker..." She was fast losing her patience.

"Chelsea, study me carefully."

"Huh?"

"As point of study, observe my bum ankle. Observe the thick layer of bandage."

Chelsea did as requested. "Doc Saunders did a fine job," she said blandly, certain this was just another delaying tactic on Walker's part.

"You don't see the problem?"

Chelsea folded her arms across her chest. "No, Walker, I don't see the problem." She gave his ankle another look, and then the nature of Walker's problem abruptly dawned on her. Her face flushed at the realization.

Walker laughed. "This is getting downright silly, isn't it, Chelsea?"

She couldn't meet his eyes. She knew they'd be sparkling with an amused, seductive glint.

"Silly, all right," she muttered. But neither of them really thought silly was the right word.

"Why didn't Doc Saunders...?" Chelsea started.

"What did you want him to have me do? Remove my trousers before he bandaged my ankle? These trousers have tight cuffs. It's the style. I'd have never got them back on over all this bandage. I would have had to exit his office in my underpants. Would you have wanted me to parade through the waiting room and then drive through the whole town in my underpants? With you beside me? The talk, Chelsea. Heavens to Betsy, we'd really be the talk of the town then."

Chelsea gave him an incredulous look. "Does this happen with every woman you meet?" she asked without thinking.

Walker chuckled. "Not in exactly the same way."

"You're impossible, Walker." And then, before he could respond, she gave him a warning glare. "And do not say that's the nicest thing I ever said to you."

Walker opened his mouth to speak, but once again Chelsea cut him off. "And don't call me sweetheart. Ever again."

He gave her a smile, this time a contrite one. Another variation from his bag of tricks. "I guess you'll have to cut off the leg—of the trousers I mean."

Chelsea grinned. "Okay, where are the scissors?"

"Check on top of my dresser."

"Nope," she said after a thorough search. "I'll check downstairs."

She returned a few minutes later with a huge set of heavy-duty shears left behind by the construction crew.

Walker feigned alarm as she approached the bed.

Chelsea grinned. "Don't worry, Walker. I'll be gentle with you."

As she knelt by his bandaged leg, Walker's hand drifted lightly to her hair. Her eyes shot up.

"Gentle, that is, unless you don't behave yourself," she warned.

"Your hair's still so wet," he said softly.

"It's still storming out." She tried to concentrate on snipping his trouser leg, distracted by Walker's hand still lightly caressing her hair.

"I'd forgotten how much I adored your hair, Chelsea."

Chelsea hadn't forgotten. Back when they were teens he'd gone on and on about her hair. He'd made her promise never to cut her hair short, never to wear it any other way.

And she hadn't.

"Walker, hold your leg steady," she demanded brusquely. But it wasn't his leg that was shaking, it was her hand. And when he let out a low grunt, she was sure she must have cut him.

"Oh no, Walker. I'm sorry. What did I . . . ?" She frantically pulled up his cut trouser leg to investigate.

Walker cupped her chin. "You didn't do anything bad to me, Chelsea," he said softly, his eyes playing over her face. "I really am a little woozy. I kind of drifted back in time for a moment." He closed his eyes. "It was a real nice moment . . ." His hand dropped from her chin and he let himself fall back on the bed. "Mmm. Very nice . . ."

"Walker, don't drift off on me now. I've finished cutting. You can get your trousers off now. Walker. Walker?" She got to her feet, leaned over the bed and peered suspiciously down at him. If this was some ruse to get her to undress him . . .

"Walker, I'm not in the mood to play games."

Walker's head flopped to one side and he opened one eye. "Tennis anyone?"

"Not funny, Walker. I'm leaving. Do you hear me, Walker. I'm going now. You're on your own now. I'm going home to get out of my own wet clothes. Do you hear me, Walker?"

He managed a limp wave.

Chelsea chewed on her lip. "Damn it, Walker, don't just lie there like a deadweight. You're... getting the bed all wet."

"Set? First set? Great set, sweetheart..."

"Not set. Wet. Wet." She might have been trying to shout to Dot Prescott with her hearing aid shut off.

This time Walker made no response. Except for some deep sighing breaths. He must be drifting back in time again, Chelsea mused. Having pleasant thoughts. Chelsea wondered if they were about her. Not too likely, she decided. Probably about him and Vanessa Harper. Van. Van, the woman who'd try anything once.

She stared down at him. Damn, there was a lascivious smile on his face. She ought to just walk out and leave him to his... nice thoughts.

But she couldn't do it. She glared down at him. "All right, Walker. I suppose it would be dumb for me to have saved you from a collapsing building only to let you lie here in soaked clothes and die of pneumonia."

She eyed him suspiciously as she began undoing his belt. "If you're not really out, Walker, you can just forget about my ever coming to your rescue again."

Walker made a low, sighing sound, a precursor to a snore.

Chelsea hesitated at his fly. Okay, she told herself, so what was the big deal? Don't make it so personal.

Ha! How was she supposed to make stripping a handsome, well-built, one-time boyfriend anything but personal?

She decided to remove his shirt first. Undo the buttons. Nothing to it. There. Just pull his shirttails out of his trousers. Last button...

Damn, Walker, she thought staring down at his broad, tanned chest, why couldn't you have gone to pot after all these years? Why do you still have to look so damn good? Better even than when you were eighteen. I thought boys were supposed to peak at eighteen.

She nudged him first onto one side then the other, getting his arms out of the sleeves of his shirt. He was deadweight. She had to laugh to herself. What would the overwrought, jealous gossips of Corbet have to say if they spied her in Walker's bedroom stripping the unconscious man down to his underpants?

I never saw anything like it. Loose morals just like her father.

Probably drinking, the two of them. And she was not about to be deprived of a good time even if he did pass out.

She wasn't fooling me with her Goody-Two-Shoes, Miss Prim and Proper act. Scandalous. Downright scandalous.

Chelsea's smile vanished. She glared down at Walker, as if somehow he were responsible for all her old hurts. At least that made it easier for her to get him out of his trousers without her mind drifting unbidden to erotic fantasies.

"There, Walker. Nothing to it," she said aloud, unfolding the blanket at the foot of his bed and tossing it over him.

He sighed contentedly at the warmth, a faint dreamy smile on his lips.

Chelsea started for the bedroom door, then stopped abruptly, pivoting round. "And another thing, Walker. I hope you are dreaming about Ms. Try-Anything-Once Vanessa Harper. Because, if by any chance you're dreaming about me, Walker Jordan, you are wasting your dreams. You don't know it yet, Walker, but that love letter you unearthed for me, just might prove to be my ticket out of this stifling little town."

Hurrying to her car out behind the house, Chelsea didn't even bother to avoid the huge puddles in her path. Her shoes, like the rest of her, were soaked, anyway. Besides, in ten minutes she'd be home, out of her wet clothes and deep in a nice hot bubble bath.

She turned on the ignition. It sputtered a couple of times and died. Okay, the car was five years old. It was finicky. It had given her a little trouble back at the medical center, too, before the engine had begrudgingly turned over. The plugs were probably wet. Her poor old car didn't like the weather any more than she did. Give it a second or two to catch its breath, she told herself, confident that it would start next time.

Chelsea gave the steering wheel a little pat. "Come on, baby. You can do it."

This time, when she turned the key in the ignition, she didn't even get a cough from the engine. Not even a sputter of hope. Nothing. Silence. She guessed that the battery was dead.

Chelsea stared out the rain-streaked windshield. Now what? She supposed she'd have to go back into the house and call Marty Cranshaw at the gas station to come jump start the car.

She turned a pensive gaze back to the house. Maybe she could dig up Walker's key and borrow his car. Damn. On the drive to the clinic, Walker had mentioned his car was in the shop for service.

Okay, no problem, she told herself during her run from the car to the back door. She'd just have to call Marty after all. No big deal. He certainly wasn't going to know that she'd just stripped Walker and tucked him into bed, for heaven's sake.

Finding the phone amidst the mess downstairs was Chelsea's first problem. Her second problem, however, was a lot more frustrating.

No dial tone. The phone was dead.

The lines were probably down from the storm. It had happened often enough during nor'easters in the past. Usually it took hours, sometimes days for service to be restored.

Now what, Chelsea thought? Visions of that nice hot bubble bath, dry clothes, and her warm cozy bed, danced before her eyes. She looked around the cluttered living room then gazed pensively up the hall stairs.

Chelsea assessed the situation calmly. She was stranded. She was wet. She was chilled. Surely, Walker would be sleeping off that painkiller for hours. He was probably out for the night. The storm would be long over by the time he got up. Her car might even start if it got a chance to dry out. And right now, for all intents and purposes, she told herself reassuringly, she was certainly as good as alone...

There wasn't any bubble bath, but the hall bathroom was in good working order and the tub was one of those big, deep, claw-legged types that Chelsea had always adored. She started the tub going and ran next door to give Walker one last check before getting undressed and climbing into a nice, hot bath.

After satisfying herself that he was still deep in dreamland, Chelsea borrowed one of his shirts and a pair of his jeans and carried them back to the bathroom with her. She stripped off her own wet things, stepped into the inviting hot tub of water and let herself slide down so that even her head went under for a couple of moments.

Chelsea soon discovered that sometimes a couple of moments was all it took for disaster to descend. While she was playing underwater nymph, someone was knocking on Walker's front door. Unfortunately, by the time she surfaced, she only heard the last knock and it didn't fully register. She assumed it was just the storm, or the house settling.

The water had risen to just the right level and Chelsea, humming to herself, shut off the hot and cold faucets.

No one locked their doors in Corbet. Lots of residents didn't even own keys. Those that had them generally only used them if they were going away for a long period of time. So it wasn't until the visitor was climbing up the stairs that Chelsea realized she was less alone than she had banked on.

"Walker. Oh, Walker, are you up there?"

Chelsea gasped. Talk about being up to your neck in hot water.

"Oh Walker, it's just me. Alice. Alice Wilson. I heard about your ankle and your phone's down...I had to see if you needed anything."

Chelsea squeezed her eyes shut. *At least that man-crazed busybody could be counted on to head straight*

*for the bedrooms. Not even Alice would just barge into
the bathroom. Would she?*

Try the bedrooms first, Alice, Chelsea prayed. If
Alice saw Walker tucked in bed fast asleep, maybe
she'd just turn around and go home.

Chelsea frowned. Wishful thinking. She knew perfectly well that Alice would see this as a golden opportunity to score points with Walker. She'd stick around,
right there at the ready, Florence Nightingale on the
spot, eager to meet the suffering Walker's every need.

Footsteps upstairs in the hall.

"Walker?"

Chelsea sucked in her breath. It sounded like Alice
had paused right outside the bathroom door. Had she
heard her?

Chelsea felt like a lobster in the pot. She was already bright red with embarrassment in preparation for
the door opening....

She stared in horror as the doorknob began to
turn...

Chapter Eight

Chelsea was about to leap out of the tub and make a mad dash for a bath towel, so at least she wouldn't be found in the buff...when the doorknob stopped.

"Who is it?" Chelsea heard Alice Wilson call out.

For a moment Chelsea thought Alice had heard her flopping about in the tub. She was about to respond and get the whole stupid mess over with, when another voice, coming from downstairs by the front door, called back, "It's me. Isabelle. Who's that upstairs?"

Well, Chelsea thought ruefully, news of Walker's visit to the medical center had certainly spread through town quickly enough. His whole fan club was descending. Soon, no doubt, there'd be a dozen love-struck Florence Nightingales buzzing around Walker's bed.

And around the bathroom, Chelsea reminded herself with alarm.

Chelsea shivered in the rapidly cooling tub water, but she was afraid to risk a move.

Hearing Isabelle Alpert's footsteps on the stairs only served to increase Chelsea's anxiety. Now, instead of one jealous gossip to worry about she had two.

"Oh, Alice, it's you," Chelsea heard Isabelle say in a plainly disappointed and irritated voice. "My my, bad news travels fast in these parts."

Chelsea sighed ruefully.

"Where's Walker?" Isabelle demanded. "How's his ankle? I hear Chelsea brought him into the medical center."

"Supposedly, she *found* him in his old barn," Alice snickered.

"Right," Isabelle said. "She just happened to be strolling by his barn out in the middle of his field during a torrential nor'easter and..."

"Shh, Walker might hear us."

Chelsea rolled her eyes.

"Is he in there?" Isabelle asked.

"I don't know," Alice said. "I thought I heard water running."

Chelsea braced herself to spring for a towel.

"How could he be in the bathroom all this time and not say a word?" Isabelle pointed out.

"I called out to him," Alice retorted, "and he didn't answer."

"He might be lying there on the bathroom floor this very minute...unconscious," Isabelle gasped.

Isabelle knocked. "Walker? Walker, are you in there? Are you okay? It's me, dear. Isabelle."

Chelsea stared balefully at the door as the knob turned again. The tension of anticipation was beginning to feel worse than the prospect of actual discovery for Chelsea. Her eyes lifted to the heavens.

Amazingly her prayers were answered. Once again the doorknob stopped moving.

"What was that sound?" Alice asked intensely.

It's my heart pounding against my chest, Chelsea answered silently.

"What sound?" Isabelle asked.

"It's from next door. Walker must be next door, in the bedroom."

Chelsea could hear the women's footsteps scurry toward Walker's bedroom. He must have woken up.

Oh, Walker, thank you, thank you, Chelsea intoned to the gods.

Of course she wasn't completely out of the woods yet. But at least she could climb out of the tub and get some clothes on. And, with luck, she could sneak out to the car. No, not the car. What was she thinking? Her car was dead as a doornail. Oh well, she could always hide out down in the basement until the two women left. Thank heavens, Chelsea thought, she'd parked her car out back. Isabelle and Alice had both come in the front door, so they wouldn't have spotted her car.

She was out of the tub and hurriedly drying off, when she heard Isabelle's voice again.

"I'll wet a washcloth for him and you go downstairs and see to the orange juice." Isabelle was a take-charge kind of woman. A take-charge woman about to walk into the bathroom.

As the bathroom door opened, Chelsea ducked behind it.

Chelsea held perfectly still behind the door as she heard the water in the sink running. Then she remembered the bathtub full of water. What would Isabelle think?

She didn't have to wait long to find out.

"Walker, dear," Isabelle called out, "you weren't thinking of climbing into a bath before, were you? Poor man. You must have been so woozy you didn't even realize you couldn't get that poor bandaged ankle of yours all wet.''

Chelsea heard the water start to drain out of the tub. *Okay, Isabelle, that's enough already. Go rush to your patient like a good little nurse.*

She heard Isabelle utter a few tsks and then finally make her exit. The fastidious woman closed the door behind her.

Chelsea's breath whooshed out. Now all she needed to do was throw on some...

Chelsea gasped. The clothes. Walker's jeans and shirt... Even her own wet jeans and sweatshirt... "No, no, she didn't," Chelsea muttered, her eyes frantically searching the room. "She couldn't..."

But Isabelle, so anxious to please, had, indeed, gathered up all the clothes in an effort to tidy up for "poor" Walker.

Now, not only didn't Chelsea have a stitch of clothes to wear, but she had to worry about Isabelle noticing that some of the clothes in that heap were hers. At least Chelsea had thought to throw Walker's sodden clothes down the laundry chute, or Isabelle might have wondered what he was doing with two sets of wet clothes lying on the floor.

Chelsea pulled herself together. She couldn't very well stand around contemplating all the disastrous possibilities. Tucking the not-so-large bath towel around her body she got ready to make a run for it.

Wait. Footsteps up the stairs again. Oh, right. Alice with the orange juice for Walker. Chelsea waited impatiently for Alice to pass by the bathroom and enter Walker's room. She pressed her ear to the bathroom door, hoping to hear the door close shut to Walker's room.

No such luck. Not that she was putting great stock in luck since hers seemed to have abandoned her almost completely. Almost.

She waited another minute. Then, her hand trembling, she nudged the door open a fraction of an inch and peeked out through the crack.

She counted to ten, edging the door open a little wider. The hinges made a low whining sound. Chelsea froze. But there was no response from Walker's room. No doubt Alice and Isabelle were too busy fussing over Walker to hear a creaky door. Still, she gave it another ten count.

And then, just when she was sure the coast was clear, she heard Isabelle coo, "Oh Walker, do be careful, dear. Where's your robe?" And then a few moments later, "Easy now. Would you like some help...?"

Walker's laugh echoed down the hall. "Thanks, Isabelle, but I've been managing this on my own since my momma took me out of diapers."

"Oh Walker, you're a terrible tease. You know I didn't mean..."

"He knows, Isabelle," Alice said with a superior tone. "He's pulling your leg."

And, Chelsea thought with alarm, he's heading for the bathroom.

Now what? She couldn't very well duck out and risk Walker's cry of surprise when he spotted her fleeing in a skimpy towel down his hall. Or his laughter. Not to mention that his two nursemaids were sure to follow him out into the hall, anyway, to see that he made it safely to the bathroom.

"Careful, Walker." This time it was Alice's turn to show her concern.

An involuntary gasp escaped Chelsea's lips as the bathroom door swung open. Fortunately the creaky door hinges masked the sound.

She managed to hide once again behind the bathroom door. Only this time Walker—requiring privacy—shut the door, leaving Chelsea fully exposed.

Walker was starting for the toilet, when Chelsea let out a low, hissing, "Don't."

Poor Walker. He almost jumped out of his skin. His crutches clanked to the tile bathroom floor as he swung around, nearly losing his balance.

Chelsea had to rush over to steady him before he could fall, nearly losing her towel in the process. She slipped her hand over his mouth.

"Walker? Walker, are you all right?" It was Isabelle at the door, ready to come to the rescue. She must have heard the crutches fall. And if Isabelle was there, Chelsea knew, Alice couldn't be far behind.

Chelsea gave Walker a pleading look. He, in turn, gave her a baffled one. It traveled over every inch of her. And then, when his gaze finally returned to her face, he smiled. One of those you-really-know-how-to-blow-a-guy's-mind kind of smiles.

"I'm fine, Isabelle. Just fine," he called out after prying Chelsea's fingers from his lips. His still-smiling lips.

"Are you sure now, Walker? There are times for modesty and then again there are times—"

Walker had to fight not to laugh as he broke in with, "Honestly, Isabelle, modesty isn't my problem."

After a moment or two, they heard retreating footsteps. Still, Chelsea cautioned him with her eyes to be on guard. She was sure the two women would be hovering nearby.

He leaned close to her, pressing his lips to her ear. "What are you doing here?"

"Dying of embarrassment," Chelsea whispered back.

He grinned, his lips still pressed to her ear. "I'll tell you, sweetheart, I think we're fated to be naked together."

She gripped his arm. "Walker, you owe me," she whispered. "Now it's your turn to save my life. Well... at least my reputation."

"Baby, I'd do anything for you. I'd give you the robe off my back, but don't you think poor Alice and Isabelle would get the wrong idea if I came hobbling back into the bedroom in nothing but my shorts?"

Chelsea went over to the sink and turned on the taps to mask the sound of their voices. Then she turned to Walker with a warning expression. "Don't go glib on me now, Walker. Get rid of them."

No sooner had Chelsea made her demands than Alice knocked on the bathroom door. "Walker, I'm just going to hop downstairs and make you something to eat. What would you like for lunch? When I got you the juice before I saw you have a few cans of tuna and some soup. Or, how about a grilled cheese sandwich? I saw cheddar in the fridge."

Chelsea gave Walker a beseeching look as he seemed to be contemplating the selection. Then he broke into a wide grin, leaned close to her again, took a little nibble of her ear and called back, "Thanks, Alice, but I'm not hungry. I think I'll just—"

"Oh, Walker, you've got to eat. You'll feel better. Why don't I just whip you up—"

Walker's eyes danced. "I really couldn't eat a thing." For a moment, his hands lightly trailed over Chelsea's naked arms. When they reached her shoulders, he guided her back against the wall beside the door, planting a not-so-light kiss on her lips. Then he picked up his crutches, opened the bathroom door and stepped out into the hall, carefully closing the door behind himself.

"I'm falling asleep on my feet," he said to Alice, who was waiting two feet away. "Thanks for coming by, but I really think what I need is to conk out for a few more hours."

"Well, I'll stick around just in case—"

"What's the matter?" Isabelle asked anxiously, joining the pair in the hallway.

"Walker needs some more sleep," Alice told her.

"Well, of course he does," Isabelle readily agreed. "I've got nothing on my agenda. I'll hang around, throw a wash in for him—"

"I was just going downstairs to make him some lunch so it'll be ready when he wakes up," Alice broke in. "I can throw in a wash as well, for heaven's sakes. No reason for both of us to—"

"You're both wonderful," Walker crooned. "But really, ladies, it's only a sprain. I'm sure, once I get some more sleep, I'll wake up feeling fit as a fiddle."

"You shouldn't be alone, Walker," Isabelle insisted. "Not with your phone line down. What if you fall or something and need help?"

"I won't be alone, actually," Walker replied blithely.

Chelsea almost choked. *Oh Walker, you wouldn't...*

"You see," Walker went on after a brief pause. "Chelsea..."

Chelsea squeezed her eyes shut, a slew of very unladylike phrases rushing through her mind.

". . . said she'd drive by later to check on me. What time is it now?"

"One-fifteen," Alice said dejectedly.

"Oh, well, she'll be by in…a couple of hours. She's bringing over some dinner for me."

"I thought you and Chelsea were still at odds over her fanatic quest to prove her theory about the battle at Fremont," Isabelle remarked archly.

"Well, you might say we've called a truce."

"Really, Walker, believe me, I'm not one to throw stones," Isabelle said cattily, "but I have to tell you Chelsea can be quite ruthless about getting what she wants. She's had too many dreams of glory to give up without a fight."

"I haven't lost many fights up to now, Isabelle," Walker said with a laugh.

"All I'm saying is, I think this obsession of Chelsea's is really out of hand."

"Of course, if Chelsea ever did prove her theory," Alice pointed out, "it would certainly perk up our sluggish economy in town. Not that I'd want to see Corbet overrun by tourists, mind you, but business and real estate would definitely pick up."

Walker yawned dramatically.

"Alice, really this is not time to go on about such nonsense," Isabelle chided. "Although I'll say one final word on the matter. Even, and mind you I say *even* if Chelsea were ever to prove that an important Revolutionary War battle did take place here, I'm willing to lay odds that the citizens of Corbet would go up in arms against her plan to turn this lovely little town into another—" She stopped, searching for the right expression.

Walker helped her out. "Three-ring circus?"

"Precisely," Isabelle said. "A three-ring circus."

"Oh, for heaven's sake, Isabelle, it wouldn't be anything like that," Alice argued. "Have you ever even been to a three-ring circus?"

"That isn't the point, Alice," Isabelle retorted.

"Ladies, ladies, please," Walker broke in. "To set the record straight, I've made it clear to Chelsea that I have a strong desire to see Corbet remain just as it is right now. A charming, friendly, quiet little haven. A...paradise, if you will."

"Oh Walker, that's so lovely," Alice simpered. "And don't get me wrong. I feel the same as you about Corbet. I was just...playing devil's advocate. If it came right down to it, I, personally, wouldn't support having this town turned into a..."

"Three-ring circus," Isabelle finished with a self-satisfied smirk.

Chelsea, trapped as she was in the bathroom, knew damn well that Walker was getting the greatest satisfaction out of the conversation she was being forced to overhear. Well, she thought, we'll just see who gets the last laugh here, Walker Jordan.

As soon as Chelsea heard the two women descend the stairs and Walker call out his final thanks, she opened the bathroom door.

Resting on his crutches, he greeted her with a broad smile.

"Wipe that smirk off your face, Walker," she snapped, clutching her towel around her as she brushed past him on her way to the bedroom.

Walker entered behind her.

"I need something to wear," she said, trying hard to avoid the licentious look she was sure Walker was giving her from behind.

"The shirt off my back, if you want it, sweetheart," he answered, still teasing her lightheartedly.

Chelsea turned around to face him. He instantly donned a sweet, innocent little boy smile.

She opened her mouth to say something cutting, but instead broke into a smile, too. "Pretty weird, the way this keeps happening to us, Walker."

"Well, at least your reputation is intact."

"You must think it's ridiculous for a single woman my age to worry about gossip."

"A few weeks ago, I might have thought so," Walker agreed.

"And now?"

"Now I understand that the gossip brings back very painful memories for you."

"And what about the gossips themselves?" Chelsea chided. "I thought you were just thrilled at the way those two women reached out to you in your time of need."

Walker grinned. "They were just being neighborly."

"Right," Chelsea said facetiously.

"What about you?" As he asked the question he moved toward her. "Is that why you decided to stick around, Chelsea? It is very neighborly of you."

In a nervous burst, Chelsea started to explain the absurd comedy of errors that had led her to be standing here in Walker's bedroom wrapped in a skimpy towel. But suddenly Walker's nearness heightened her feelings of vulnerability and she started tripping over her words, unable to concentrate on what she was saying. Walker's sympathetic murmurs weren't helping matters any. She could have stepped back, gained some much needed distance, but some unseen force held her in place.

Walker was having an equally hard time concentrating on what Chelsea was saying. Her body looked so velvety smooth, the lines and curves so elegant. His eyes strayed to her hair, falling in damp waves down around her slender, delicate face to her shoulders where the drying ends curled wispily. She was a sea nymph, sleek, ravishing, enticing. He wanted her. And it wasn't smugness that told him that with a little effort he could have her. The attraction between them was charged. It was also rife with complications.

Walker reminded himself that Chelsea was a woman with one foot in Corbet, the other poised on the ladder to success. And Walker knew better than most how ambition, the drive to make a name for yourself, tended to be all consuming. He also knew how the ones who loved you were inevitably the ones who ended up getting trampled in your upward climb.

Walker had been trampled, and he'd done some trampling of his own. But that was the old Walker. This was the new Walker. And this incredibly alluring woman, he forced himself to remember, was the new Chelsea. Caution and common sense worked better than a cold shower.

"I better get you some clothes," he said in such a brisk tone that Chelsea flushed.

"Yes...please," she muttered awkwardly, clutching her towel with renewed vigor.

He started to hobble over to his closet, but Chelsea stopped him.

"Why don't you get off your feet," she said quietly. "I'll just take a pair of jeans and a flannel shirt, if that's okay?"

"Sure, help yourself," he said cavalierly, making his way over to the bed.

"Is this okay?" Chelsea held up a worn pair of jeans and a gray-and-red-plaid flannel shirt.

"Yeah, fine."

"I'll just put these on . . . in the next room . . . Then I'll toss my wet clothes in your dryer for a . . . few minutes, change again and be on my way."

Clutching the clothes, she hurried toward the door, then hesitated, looking back over her shoulder. "Are you okay, Walker?"

He cast her a sober look. "Never better."

She gave him an edgy, doubtful smile and exited, closing the door behind her.

A few minutes later she knocked softly on Walker's bedroom door.

"Yes?" he called out.

"I need a belt."

She opened the door. Walker was stretched out on the bed, his arms bent behind his head. At the sight of her in the oversized clothes, he flashed one of his now familiar jaunty smiles.

Chelsea observed that a bit of time and distance seemed to have helped Walker regain his equilibrium as much as it had helped her. Being dressed was a big help, too.

"How about a pair of suspenders?" Walker suggested. "I've got some great red-and-blue-striped suspenders hanging on a hook inside the closet."

Chelsea got them and began adjusting them so they would fit her.

"Come here," Walker said. "I'll snap them on in back."

Obediently Chelsea approached Walker. Because she didn't want him to have to move around she sat down on the edge of the bed to be within his reach.

Her back was to him. She snapped the suspenders in front, tossed them over her shoulder and waited for him to do the back. But he made no move.

Finally, uneasily, she turned to face him. "Isn't it going to work? Is there a problem?" she asked awkwardly.

His eyes were fixed on her back, but he wore a perplexed expression.

"What is it?" she asked.

Slowly Walker lifted his gaze to meet hers. "I was just remembering something you said outside the barn before. About...having Henry Cotton and Abigail Fremont to thank for your being in the right place at the right time. What did you mean?"

Chelsea hesitated.

Walker's gaze took on a heightened intensity. "Was it something about that love letter that led you to my barn, Chelsea?"

She nodded, feeling distinctly uneasy, especially given that she was having this conversation with Walker on his bed.

Spontaneously Walker's hand came up to her face and smoothed her tangled hair back from her cheek. "Me too," he murmured. "Something propelled me to the barn, too, after you told me about Henry and Abigail last night. I can't explain why. I had no real reason for it, but I just...got this feeling that our lovers had held their last tryst in that barn."

Chelsea stared at Walker, stunned by his instinctive and accurate guess. "You were . . . right," she said in a breathless whisper. "I . . . stayed up all night . . . deciphering more of Abigail's letter. She mentioned . . . the barn, their . . . passionate moments there, the longing to be there with him again. And the hopelessness of that desire . . . under the circumstances."

"The war," Walker whispered, enchanted by the heightened color in Chelsea's cheeks.

There was more to tell, but Chelsea hesitated. Walker's hand remained pressed against her hair. Its warmth seemed to seep through her skin. She knew she was allowing her renewed feelings for Walker to sway her from telling him the most important part, the part that would correct a certain aspect of the myth about Abigail and Henry.

"Walker . . ."

"Chelsea," he broke in, "there's something I have to confess." His voice sounded a little raspy. His gaze searched her face. Both his hands were in her hair now.

She swallowed hard. "There is?" She felt uneasy and aroused all at once.

"When I was up there in that loft, I . . . visualized them—Abigail and Henry—making love in the hay. Only . . . it wasn't them, Chelsea."

Chelsea's lips fell open. She took a shallow breath. Her last before Walker's lips descended.

It wasn't as if she hadn't seen it coming. Still, the instant his lips touched hers something changed within her. A trigger, poised for weeks now, was pulled. Blood thudded in her ears.

She wanted him. She'd wanted him at sixteen, too, but they'd both been scared then, inexperienced, unsure of themselves. And they'd believed it was wrong.

Chelsea still believed it was wrong, but for different reasons. Wrong for her to let her priorities get obscured. Wrong for her to get involved with a man whose view of life was so different from hers. Wrong for her...

His arms came around her, gently drawing her down on the bed with him. Her lips parted, allowing the warm touch of tongue upon tongue.

Hadn't it been wrong for Henry and Abigail, too? A man and woman on opposite sides of a war? Had it stopped them? Not until it was too late.

It was almost too late for Chelsea too. Until she heard a voice calling her name.

She broke away from Walker with a start just as Ned Hunt appeared at Walker's open bedroom door. It was a toss-up which of the three of them looked more embarrassed.

Chapter Nine

Walker, Chelsea and Ned sat around the cleaned-off table in Walker's dining room, ignoring the clutter of sawhorses, wood planks and sawdust around them. They were finishing up mugs of tomato soup and grilled cheese sandwiches, while Chelsea held court, regaling Ned with the events of the afternoon—discreetly leaving out certain items and "what ifs." Ned was laughing so hard, tears ran down his cheeks. Walker got his chuckles for the second time. Even Chelsea could laugh, now that she'd gained some distance from the whole comedy of errors. It almost seemed like something out of a TV sitcom.

"But you still never said how you knew I was out here," Chelsea said to Ned when she'd finished.

An amused glint in his eyes, Ned looked across the table at Chelsea. "Well now, of course I heard in town how Walker here got trapped in the barn and how you happened along to rescue him, brought him in to Doc Saunders and then drove him on home," Ned began laconically. "When I dropped by your place later to see how you were faring in the storm I saw your car was gone, and took it from there."

Walker interrupted. "I know all about word traveling fast in a small town, but this news must have been posted on a blimp. Why, Chelsea and I couldn't have been back from the medical center for a half hour when two angels of mercy descended. What gives?"

Chelsea laughed ruefully. "I can give you the answer in two words. Joanie Storch."

Ned grinned, explaining further. "Joanie Storch is Doc Saunders's daughter. She keeps house for him. She's also the town clerk."

"Oh, yes," Walker mused. "I met her when I went to pay my resident tax. She's the one with the frizzy brown hair..."

"Don't ever let Marge Horton hear you call it frizzy?" Chelsea teased.

"Who's Marge Horton?" Walker asked, bemused.

"Why, Joanie Storch's beautician over at To Dye For," Chelsea edified with a giggle. "And Joanie's first cousin."

"By marriage," Ned corrected.

Chelsea gave her old friend a nod, then looked over at Walker. "I'd lay odds Marge was the first one Joanie called with the news about your ankle."

Ned disagreed. "My bet is she told old Mrs. Jarvis next door first. And then the old lady phoned her daughter, Barb..."

"Hold it," Walker interrupted again. "How could she phone? Chelsea told me the lines are dead because of the storm."

"Your line's dead, Walker," Ned clarified. "Probably all the lines this side of town are out. The Madison place, the Cooksons', Shanks' farm. That's because of the way the storm blew in. But the rest of the town still has phone service."

"Okay, okay," Walker muttered, "I get it."

Ned grinned. "You gotta understand, Walker, most of the time life's pretty quiet and kinda dull around here. Lean pickings in the gossip department."

A shadow fell across Chelsea's face, her good humor evaporating. She was immediately propelled back sixteen years to the last really juicy gossip this town had spread. She'd been in the limelight then, as well. "Yes," she said contemptuously, rising and briskly gathering up the dishes, "it's been years since they had anything as juicy as us to gossip about in Corbet."

Walker watched her stride out of the room into the kitchen, shoulders squared, chin lifted in an I-dare-anyone-to-take-a-swipe pose.

Ned moved some crumbs around the table, then looked across at Walker, giving him an awkward half smile.

"Was it really that bad for her?" Walker asked softly.

"When your momma takes her own life, son..."

"No, of course that was terrible. Just unimaginably awful. I meant...the gossip."

Ned sighed. As he heard the water start to run in the kitchen sink, he leaned forward, resting his elbows on the table, his chin cupped in the palms of his hands. "Gossip always hurts. Especially when there's more than a grain of truth to it. But, don't get this town wrong, Walker."

"What do you mean?"

"There were plenty of kindly folk reached out to Chelsea when all that sorrow happened. Plenty who didn't gossip. Plenty who felt nothing but plain outright sorry for her." He hesitated. "If you ask me, son, they're the ones she had the hardest time with. Chelsea's pride can really get in her way."

"I wish now I'd known how bad it was for her. At the time, when the whole affair between her father and that woman surfaced, and her mom caused a scene in public, I just thought...it would be old news before the week was out. I figured her folks would iron things out. Or get divorced."

"Takes a while for that kinda stir to die down in a town where everyone knows each other. And Chelsea's mom couldn't face the shame of divorce."

"And then, after her mother died, her father started drinking more?"

Ned nodded.

Now Walker pushed some crumbs around the table. "I wish...I'd been more understanding. I took her dad's affair so lightly. I didn't realize..."

"You were a kid, Walker. A kid from the big city."

"I was in love with Chelsea. Our summers together seemed so magical, so perfect. I think that when the business about her dad's affair came out, a part of me..." Walker paused.

Ned nodded. "Resented the intrusion into your idyllic romance?"

Walker flushed. "I'm ashamed to admit it, but... yes. Everything changed after that. Instead of idyllic romance as you so aptly put it, we had harsh realities."

"That's true enough," Ned reflected.

"I didn't know what to say to Chelsea. I wanted to fix it, so we could go back to being the way we were. Man, was I selfish. I just walked out of her life and left her to face it all alone."

"You were...what? All of eighteen? Yale beckoning? Don't be so hard on yourself. Besides, I happen to know you wrote her, even called a couple of times, anyway."

"Don't go easy on me, Ned. Chelsea saw right through me. She probably knew I'd just toss her a few platitudes, and then pat myself on the back for doing the right thing."

"I don't think Chelsea was all that perceptive about you when she was sixteen, Walker. What I think is, Chelsea just didn't want anyone, you included, feeling sorry for her. She was feeling so bad herself, so ashamed, hurt and angry, she just couldn't handle sympathy. Any more than she could handle all that her momma and poppa had done."

"Maybe if there hadn't been so much gossip, her folks would have been able to work things out. It's easy enough to understand why Chelsea resents all the gossipmongers."

Ned nodded. "Yeah, it's easy enough to understand. But there's something else you need to understand. Not just about Chelsea. I'd say it's more about human nature."

Walker gave him a puzzled look. "What's that?"

"I'll put it this way. Let's say you have this job and the boss is always giving you a hard time, making life miserable for you. You feel this rage growing inside, but you're scared to lose your job so you tell yourself there are just some things in life you gotta accept and pretend don't really bother you."

Walker sighed. "I've been there myself."

"Sure. We all have. But, my point is—" Ned grinned "—Chelsea's always on my case for taking so long getting to my points. But here it is. One day you leave your office, come home and you find a water pipe burst and your basement's flooding. There you are, ankle deep in water, ranting and raving about how that dumb pipe is the cause of all your problems, all your grief..."

Walker's eyes strayed to the kitchen door. "So you think Chelsea focused in on the gossipmongers because she was too scared to admit how angry she was at her parents?"

"And herself," Ned finished softly. "She talked about leaving then, too, but in the end she got tangled up in duty and pride. She stayed put, defying the gossip, turning her back on most of those offering sympathy, looking after her daddy, even though the poor fellow was soused so much of the time he didn't hardly know she was around."

"I guess I can understand why she still wants out. She'd be free of the gossip."

Ned raised a brow. "But not of herself. You can't escape yourself no matter where you go or how successful you become."

Chelsea came back into the dining room, eyeing the two men suspiciously, guessing they'd been talking about her. Both men acted a little awkward and Ned rose from the table a might too fast.

"So, ya want me to try to jump start your car now, Chelsea?"

She hesitated, her gaze skidding across Walker's face before answering. "Yes. Great. I've stayed around here longer than I planned, that's for sure."

THE RAIN, if possible, was falling even harder as Chelsea rode home beside Ned, her own car simply having refused to start. "Just as stubborn as its owner," Ned had teased her.

When Ned pulled up in front of her house, Chelsea turned to him. "Can you come in for a few minutes? There's something I want to show you."

"Sure." He looked across at her, caught her enigmatic smile.

They made a run for the porch, Ned in his high rubber boots and hooded rain slicker, Chelsea with Walker's borrowed trench coat flung over her head.

"First things, first," Chelsea declared as soon as they were in the house. "I've got to change into...other clothes."

Ned chuckled, but he knew better than to make a comment about how darn cute she looked in Walker's oversized clothes. Instead, he offered to put up a pot of tea.

Chelsea caught a glimpse of herself in her bedroom mirror before she changed. A faint smile curved her lips as she zeroed in on the red-and-blue-striped suspenders. Walker must have picked them up at Sawyer's General Store. She tried to picture him wearing them. It was an altogether appealing picture.

Shaking off the vision, Chelsea hurriedly changed. Dressed in her own clothing, she felt more like her old self. But not completely. The truth was, she hadn't felt completely like herself since Walker'd fallen on top of her in that ditch all those weeks back.

As she brushed her hair, she found herself wondering if she was relieved or sorry that Ned had shown up when he had at Walker's bedroom door. She had no doubt where things would have progressed had Ned not materialized just then.

Again she told herself that what she was feeling for Walker was purely physical. But this time she couldn't buy it. Not that the physical attraction wasn't there in spades. But there was something more. For all of Walker's glib facade—not all of it acquired in L.A. as she remembered him being pretty slick at eighteen—there was a tenderness, a sweetness, a vulnerability about Walker now that she hadn't seen in him before. He was also, she was quick to remind herself, still stubborn, opinionated, obstinate and an impossible tease.

She left her bedroom having concluded that Ned's appearance at Walker's had definitely been for the best. Of course, that didn't exactly resolve the issue of how she felt about doing what was best.

"Water's just coming to a boil," Ned said cheerily as Chelsea entered the kitchen.

"Leave it for a minute. Come in here."

Ned followed Chelsea into the living room and watched her carefully remove a plastic-encased letter from her drawer. He walked over.

"Walker gave this to me yesterday. He found it up in his attic under an old trunk. It's a love letter from Harmon Fremont's daughter, Abigail, to her Loyalist lover, Henry Cotton."

"Well, well, well. And Walker just gave it to you?"

Chelsea cast Ned a wry look. "Yes, but I doubt he would have if he'd been able to read it through."

Ned squinted at the faded, blurry print. "Can't say as how anyone could read much of it. Just a couple of lines..."

"I spent half the night on this letter, and managed to decipher a fair amount of it," Chelsea said in a low voice.

Ned gave her an appraising look. "What did you find that would have kept Walker from giving it to you?"

Chelsea's eyes lit up. "You know the story of Abigail and Henry as well as anyone."

"I suppose," Ned agreed.

"We all believed that Captain Henry Cotton fought under Burgoyne up in Canada, right?"

"Right," Ned said cautiously.

"And the story goes that the captain snuck down from Canada to meet with his lady love, Abigail Fremont."

"We already agreed I know the story, Chelsea."

Chelsea grinned. "I'm getting to the point, Ned. And the point is, according to this letter, he wasn't sneaking down from Canada when he and Abigail met for their trysts at the Fremont place. Or, more specifically, their trysts in the Fremont barn. Abigail makes direct reference—"

"So that's what you were doing out there. And Walker."

"The weird thing is, Walker didn't know for a fact that Abigail and Henry rendezvoused in the barn. He just had a sixth sense about it and went out there to nose around. Needless to say, it was a toss-up which of us was more surprised at spotting the other one out there."

Ned grinned.

Chelsea went on excitedly. "Anyway, the important thing here, Ned, is that Abigail actually refers to Henry being in a Loyalist camp right in this area. Look closely." She pointed to the line. "Right here, you can make out East Hoseck. See? Do you realize what that means, Ned?"

"Well now, wait a minute, girl. Don't go running away with this. We all know there might have been some Loyalists camped over near East Hoseck, skulking around our fort there. Makes sense, considering it was a major ammo dump. But that still doesn't mean there was an actual battle in Corbet. Or at the Fremont property to be specific."

"But, it could mean just that, Ned," Chelsea said fervently. She picked up the letter carefully. "Look. I can't make out the whole sentence, but right here Abigail makes a reference to bloodshed at her door."

Ned could just barely read the words, now that she pointed them out, but he remained skeptical. "She might as easily have been referring to a wound inflicted on Henry by the farmer who discovered a Loyalist in the barn of a Green Mountain Boy. With that Green Mountain Boy's very own daughter."

"You're just being obstinate, Ned. I wish you were on my side on this. I'm getting closer, Ned. And I think I might find some more clues out in that barn."

Ned gave her a sharp look. "That barn belongs to Walker Jordan, Chelsea. And you already know how he feels about you—"

"Digging up his property," she finished the sentence with an all-too-familiar defiant look in her eye. "I wasn't going to dig up his barn. I was simply out there as... as a representative of the Historical Society, checking out one of our duly registered historical landmarks."

"Chelsea..."

"Oh Ned, I wasn't going to remove anything from the premises. I was just going to look around. If I dug anything up... scratch the word *dug*. If I came upon anything, I would have certainly given it over to

Walker. But don't you see, if I could establish solid evidence of the battle up here, I could get some strong support behind me."

"You mean from the town?"

"That, too. But I'm talking about other experts in the field. Next weekend I'm going up to Burlington to attend the New England Conference on Revolutionary War Strategy and Defense. Jack Scheurer from Danbury is one of the guest speakers. He's the American history professor I've been corresponding with, the one who thinks I may be onto something. Wait till he sees this letter."

Ned slowly shook his head. "Wait till Walker Jordan finds out about it."

"Walker gave me this letter, Ned. No strings attached," Chelsea retorted, and her voice lacked conviction. She knew perfectly well that Walker would never have blithely handed over the letter if he knew it might lend more credence to her theory of a Revolutionary War battle right at his front door.

"Well, if you ask me, you're stirring up a hornet's nest, Chelsea. You're gonna end up with half the town ready to take up arms to keep this business from gettin' outta hand."

"I'll have plenty of folks on my side as well, and you know it, Ned," Chelsea protested.

"So, what are you hoping to do here? Start the second battle at Fremont? Cause that's what'll happen, Chelsea. And Walker'll be the enemy this time."

"Really? A smart city type like him. All Walker would have to do is sell at a huge profit, let you find him another piece of . . . paradise and pocket the handsome difference," Chelsea pointed out.

"Is that what you think he'll do?" Ned prodded.

"Why, you've got a good half dozen listings in the area for gentlemen's farms that would suit Walker just as well. Better. Maybe I can't persuade him by myself, but if enough people—"

Ned's voice was unexpectedly harsh. "And what if Walker gets mad enough to pack up and find himself another piece of paradise somewhere else altogether? Or maybe he'll just get fed up with the complications of country life and head on back to L.A."

Chelsea stared down at the letter, not responding. She didn't look back up at Ned until she felt his comforting hand on her shoulder.

"Walker and I..." she started, then stopped, looking for the right words, but not finding them.

"He's a good man, Chelsea. And it's as plain as the nose on your face that he's smitten with you."

She couldn't look her old friend in the eye as she muttered, "Oh Ned, nobody uses that word anymore. It's archaic."

"I still say he's smitten," Ned said with a smile.

Chelsea laughed dryly. "If Walker's smitten with anyone, it's his ex-fiancée. He was so...so smitten, he even defended her on an embezzlement charge a few years back. Knowing full well she was guilty."

"Is that what he told you? That he knew she was guilty?"

"Lawyers don't only defend innocent clients, Ned."

"That isn't what I asked you."

Chelsea hesitated. "No, he didn't exactly say it, but I can read between the lines. My guess is he hoped that by getting her off, she'd change her mind about marrying him."

Ned scratched his head. "Why'd she break off their engagement in the first place? Seems to me Walker'd be a good catch for any woman," he reflected, giving Chelsea a meaningful look.

"I haven't the faintest idea. But the point is, even after Walker got her off, he didn't get her back. And I bet he made a fool of himself over her and suffered some ridicule for it as well. He practically said as much. It may have happened years ago, but the man's still carrying a torch for her, that much is obvious."

"And so that little...um...scene I innocently barged in on up there in Walker's bedroom..."

Chelsea's whole face reddened. She turned from Ned and made a production out of putting away the valuable letter. "I'm just a... diversion to Walker, that's all."

Ned Hunt chuckled.

Chelsea spun around and glared at Ned. "Well, it's true. Just as it was true sixteen years ago."

Chelsea's retort didn't temper Ned's grin. "I'm sure Walker Jordan could come up with quite a colorful assortment of descriptions for you, girl, but I doubt *diversion* would be one of them."

THE RAIN WAS still coming down in huge sheets. Walker stretched out on his bed, listening to the storm beating down on the roof, a smile on his lips.

Quite a day, he reflected. If he'd stayed put in L.A. he'd never have had one anything like it, that was for sure. He'd never have gotten trapped in a broken-down barn, never have been rescued by a chestnut-haired beauty, certainly never have been surprised in his own bathroom by that very same beauty, clutching a bath towel and desperately trying to preserve her dignity and her reputation. His smile deepened. For all the pain in his ankle, he wouldn't have traded this day for anything.

The question was, where would this day lead? Walker wasn't sure what he was hoping for when it came to Chelsea. A simple, uncomplicated physical relationship? He grinned. No way. It had definitely moved past that stage. It had moved past that stage after the first half hour he'd been with her. He was at least smart enough to know that.

Walker sighed. He'd come here to his little patch of paradise seeking tranquillity, freedom, contentment. Chelsea was so ambitious—if he had to find himself fiercely attracted to a woman, why did it have to be to one who represented everything he was escaping from?

He felt a disquieting sense of déjà vu. Chelsea's drive, even her determination to bury her past, reminded him of Van. Van had come from a broken home. She was raised by a mother who had been anything but discreet when it came to men. At seventeen, she had run away from home. She worked her own way through college and law school. She wanted success so badly she was willing to do just about anything to get it, no matter how callous and self-serving she had to be in the process.

Not that Walker believed Chelsea could ever be that ruthless. Still, a disturbing prickle scratched at his mind. He had a vague, foggy memory of Chelsea saying something to him about that old love letter. Something about it being a ticket? What had she meant by that?

CHELSEA HELPED Julie Martin off with her dripping wet rain slicker.

"Thanks for the dinner invite," Julie said cheerily. "The electricity went just a minute after you called, so I would have had to make a dinner of cold tomato soup at home."

"Is it letting up at all?" Chelsea asked.

Julie laughed. "Yeah, instead of raining cats and dogs it's only raining mice and puppies."

"I've got a fire going in the living room."

Julie headed in there ahead of Chelsea. "Only in New England can people have fires going in May. Martinique can't come soon enough for me."

Chelsea gave her friend's shoulder an affectionate squeeze. "Not long now, and I don't know a single divorced couple who honeymooned on Martinique."

Julie grinned. "Neither do I." She flopped down on the couch. "Which means it's a safe bet for you and Walker, too."

Chelsea rolled her eyes. "I merely lifted a timber off Walker's leg and took him to the doctor."

"And just what were the two of you doing in that old barn before the walls of Jericho came tumbling down?" Julie asked with a sly smile.

Chelsea sat down beside Julie. She wore such a heartsick expression that Julie regretted her teasing inquiry. "That's it, isn't it, Chelsea. You're still hooked on the guy."

Chelsea managed a limp shrug. "I don't know what I feel." With a quiet sigh she folded her arms across her chest. "Until Walker stumbled back into my life, everything was so clear. I had it all worked out. I knew exactly where I was going and I was forging full steam ahead. Now..."

"Now?" Julie gently prodded.

Chelsea's mouth went dry. "Now ... I've practically got the ticket in my hand, but if I use it, I may be burning more bridges behind me than I want to burn."

Julie gave Chelsea a tender study. "Especially that cute little bridge out by the brook on Walker's property?"

"I don't know why I'm so ... attracted to him. We don't see a single thing in the same way. We don't have anything in common. We have utterly different goals, dreams, plans. We're never on the same wavelength at the same time. And to save the worst for last, he's obsessed with preventing Corbet history from having its due. And you know how I feel about that."

Julie gave Chelsea a shrewd but caring look. "And aren't you obsessed with seeing to it that history doesn't repeat itself?"

Knowing perfectly well that her friend was not referring to American history, Chelsea didn't answer.

Julie hadn't expected a reply. She only hoped her message would sink in. Pulling off her cardigan, now that the fire had sufficiently warmed her, she let a few silent moments elapse and then turned to Chelsea. "Okay, so now tell me the real reason you invited me over for dinner tonight."

Chelsea had to laugh. "I can't ever put anything over on you, can I?"

"Nope."

"Okay," Chelsea admitted, "I did have another reason. You know that conference up in Burlington I'm attending next weekend?"

"You're not going to try to talk me into going up there with you again ... ?"

"No, I'm going to try to talk you into helping me write a paper I want to present during open forum."

"What's the paper about?"

"Well, you might say, it's a love story...."

Chapter Ten

"Interesting paper, Ms. Clark. Very interesting. That letter was quite a find."

Chelsea smiled at the renowned, gray haired history professor from Boston's Danbury College as they stood outside the conference room of the Burlington Hedgemont Hotel. "Thanks, Dr. Scheurer."

He took her arm, guiding her away from the door. "It seems clear from that letter that your theory about a Loyalist encampment in your area definitely has some merit." He paused. "And you say East Hoseck is ... what? Ten miles from Corbet?"

"Nine and a quarter miles," Chelsea clarified. "And what's significant here, Dr. Scheurer, is that at the time of the Revolutionary War there was a carriage path that ran from East Hoseck right through Corbet and then north to the Canadian border."

"And your premise is that a party of British was sent down from Canada by Burgoyne to raid the fort at East Hoseck for arms and provisions?"

"And move them right through Corbet to join up with Burgoyne's troops north of Saratoga," Chelsea finished excitedly. "My theory is that the British succeeded in overtaking the fort, captured the arms and provisions and set out to bring their cache up to Burgoyne.''

"But it's your contention that a group of Green Mountain Boys got wind of the plan, gathered at Corbet and stopped the British from moving the supplies up north.''

"Yes. My best guess at this juncture is that the Green Mountain Boys, headed by Harmon Fremont, hid in a barn on the northern end of his property and waited for the British to cross the brook and start down the road past the barn,'' Chelsea went on excitedly. "It's the perfect spot for an ambush. I believe the British were caught off guard, a battle ensued and the Green Mountain Boys drove the Loyalist band off and recaptured the stolen supplies.''

Professor Scheurer ran his thumb across his lower lip in thought. After a moment, he said, "Of course you know that if you're right, Ms. Clark, the loss of those supplies would have been a crucial blow to Burgoyne's assault plan.''

Chelsea knew it in spades. "I believe that the success of the Green Mountain Boys at Corbet was a critical factor in forcing Burgoyne's surrender at Saratoga. Burgoyne's army had already been greatly reduced since its departure from Canada. That much has long been documented. Still, had they gotten those arms and provisions from East Hoseck, they might have pushed south of Saratoga, and...''

Dr. Scheurer smiled. "And the course of history could have been greatly altered.''

Chelsea's eyes sparkled. "Precisely. Now you understand why I can't let this slip by me. Abigail Fremont's letter opens the door.'' Now, Chelsea thought, the question was would Walker Jordan ever let her step through it.

"Did you happen to bring the letter along?" Scheurer asked.

"No, just a copy. The actual letter is on file at the Corbet Historical Society along with some other very interesting supporting documents."

"I'd love to stop down there and have a look on my way back to Boston."

Jack Scheurer's response was precisely what Chelsea had hoped it would be. "That would be great. I'm driving home right after the closing meeting at noon tomorrow. I'd be glad to give you a lift, unless you've got your own transportation."

"I'd love to drive down with you. I came up by train, but I was going to rent a car to drive back. Take the scenic route."

"Well, Corbet's about as scenic as it gets."

"Yes, so you mentioned in a couple of your letters to me. Corbet sounds incredibly beautiful and idyllic. Sometimes, I have to tell you, Ms. Clark, I dream of chucking it all in and settling in a place like Corbet. It sounds like paradise."

Chelsea's heart lurched. Paradise. Couldn't Scheurer have picked any other word?

"I suppose," she said slowly, uncomfortably, "if I ever do find solid evidence of that battle, Corbet would go through . . . some changes."

Scheurer gave her a thoughtful look. "Yes, I suppose it would." He winked at her. "Maybe I ought to buy myself a piece of property there now, before you go and put Corbet on the map and it gets too pricey for me."

"Right," Chelsea muttered, manufacturing a half-hearted smile.

LITTLE DID CHELSEA realize that change was already afoot in the little piece of paradise known as Corbet—thanks, or no thanks depending on one's outlook, to a local carpenter by the name of Wes Moore.

Wes Moore was one of the four men Walker had hired to shore up the barn. It was quite an undertaking, requiring among other things, digging to repair the old foundation. Wes was assigned to dig out behind the north end of the barn. When his shovel struck something solid, Wes thought at first it was a large rock.

He soon discovered what he'd actually hit was a musket.

Carter Simpson, one of the carpenters on the job, saw it and let out a low whistle. "Nice little souvenir."

Wes scratched his scalp. "Ought to turn it over to Jordan. By rights, it's his."

"True," Simpson mused. "But I hear he's gone for the weekend. Maybe you better hold on to it until he gets back."

Wes's nose twitched. "I don't know. Don't really want to be responsible for it if it's anything... valuable. Maybe I'll leave it off at my Aunt Norma's house."

"Good idea. She's a teacher. Maybe she'll know something about it."

"Or she could show it around at the Historical Society. She just got appointed to the board last month."

"WELL, CERTAINLY it's of historical significance," Graham Sawyer agreed. "I'm all for asking Mr. Walker to donate the musket to the society. We can put it on display in a nice showcase, let the kiddies have a gander at it."

"Our children deserve more than a gander at a musket, Graham," Norma Lund argued. "They deserve to know the entire truth about Corbet's place in history. You know very well that this find is the first solid piece of evidence that Chelsea's been right all along. I'm sure when she gets back from Burlington and learns about the discovery, she won't rest until we find out just how extensive a find we have here."

"*We* don't have a find," Isabelle Alpert emphasized. "That musket is in our temporary possession. It belongs to Walker Jordan."

"Besides," Alice Wilson added, "the musket hasn't even been authenticated. It's only our supposition that it dates back to the Revolutionary War."

"Well then," Nan Prescott Green piped in, "I think we ought to proceed to have it authenticated."

"We can't proceed to do anything," Ned Hunt spoke up for the first time. "As Isabelle pointed out, that musket isn't our property."

"Then I say that Jordan should be approached—" Nan began, only to be cut off by her sister.

"I think Chelsea's the one to approach him," Dot Prescott spoke up. Today, she had her hearing aid not only turned on, but turned up, the cost of new batteries be damned. "We all know those two are as thick as thieves."

CHELSEA WAS ELATED when she left Jack Scheurer. He'd as good as promised to arrange a lecture series for her at the distinguished Danbury College if her work on the Fremont battle was supported. And he suggested that she'd have the basis for a very fine book-length treatise on the subject. He'd even given her the name of his literary agent.

She was heading past the hotel's coffee shop when she realized she hadn't eaten all day. The conference luncheon had been served just before open forum, and she'd been too preoccupied with how her presentation of her paper on the Abigail Fremont love letter would go over, to eat. It was now close to five o'clock, and the conference dinner wouldn't be served until eight.

Chelsea stepped into the coffee shop, pausing by the sign requesting customers to wait to be seated. The hostess was just coming over to her as Chelsea caught sight of a familiar face twenty feet away at a window table. She let out an involuntary gasp of surprise which coincided with the hostess's approach.

"Is there something wrong?" the trim, smartly attired hostess asked with concern.

Chelsea slowly shook her head, walked past the puzzled woman and headed for the window table.

A minute later she was eyeing Walker Jordan warily. "What are you doing here?"

Walker gave her a brief, disinterested glance. "Eating a hot turkey sandwich with all the trimmings. Take a seat and I'll give you a taste."

Chelsea slid into the seat across from him. "Seriously, Walker—"

"Seriously, Chelsea," he countered, a distinct edge in his voice, "that was some paper you presented."

Chelsea's eyes widened. "You . . . were there?"

"Open forum. I even managed a front-row seat."

"I didn't see you."

Walker gave a brief, dry laugh. "That's because you were too busy eyeing some slick-looking, gray-haired guy on the other side of the room. The same one you were chatting with so animatedly outside in the lobby."

"That was not just some guy, Walker. That was Dr. Jack Scheurer, a professor at Danbury College and one of America's leading Revolutionary War historians."

Walker raised one brow. "I'm duly impressed." He sliced into the turkey, speared it with his fork and extended it in Chelsea's direction. "Here. Take a bite. It's delicious. You'll be duly impressed."

"Walker..." But as she parted her lips to say more he deposited the forkful of turkey into her mouth. There was nothing for it but to chew.

A waitress approached with a menu for Chelsea, just as Walker was presenting her with a second bite. "Will you be ordering, miss? Or... sharing?"

Chelsea gave Walker a sharp look. "Definitely not sharing," she said tightly, taking hold of the menu.

"Right," Walker said in a low, chilly voice. "I forgot. Sharing isn't your thing." Without another word, he dug his hand in his pocket, pulled out a large bill and plunked it on the table. Then, grabbing up his crutches, he rose from his chair. "Go on, have dinner on me, Chelsea. Or just take mine. I don't seem to have much of an appetite, after all. Whereas yours is obviously voracious."

He spun around rather adeptly on his crutches and started for the exit. Chelsea jumped up and headed after him.

"I know I should have told you about the contents of the letter," she admitted, catching up with him.

Walker kept heading toward the front door of the hotel.

"Where are you going, Walker? Why can't we sit down and talk about this like two rational adults?"

The electronic doors slid apart. Walker headed outside, Chelsea on his heels.

He started across a wide patch of green lawn.

"Oh come on, Walker. Where are you running off to?"

"To the bus depot."

Chelsea grabbed hold of one of his crutches. "In the meantime, look what you're doing. The sign says, keep off the grass."

Walker gave her a contemptuous sneer. "Since when did you go by the rules?"

"I didn't commit a crime, damn it. You gave me that letter."

He pulled the crutch from her grasp and continued across the lawn.

"It still doesn't prove anything conclusive, Walker," she argued, keeping up with him.

"No, but you'll keep pressing, Chelsea." His lips curled derisively. "You'll go as far as you have to, all the way if necessary, in order to get what you want."

Angry at the implication of his remark, Chelsea started to turn away.

As Walker turned to add one last remark, he caught one crutch in a hole and stumbled. Before she could reach out to steady him he lost his balance and fell to the grass. He let out a sharp groan on landing and Chelsea dropped to her knees beside him.

"Walker. Are you hurt? Is it your ankle?"

He slowly rolled over, propped himself up on his elbows and looked up at her. "Relax, Chelsea. It's only my dignity."

She sat down on the grass, mindless of the stains it was likely to leave on her pink cotton skirt. Absently she plucked a blade of grass and ran it through her fingers.

"Did Ned tell you about the letter?" she asked quietly. "Is that why you came up here?"

Walker smiled. "No. Ned didn't say a word about the letter."

"No," Chelsea murmured, her eyes meeting Walker's. "No, he'd want to tell you, but he wouldn't."

"He just told me you were up here for the weekend. And I thought..." He laughed wryly. "I thought I'd get you to give me another history lesson."

Chelsea gave him a contrite look. "I'm sorry, Walker." She hesitated. "I should have told you I'd deciphered more of the letter. Especially the part about the barn being where Henry and Abigail met. That's why I was down there last week."

"Well, I guess I can't be too mad at you since that letter was directly responsible for your being in a position to save my life."

They continued looking at each other as they sat there on the soft grass. A gentle spring breeze toyed with Chelsea's earrings so that the light silver loops swung against her jawline.

Walker stretched out a hand and touched the point of contact. Then, with his fingers, he traced the line of her jaw.

"You've avoided me like the plague ever since that nor'easter last week."

"I called to find out how you were," Chelsea protested shakily, Walker's sensuous touch speeding up her pulse. "Twice."

"Two brief, formal, obligatory calls. A fifty-cent get well card would have been warmer."

His fingers had progressed to the back of her neck. "They...don't sell cards for...fifty cents anymore, Walker." She swallowed hard as his fingers twined in her hair.

"What I want to know, Chelsea, is were you avoiding me because of a guilty conscience over that letter, or because of...temptation?"

"I didn't feel guilty," she protested. And then, realizing where that left her answer, she reddened. "Oh Walker, I can't seem to think straight when you're near."

"Same goes for me," he admitted. "Even after all these years, Chelsea, my heart seems to go haywire around you."

She saw the glitter in his dusky gray eyes, the aggressive angle of his jaw. She knew what was on his mind. It was on her mind, too. "Walker...it would be dumb for us to start something..." She could feel his fingers sliding through her hair, shifting the strands as he cupped the back of her neck. Her pulse beat erratically.

"Why must we be so smart, Chelsea?" he murmured as his face came toward hers.

Just as their lips met the sprinkler system went off, frigid jets of water engulfing them. Gasping, sputtering, they broke apart in astonishment. And then, both of them already drenched to the skin, they broke into gales of laughter.

Finally catching her breath, Chelsea got up and gave Walker a hand. But before she could bend down again to get his splayed crutches, he grabbed hold of her and drew her to him.

"Walker," she protested in a smoky voice, "look at us."

Walker's gray eyes sparkled. "Guess there's nothing for it but to go upstairs and get out of our wet things."

EVER ON GUARD against rumors, Chelsea made Walker use a delivery entrance to the hotel and sneak upstairs on a service elevator. What would her distinguished colleagues think if they saw her and Walker parading dripping wet through the lobby?

When they stepped into the empty elevator, Walker pressed the button for the seventeenth floor. Chelsea's room was on the fourteenth floor, but she didn't say a word. Partly because she was trembling. Partly because she was struggling with an attack of nerves. Partly because she wanted him so badly.

This is a diversion, her mind kept repeating. But a diversion for which one of them? Suddenly she wasn't only worrying about Walker's intentions, but her own.

Walker was leaning against the wall of the elevator, not really using his crutches for support. His damp shirt and trousers clung to him, accentuating his lean, muscular physique. His eyes rested on her, those sensuous, amused, smoky gray eyes that held the same allure for her as they had sixteen years ago.

Nervously she looked away, fixing her eyes on the numbers lighting up in sequence as the elevator ascended.

Nine blinked on. She looked over at him again.

"Walker..." Could he hear the edge of panic in her voice?

He reached out for her. She couldn't resist the pull of his hand.

He smoothed back her damp hair and put a finger on her chin, then pressed his lips to hers for a mere breath of a kiss.

She went limp. The faintest touch of his lips and she was already turning to liquid. And feeling reckless. She kissed him back with an urgency that took them both a little by surprise. This was some diversion!

When they stepped silently into Walker's room, an unwelcome blast of cold air from the air conditioning made them shiver. Walker went over to the unit under the window and switched it off.

They stood across the room from each other, the sudden silence holding them frozen in place.

Walker turned to her slowly and smiled. Not a typical Walker-type smile. This one didn't seem plucked from his nifty grab bag of smiles for every occasion. This smile was from the heart—awkward, tender, uncertain, needy. Balancing most of his weight on his good foot, he dropped his crutches and slipped his wet jersey over his head. Still he made no move toward her.

Chelsea slowly lowered her gaze, then met his eyes again.

"Oh Walker," she said softly, crossing the space separating them. With each step she undid another button of her blouse. When she got to him she let the damp garment slip down her shoulders to the floor. "We never do seem to manage to keep our clothes on for very long around each other, do we?"

Walker took her in his arms. She twined her fingers around the back of his neck. He undid the clasp of her bra.

Her head lifted. She gave him a helpless look.

"This could be risky. We're on opposite sides—"

Walker's lips captured the rest of her words. Then he said softly, "Think of Abigail Fremont and Henry Cotton. They were certainly on opposite sides, but it didn't stop them from wanting each other." He strung a necklace of kisses across her neck. "This is just history repeating itself, Chelsea."

"But," she mumbled breathlessly, "look at how history treated poor Abigail and Henry."

Walker gently drew her bra straps off her shoulders. "Who knows? Maybe, after the war was over, Henry switched sides and found his way back to Abigail's arms."

"That's a nice fantasy, Walker," Chelsea whispered, the bra landing next to her shirt on the mauve carpet.

As they slowly, seductively helped each other off with the rest of their damp clothing, Chelsea could feel every one of her nerves tense with anticipation and almost uncontrollable excitement.

When they fell together naked on the bed, Walker emitted an involuntary grunt as his taped ankle collided with the bed post.

"Are you . . . okay?" she asked breathlessly.

He pulled her close. "I will be," he murmured, smoothing her hair to one side, kissing the sensitive skin behind her ear.

"Mmm," she murmured, "you're better at this now than when you were eighteen."

He laughed softly. "Yeah, but what we lacked in experience then, we made up for in youthful exuberance."

"I was wild about you, Walker," Chelsea confided.

He stroked her hair. "I was a shallow, selfish jerk. The crazy thing is, those summers with you in Corbet were the happiest times of my life. I wish I'd realized it then." He fixed his gaze on her. "Is there a statute of limitations on apologies?"

Chelsea smiled. "I think you can still get in under the wire."

"Good."

"And am I forgiven for not telling you that Abigail's letter confirms my theory that there was a British garrison—?"

Walker pressed his finger to her lips. "Let's not talk about any more past history now," he murmured as he arched against her. "Let's make some history of our own."

"Only...sixteen...years in the...making," she whispered breathlessly as he began planting a string of kisses down her body.

Walker smiled. Sixteen years to come full circle. Sixteen years to finally hold Chelsea naked in his arms. Sixteen years to claim her. But he was no longer claiming a lovely young girl. He was claiming a woman whose beauty had blossomed, as had her spirit. He might rail against her ambition but he was falling hopelessly in love with her irrepressibility, her determination to claim her due, to fight for what she believed in.

As he came into her, Chelsea thought, I love this man. I have always loved him. It was a startling thought. She tried to unthink it but her weak attempt at denial faded instantly under the passionate intentions of her body and the depth of her true feelings. For the first time in a long time she wasn't thinking *no.* She was feeling *yes.*

The physical attraction between them was so powerful that at first it overwhelmed them both. They were driven by desire and urgency. And the need had been building so long, neither of them could prolong their release.

But later, as they held each other close and Walker stroked her gently, they both felt a deeper bond enveloping them.

"It's been a long time for me," Walker said softly.

Chelsea gave him a playful look. "Really? How long?"

"A dozen years. Maybe more."

Chelsea laughed dryly. "You're telling me you haven't had—"

"I haven't felt this good in that many years," he said with an inimitable Walker smile.

But Chelsea believed him. "It's been a long time for me, too."

"How long?"

Her lavender eyes darkened. "Sixteen years." She brushed her lips against his. "Sixteen years since I felt this good."

He held her closer, wanting his embrace to somehow soothe all the hurt and pain she'd gone through even though he knew it was impossible.

"After my mother died," Chelsea confided, "I felt as though my whole world had come unglued, like something inside of me had shifted, permanently destabilized. If it hadn't been for my studies, for my growing fascination with local history, I don't know how I would have survived."

"History was your escape."

Chelsea turned on her side to study him. "Only at first. Then it became my passion. It ... still is."

Walker smiled. "Not your only passion anymore."

Chelsea felt a disquieting flash of anxiety. "Walker, this doesn't change anything. I'm still going to do everything I can to prove that battle took place on Fremont soil." Her eyes searched his for understanding. "I've got Jack Scheurer coming down to Corbet tomorrow to actually look at my papers. It's taken me years to get someone of his caliber to even consider my theory. If he takes an active interest, why . . . my future would be set. He can open so many doors for me. . . ."

"Yes, influential people are certainly an asset when you're seeking fame and fortune," Walker said dryly.

Chelsea gave him a sharp look, but something in Walker's eyes told her his reflection was more personal.

Hesitantly, she asked, "Van?"

He studied her in silence before nodding slowly.

"Tell me about her," she said softly even though she felt some trepidation.

"Tell you about Van?" Walker rolled over on his back, separating himself from her, and looked up at the ceiling. For Chelsea the distance between them became more than just a few inches on a double bed. She waited with tense anticipation to learn about the woman Walker Jordan had wanted to marry.

"Van was the most dynamic, scintillating woman I'd ever come across," he began quietly. "And she had the most exuberant disdain for mediocrity." He cast Chelsea a wry glance. "Mediocrity as in those who do not aspire to the top rung. And then reach it, of course," he added cynically.

"Is it so terrible to want to do your best?" Chelsea asked, propping herself on her elbow as she studied him.

Walker sighed. "I guess it boils down to how you ultimately define *best*. For Van the end always justified the means." He paused. "I'm not proud to admit it, but then I was all too eager to follow in her footsteps."

"So, what happened?"

"She kept stepping on my toes. The way I saw it at that time in my life, I had only one choice. Step faster. Get ahead of her. For months we had ourselves quite a little relay race."

"That doesn't sound very romantic," Chelsea reflected.

"Ah, romance was never the name of our game, Chelsea. Excitement maybe, one-upmanship definitely. Van loved every minute of it. Until I got more than a few steps ahead of her and she started having trouble catching up. Things fell apart after that."

"She broke off the engagement?" Chelsea asked, thinking she understood.

Walker eyed her with amusement. "Who told you she broke it off? Who told you we were even engaged?"

"Don't get that cocky look in your eye, Walker. I wasn't keeping track of your escapades. My friend Julie used to read the society columns. And she mentioned the other day that you'd been engaged to a very successful, high-powered lawyer."

"Well, she couldn't have read that Van broke it off, because I did."

Chelsea's expression didn't mask her surprise. "You decided you didn't want to marry her after all? You weren't in love with her?"

Walker hesitated. "I thought I loved her. The problem was…I realized I didn't like her." He looked back up at the ceiling.

"But then, later, you…defended her. I thought…you were trying to win her back," Chelsea murmured.

"Julie again?"

Chelsea shrugged. "She told me about the trial. The rest…I kind of guessed at."

"I can be a fool, but not that big a fool," Walker said with a self-deprecating smile. "Oh, believe me, by then I knew Van was ruthless, that she'd go to great lengths to survive at the top. But I still didn't believe she'd ever do something downright illegal. I thought she was too clever. And she swore she was innocent."

"If she'd admitted her guilt, would you still have defended her?" Chelsea asked.

"Like I said, I was a fool. I was dumb enough to think that if she were guilty she would admit it to me."

"So, you got her off and then found out she really had embezzled funds?"

"Let's just say I was the laughing stock of my so-called friends and colleagues for quite a while. A lot of ugly gossip circulated about my motives. There were even rumors that I was involved in Van's underhanded activities. There was never anything tangible. Just the fact that we'd been an item, that I was starting to make a name for myself. Plenty of people thought I'd taken a ride on her coattails and my defending her was nothing but payback."

"Oh Walker, that must have been awful for you."

He met her gaze evenly. "Don't paint me golden, Chelsea. The gossip hurt most because some of it was true. I didn't consciously set out to use Van, but I did let her open doors for me. Through her I met the right people, made important connections. That's the name of the game. And I was tops at it. So much of a pro, that I figured the way around the gossip was simply to get so powerful, so successful, so influential, that no one would risk gossiping about me again."

"And . . . did it work?"

"Yeah, it worked. But what did I really achieve? I was rich, successful, and . . . alone."

"You didn't have to be alone. There must have been women—"

"Plenty of women. Most of them clones of Van. Or wishing they knew how to be. I was looking for...something else. I think way in the back corner of my mind, I was looking for someone just like that wide-eyed, chestnut-haired girl with the infectious laugh who took utter joy in racing with me through daffodil-covered meadows, who pointed out the constellations to me on starry nights, who taught me how to fish, who teased me unmercilessly about being a flatlander."

"Oh Walker . . ."

"Chelsea, it's almost Independence Day. Almost time to celebrate victory. It could be our victory, too. It's only fitting. After all, we first met on Independence Day. We could have ourselves one wallapallooza of a celebration. What do you say?"

Tears made her blink. "No one says wallapallooza anymore."

Walker kissed her full on the lips. "I'm just a country boy. What do I know?"

Chapter Eleven

Independence Day might still be six weeks off, but right now there was an internal battle raging inside Chelsea, and the prospect for peace looked dim. For one thing, she couldn't imagine any way to reconcile her intense feelings for Walker with her basic cynicism about the durability of intimate relationships. For another, she saw no way to reconcile Walker's cynicism about the basic emptiness of success with her quest for professional achievement. To complicate matters...well, she had certainly complicated them yesterday afternoon in Walker's hotel room. And then spent a sleepness night in her own room feeling overwhelmed, frightened, confused and frustrated because she still wanted him. She tried to blame her burning desire on having been chaste so long. When that didn't work, she blamed her longing on Walker. If he hadn't come up to Burlington... If they hadn't gotten caught under the lawn sprinklers... If either one of them could just manage to keep their clothes on around the other...

Now, to further complicate matters, she was stuck driving all the way back to Corbet with the two men who represented the opposing sides of her private battle. Sitting beside her was Walker, looking incredibly alluring. And rested, damn him. There in the back seat was Professor Jack Scheurer, the man who could open all those doors for her.

The two men were talking companionably, but Chelsea was too tense and too distracted to join in. She was surprised that Walker seemed perfectly agreeable to discussing his purchase of the Fremont estate, and the letter he'd found from Abigail Fremont. Walker and Scheurer even got into a discussion of the contents of the letter. Chelsea was grateful to Walker for not mentioning that he'd only learned the details after sitting in on the open forum.

"Abigail must have been madly in love with Henry to sleep with the enemy," Scheurer mused. "And likewise for him."

"Ah, the fire, the ecstasy they must have shared up in that hayloft," Walker murmured in a low, seductive voice. "He was her foe, he stood for everything she and her revolutionary compatriots were fighting against, but still she couldn't resist him. A daring, independent-minded young lady, our Abigail. And, I imagine, extraordinarily desirable. I can just picture those passionate encounters. Abigail, exquisite, sensuous, innocent, aroused beyond the limits of her control, a captive of ecstasy . . ."

"Walker . . ." Chelsea could feel her cheeks heating up. She stiffened, her hands gripping the steering wheel more tightly, her eyes straight ahead. *Damn you, Walker.*

Scheurer chuckled. "Nothing wrong with having a wild imagination. A captive of ecstasy. A bit melodramatic, but certainly colorful." The professor leaned forward.

"I'd really love to have a peek around that barn of yours, Jordan," Scheurer said. "If those two met up there in the hayloft on a regular basis, we might unearth some further evidence..."

"The barn's off-limits," Walker said brusquely.

Wanting to temper Walker's rude reply, Chelsea quickly added, "What Walker means is that the barn is in the process of being renovated."

Walker smiled blithely. "That, too."

Chelsea shot him a chilly look.

Walker merely stretched his left arm idly across the back of Chelsea's seat, without quite touching her. Chelsea was acutely aware of that inch between their flesh. She inhaled sharply.

A faint smile played upon Walker's lips as he went on to explain his position to Scheurer. "Don't get me wrong, Jack," he said amiably, "I've got absolutely nothing against history being told. I just object to it being hyped. As far as I'm concerned, I'd just as soon leave crass commercialism to the cities and save a few oases of tranquillity for those of us seeking to live quiet, peaceful, contemplative lives."

"Believe me, Jordan," Scheurer countered, "I'm not a proponent of crass commercialism or hype. But the point here that Miss Clark is researching is what could well turn out to be one of the most significant and decisive battles of the Revolutionary War. All other considerations aside..."

"That's my point, Jack. Those considerations can't be brushed aside," Walker argued. "You've got to look at the whole picture. History doesn't exist in a vacuum, especially today. If there's money to be made off of it, history becomes simply another commodity, an item to be successfully marketed, promoted."

Chelsea bristled. "Walker's convinced that if I prove my theory, Corbet would be ruined, his land trampled on by hordes of tourists, the main-street shops turned into tacky souvenir emporiums—"

"Tell me something, Jack," Walker cut in, "did you ever hear of Jessica the Hereford cow?"

"Jessica...the cow?" Scheurer echoed. "No, I don't think..."

But Chelsea had. "That's not the same thing, Walker. It has nothing to do with historical documentation."

"Oh wait, I think I remember," Scheurer mused. "A few years back, wasn't it? Something about a moose who took a fancy to a cow up on a farm somewhere here in Vermont. Yes, it made a big splash in the national media. I think there was even a picture in the papers..."

"*A* picture?" Walker sneered. "A few hundred pictures more likely. Which means quite a horde of photographers and reporters. Not to mention a few thousand tourists clogging the roads, trampling fields, overrunning some poor farmer's property. A remote little village was turned topsy-turvy over a moose falling for a cow. The courtship lasted all of a month, but that was plenty enough time for the hucksters to cash in with T-shirts, bumper stickers, coffee mugs, you name it."

"Okay, okay," Chelsea muttered, "things were a little crazy for a while..."

"Crazy?" Walker laughed dryly. "Busloads of people, traffic jamming the roads, reporters from every newspaper, radio and TV station. They'd arrive at dawn, or after dark, shining their headlights on the poor animals. The farmer had to divide his time between crowd control and putting up No Hunting signs. People were suggesting the farmer sell admission tickets. Vendors tried to set up concession stands. It was a regular sideshow.''

Chelsea grit her teeth. ''And it all blew over. If you drove into Shrewsbury today you wouldn't know there'd ever been a fuss.''

Walker grinned. ''Ah, that's only because that old moose was fickle.''

''They usually are,'' Chelsea muttered under her breath.

Walker, however, caught the remark and cast her a wry look. ''Maybe the moose got turned off because Jessica was too high-minded for him, gave him too hard a time, had other fish to fry.''

Chelsea glared at him, and the air seemed to bristle with tension. Only Jack Scheurer seemed oblivious to it, his mind running to more scholarly thoughts.

''I'll tell you what I think,'' the history professor from Danbury offered. ''It's all in the way these things are handled. Miss Clark is an historian, a scholar. I'm sure she's not interested in turning Corbet into a tourist mecca. There's no reason why she can't go about her research in a quiet, unobtrusive way. And, let's face it, Jordan, you may be worrying for nothing. While I certainly agree that Miss Clark has made a credible start, she may never turn up any tangible evidence.''

Walker's gaze was fixed on Chelsea as he replied, ''You're certainly right about that, Jack,'' he said with a smile.

Chelsea recognized that particular smile. It was the one he donned when he was being most stubborn, obstinate, impossible.

THERE WAS A FULL TURNOUT for the luncheon meeting at the Chamber of Commerce where Bill Laird, the landscaper, was addressing the group of businessmen and women of Corbet.

"Nothing this exciting has happened to Corbet in two hundred years. We have ourselves a gold mine here, friends. Let's face it. We've been tiptoeing around a recession for the past two years. Most of us are reporting bigger losses each quarter. Now just imagine our financial outlook if we can claim Corbet as the site of one of the most decisive battles of the Revolutionary War. Think of the boost that would be to our inns, restaurants, shops..."

"Aren't you jumping the gun, Bill?" Arthur Newcomb, of Newcomb Pharmacy, queried. "What did your boys dig up out there anyway? One musket?"

"Not just any old musket," Laird emphasized. "Red Gilman had a look at it this morning, and he says it's a Loyalist firearm. Stands to reason there were Loyalists crossing that field. Or trying to cross it."

Hal Opheimer, a contractor, chortled. "Maybe it was Henry Cotton's rifle. He might have dropped it racing to clear out of that barn after foolin' with Fremont's daughter."

"I agree with Bill that this find is significant," Freda Lynch, a Realtor argued. "We all remember Chelsea's presentation last fall. And we all were quick enough to put down her theories then."

"And we were equally quick to reject her proposal to form a cooperative to purchase the Fremont property." Bill pointed out. "Just think if that land belonged to us now."

Opheimer was swayed. "Maybe we can keep the find hush-hush for as long as it takes to make Jordan a quick but *generous* offer. Say ten thousand over what he paid. That's a tidy profit for a less than sixty-day investment. Jordan's smart enough to see—''

"He's smart enough to see when someone's trying to pull the wool over his eyes," Freda Lynch countered.

"Besides, word of that musket's already spread like wildfire," Bill Laird pointed out.

Jed Howell, vice president of First National Bank of Vermont, tapped his gold pen on his embossed black leather portfolio. "Look, Jordan's no country yokel. And he's not going to do flips if we offer him a little hedge on inflation. But, Hal's got the right idea. Money talks. If we want to move on this opportunity we've got to be willing to dig into our pocketbooks in a serious way and offer Jordan a deal he can't refuse."

Bill Laird scratched his head. "I don't know, Jed. This Jordan guy's not so easy to figure out. He's real gung ho on settling in here, and he might not be so quick to sell, even for big money. You know what they say about converts. Well, he's sure a convert to country life. You should have heard him talking to me about how his land was like some pastoral haven, his escape from urban pollution, overcrowded, crime-ridden streets, and on and on. He's got it in his head that he's reclaiming his soul or some such notion, by breathing pure air, having a kinship with nature, eating wholesome food..."

"Uh-oh, this is serious," Hal said with a frown. "When they start waxing poetic about the country life they aren't easy to budge."

"Or when they fall for a country gal," Bill pointed out. "Everyone knows Jordan took himself up to Burlington this weekend. And who else do you suppose was up in Burlington this weekend?"

Jed Howell rubbed his gold pen along his jawline. "Well now, that could be a plus, not a minus."

"True," Hal reflected. "If anyone can persuade Jordan to sell, or at least let the investigation into the truth of this battle proceed, I'd say it was Chelsea."

"I still don't think Jordan's gonna sell," Bill Laird said stubbornly. "And he's already made it clear he doesn't want Chelsea or anyone else digging on his property. One musket isn't enough to prove the battle. That whole field behind Jordan's barn is gonna need to be torn up."

"Well, if Chelsea can't persuade him that Corbet deserves its rightful place in both history books and the guidebooks, perhaps a large enough group of concerned citizens can help him to see it's his civic duty to give history its due," Jed Howell suggested.

"Group pressure, huh?" Bill Laird reflected. "I don't know. Sure, we can get support for our position, but the problem is, there are some folks in town who'd be just as quick to support Jordan in his efforts to preserve the...uh...quiet integrity of Corbet, as he'd probably put it."

Opheimer cleared his throat. "Fact is, I can...kinda see his point. I mean, sure I'd like to see Corbet's fiscal outlook brighten, but..."

"No buts," Howell said, slapping his hand on the table for effect. "You've got to be clear minded and strong-willed on this, Hal. We have to present a solid front. Look at it this way, friends. Should some flatlander come waltzing into our homeland, the soil of our fathers and their fathers before them, and deny us our very heritage? Our forefathers, those brave, young Green Mountain Boys, spilled their blood on this land for freedom..."

"SEEMS TO ME," intoned Graham Sawyer to a bunch of his cronies at Mort's Coffee Shop, "that no good is gonna come of causing a rumpus over this business. Before you know it, we'll have those sleazy tabloid reporters nosing around up here, television crews, a slew of tourists, flatlanders buying property and forcing us out of our homes."

"We got enough outsiders around as it is," Gladys Durkee, one of Corbet's finest quilt makers, stated. "Why, just the other day I had this couple pull up in some big foreign car, brazenly prance up my walk and ask me bold as day what I'd sell my house for."

"And that's before we get labeled an historic landmark," Graham pointed out.

Russ Shanks, who owned the farm next to the Fremont property, was especially concerned. "I sure as heck don't want to see the old Wicker Road all clogged up with traffic, people trespassing over my property, scaring my animals, polluting the air with gasoline fumes. We don't need any of that, that's for sure."

"Traffic jams in Corbet! The very thought makes me shudder," Gladys muttered.

"Why, we have our bikathon for mental health coming up right after July fourth," the waitress pouring second rounds of coffee, announced. "The route goes right down Wicker Road."

"And talking about July fourth," Graham said, stirring sugar into his coffee, "can you just imagine the bedlam if Corbet was proclaimed the site of an important Revolutionary War battle. Look at Lexington and Concord. Those towns are overrun with tourists, hawkers and all that folderol. Do you think the folks in those towns can walk around leaving the cars unlocked? They're locking up everything, putting in fancy alarm systems..."

"Of course," Russ Shanks reflected, "you can't very well cover up historical evidence...."

"What evidence?" Graham sneered. "One rusty musket? Big deal. I can think of plenty of reasons why that musket was buried out by the old Fremont barn."

"Coulda been Henry Cotton's musket for one thing," Gladys suggested.

Russ who also happened to be a Revolutionary War buff, offered another explanation. "It was most likely a souvenir Harmon Fremont himself picked up while fighting down in Bennington."

Gladys frowned. "Okay, maybe we can explain one musket away, but what if more get dug up out there?"

Graham Sawyer raised his thick, gray brows. "I've got a feeling that once Walker Jordan gets back, he'll put a quick stop to the digging."

"I don't know," Gladys reflected. "I heard he went up to Burlington this weekend. And we all know who else is up there. He may be coming back here with a whole different perspective on things."

"Well, if that's the case," Graham said pointedly, "it's up to us concerned citizens to see to it that he changes his perspective back."

"I'M TELLING YOU, I was sitting at the very next table, eating a hamburger," Caroline Berkenkamp, a second-grade teacher, declared to Norma Lund in the teachers' lunchroom in the elementary school. "And everyone knows how Graham Sawyer's voice carries. They are going to try to prevent the truth from being told. It's as good as a cover-up. There's no two ways about it."

Norma Lund shoved aside her turkey sandwich. "Well, we'll just see about that. I'm certain the parents and teachers of this community will not sit idly by and let that happen. I always did say that Chelsea Clark's theories made a lot of sense. I may not have spoken up forcefully enough when she wanted the Historical Society to purchase the Fremont estate, but I wasn't one to nix the proposal outright."

Caroline Berkenkamp seemed to recall that Norma had ridiculed Chelsea's Battle-of-Fremont theory on more than one occasion, but that, she decided, was neither here nor there. "I think we should call a special meeting of the PTA. What do you think?"

"I BELIEVE," declared Isabelle Alpert to her preservation group, "that we have a very serious problem here. If our town is overrun by sightseers and local properties are bought up by a bunch of wealthy flatlanders who want to put in tennis courts and swimming pools and the like, just think of what that will do to the gentle, delicate balance of nature we've worked so hard to protect all these years."

The members of the group all looked distraught. "Will any of them care that maidenhair spleenwort grows on ledges? Or that there are sixty-six distinct species of fern native to Vermont? And over twenty hybrids?" One member spoke up.

"We'll be lucky if there'll be six species left after the influx," Everett King, a sugar maker for more than fifty years, muttered.

"Tourism won't hurt your business, though, Ev," Isabelle pointed out. "Just think of all the maple sugar products you'll be able to sell. Why, you could even charge folks to come over to the sugar house and watch the boiling down."

"I won't argue the point that there's money to be made on tourism," Ev said. "But I make more than enough to satisfy my needs selling my syrup through my little catalog. I'm a simple man. And, like the rest of you, I'm more interested in preserving the environment than in making a quick buck. Back when I was a boy, my father and I hiked the Bow Trail up here in these mountains, fished the brooks, cooked out over open fires, took pictures with his old Graflex of fox, owls, flying squirrels and deer out in the fields and forests. Still got those pictures. Still hike and fish the same spots with my grandchildren. And I want my grandchildren to have the joy of doing the same with their children."

A newcomer to the group meekly raised her hand. "I know most of you consider me a flatlander even though I've lived here in Corbet for nearly eight years. But I came here, settled here with my two sons, because I wanted to raise them in a community where everyone knew and respected each other, where I could walk into the general store, pick up a stovepipe and underwear and check out the wedding and birth announcements posted right on the bulletin board outside. I wanted a community rich in tradition, where my kids could hike and fish and explore nature, just like Ev and his family." She cleared her throat. "I have nothing against other flatlanders like myself... or like Walker Jordan moving to Corbet. I see us as... conscientious citizens who aren't out to change the character of the town, but to preserve all that's fine about it."

This emotional speech was greeted by a hearty round of applause.

Isabelle closed by reminding the group how effective they'd been as lobbyists two years ago when a highway construction plan had threatened important wildlife areas on the outskirts of the town.

"We've used our influence and force to good effect in the past," she concluded, "and we can do it again."

As CHELSEA and her two passengers arrived back in Corbet mid-afternoon, the divisions of opinion had already grown sharp and bitter, each side secure in the belief that he or she had only the best interest of the town at heart.

Several representatives of those two groups were parked out by the Fremont house. They were milling about the front porch eagerly awaiting Walker Jordan's arrival, all anxious to present their views and secure the support of the new owner of the Fremont property.

"What's this? A welcome-home party?" Chelsea asked, spotting the half dozen cars as she approached Walker's place.

Walker chuckled. "Or else plans are afoot for a shotgun wedding," he teased as he saw Ned Hunt hurrying down to the end of the driveway to greet them.

Chelsea ignored Walker's little joke, but she was concerned by the grim look on Ned's face as he waved her to a stop.

Chelsea braked and rolled her window all the way down as Ned approached.

"What is it? What's wrong?" she asked anxiously.

Ned leaned down, quickly and quietly took in the two passengers, then focused his attention on Chelsea.

"Seems history's come full circle. We've got another battle on our hands, right on Fremont soil."

"*Another* battle?" Chelsea gave Ned a questioning look.

Ned's gaze shifted to Walker. "Seems one of the work crew out at your barn unearthed a musket."

Chelsea's breath caught. Jack Scheurer shot forward in his seat, his face lit with alert excitement. Walker felt a little like he imagined those Green Mountain Boys of yore felt right before entering a battle.

Chelsea found her voice first, but only to utter one word. "British?"

Ned nodded. "Seems to be."

Walker looked ahead at the half dozen parked cars. "What are they doing here? Waiting for permission to pan for gold?" he asked sarcastically.

"Some of 'em," Ned acknowledged. "Imagine there'll also be a few people looking to buy. People have been ringing my office all afternoon, wanting me to pitch you offers." Ned smiled. "I figured you wouldn't be selling and told 'em so. Wasn't wrong, was I?"

"You weren't wrong," Walker said firmly.

"Of course Isabelle and a couple of her pals are here to speak out for preservation and make sure you don't give in to the pressures of what she's calling the Corbet money grubbers."

"Oh, that makes me so mad," Chelsea snapped, clenching her hands around the steering wheel. "Everyone is missing the point."

Walker regarded her warily. "I'm worried about getting stuck with the point."

Scheurer, oblivious to the battle going on in the front seats, opened his door and stepped out of the car. "Is the musket up in the house?" the professor inquired excitedly. "I'd love to have a close look at it."

"No, it's over at the Historical Society," Ned said.

Now Walker leapt out of the car. "What's it doing there? Who gave anyone permission to remove any of my property?"

"Take it easy, Walker," Ned soothed. "It wasn't like that. It got brought up there for safekeeping." He frowned, glancing back up at the house. "Uh-oh, they've spotted you now, son. Here they come."

Walker scowled. "Looks like I'm going to be in the market for a bunch of No Trespassing signs," he muttered.

Chelsea wished she'd put some of those signs up herself. On her heart.

Chapter Twelve

When an exhausted Chelsea dragged herself into her office at the Historical Society the next morning, she was taken aback to see Jack Scheurer sitting there. Behind her desk, no less.

"Ah, good morning, Miss Clark."

"Oh...Dr. Scheurer. You're still...here." And making himself quite at home, she noted. To her consternation she also saw that he had the Abigail Fremont love letter in front of him. She frowned.

Scheurer merely smiled as he followed her gaze. "I hope you don't mind. Things were so chaotic yesterday I wasn't able to give your documents my full attention. One of the other board members...Norma Lund, I think she said her name was...was kind enough to let me into your office and provide me with access to your files." He smiled brightly. "You can certainly count her as one of our supporters."

There was something about the way the noted history professor said *our* that rubbed Chelsea the wrong way. She quickly chastised herself for her proprietary feelings about her Battle-of-Fremont research. After all, she was the one who'd spent months trying to get Scheurer involved. She should be thrilled that he was finally so enthused. Really, what was the matter with her anyway?

One thing that was the matter was that Scheurer was still sitting in her seat. And seemed quite content to remain there.

Standing inside the door, coffee thermos and briefcase in hand, Chelsea debated whether to politely ask the renowned professor to find another seat or find one herself.

"I thought your plan was to...uh...head back to Boston...last night," she said, setting her briefcase on the floor and pulling another chair up beside the desk. She sat down feeling inarticulate, adolescent and displaced.

"You didn't expect me to leave you to cope with this dilemma on your own, did you?" He gave her a confident smile.

Dilemma. She rolled the word over in her mind. It was certainly that, all right.

"I stayed over at the Picadilly Inn on Grove Street. Charming little B and B. Mrs. Kellerman, the owner, and I had a delightful chat over breakfast. She's already making plans to redecorate and very likely expand."

"Expand?" Chelsea muttered weakly. She'd always had a special fondness for the cozy charm of the Picadilly.

"She's got a good strip of land behind the place. Room for at least a twelve-unit motel. And if she's able to grab up the lot across the street..."

"Motel?" Chelsea echoed bleakly.

"Oh, nothing garish, certainly. But, as Mrs. Kellerman herself knows, while some tourists find inns charming, others prefer less intimate accommodations when they're traveling. Having both to offer is a wise business move."

"Don't you think Mrs. Kellerman is being a bit... premature?" Chelsea argued. "This whole town is jumping the gun, if you ask me. It was just... one musket. And if Walker Jordan has his way, it will be the only one."

Scheurer made light of her concerns. "I wouldn't worry about Walker Jordan, Chelsea. We'll persuade him, or get around him, one way or another. With the unearthing of that musket I feel we're really getting hot now. Why the shot from that musket could be one that will be heard around the world."

She was quick to take note that the esteemed professor had progressed to calling her by her first name. And he was sprinkling the *we*s in his conversation quite liberally. For all her gratitude for his interest and support, she couldn't help finding his authoritative demeanor irritating. She shifted in her chair. Her office suddenly seemed overcrowded.

Scheurer appeared oblivious to the effect he was having on her. "I'd most like to get another look at that musket, but Jordan's reclaimed it, and when I spoke to him this morning he was adamant—"

Chelsea set aside her concerns about Scheurer muscling in on her territory. "You spoke to Walker?"

The professor merely shrugged. "I'll give him a while to settle down. Meanwhile I thought we could spend the morning going over your collection of Fremont papers. Really pull it all together."

"You mean Walker was angry when you spoke to him?" Chelsea persisted.

Scheurer was already reexamining the love letter and gave her a distracted grimace that didn't tell her much.

"You spoke to him on the phone?"

"What?" Scheurer had plucked a magnifying glass from the desk and was peering through it at the letter.

"I asked if you—"

"I stopped at his place. I was hoping he'd give me another glance at the musket."

"What did he say?"

But instead of answering her question, he remarked, "I understand Jordan was a hotshot lawyer out in L.A."

Chelsea found Scheurer's use of the word *hotshot* irritating, even though she'd probably used the very same word herself once upon a time.

"Walker was a very successful corporate attorney." She said each word carefully.

"Hmmmm," Scheurer mused.

"Hmmmm, what?" Chelsea's eyes narrowed.

Scheurer looked across at her and smiled congenially. "I was just wondering what would make a very successful corporate attorney chuck it all in for some rural out-of-the-way spot in Vermont?" He studied Chelsea thoughtfully. "Unless there was some way of his knowing he could make an eventual killing on a piece of property that he'd be able to pick up for a song."

Chelsea bristled at Scheurer's inference. "Walker's not out to make a killing. And he had no idea that his property was the possible site of a Revolutionary War battle. He bought the Fremont estate because he...fell in love with it."

Scheurer dismissed her response in much the way a parent dismissed a naive child.

"My instinct tells me, maybe we need to look for the answer back in L.A.," Scheurer said reflectively.

"We?" Chelsea was getting fed up with that particular pronoun.

"I don't mean *we* in the literal sense, Chelsea. What I'm thinking here is that it wouldn't hurt to hire ourselves a detective..."

Chelsea was truly shocked. "You can't be serious."

"This is a serious matter, my dear. We've got to get some leverage here to influence Jordan to change his position. He's deliberately obstructing the resolution of a great historical issue. The Battle of Fremont could explain the surrender of Burgoyne. Do you realize what it would mean to bring such an historical event to light?"

"Well, of course I do," Chelsea said sharply. "This project has been my... my life. I've devoted myself to this work. I've been willing to do almost anything..." She paused, her mind flashing on some of the more embarrassing moments she'd suffered in her quest to prove the existence of the Battle of Fremont.

"The point is," Scheurer stepped in on her pause, "if Jordan was involved in any underhanded activities that we could use as a bargaining chip..."

"That's despicable," Chelsea said, outraged.

"Lawyers are not all honorable, Chelsea." Scheurer proffered a condescending smile.

"I wasn't talking about lawyers," Chelsea deadpanned. "I was referring to historians."

Contrary to being insulted, Scheurer observed her with a modicum of newfound respect. "No one chooses to relinquish the moral high ground of academia for the gritty and often harsh reality of what it takes to maintain such a lofty position. Unfortunately there are times when we must step down from our ivory towers and get tough."

"Even if it takes blackmailing someone who stands in your way?" Chelsea queried with icy calm.

Scheurer shrugged, a deprecating smile playing on his lips. "Don't be melodramatic. I'm not out to start any scandals. I just want a little leverage to help Jordan see compromise is always the wisest choice." He pressed his palms together. "In our profession, Chelsea, it's publish or perish, as you already know. Now, you impress me as a woman of drive, vitality and intelligence who has no desire to spend her life undercompensated, unappreciated, teaching in a dead-end community college, languishing behind a desk, shuffling historic papers of questionable value in a dreary Historical Society office and, in short, living a life of obscurity."

"There are worse fates," she retorted, her voice full of righteous indignation. Oh, if Walker could hear her now.

Scheurer laughed dryly. "If I can remind you of the positive glow in your cheeks when I mentioned the possibility of a lecture series at Danbury..."

"Of course I glowed," she countered. "I'm not saying I don't want to make my mark in my field." She rose abruptly from her chair and started sweeping up the Fremont papers together on her desk. "I just don't want to...to destroy anything or anyone to get there." She grabbed her briefcase and started putting the Fremont papers inside.

Scheurer gave her a baffled look. "What are you doing? I thought we'd go over those papers?"

"I have a class this morning. Over at my obscure dead-end college. I just dropped by my office here to get these papers for a group discussion on the ethical considerations of historical research and documentation." She turned abruptly and headed for her door, but stopped as she got there. "Oh, and Jack, I should mention that there's a tack that sometimes works its way up through that seat. Next time you should use one of the other chairs."

CORBET WAS RAPIDLY becoming a town under siege. The majority of the residents had split into two opposing camps, those who coined themselves the Preservationists and stood solidly behind Walker's position to let sleeping muskets lie, and those colorfully calling themselves the Sons and Daughters of the Green Mountain Boys, determined to bring the historic battle to light, some hoping to reap as many personal benefits as possible in the process. The few townspeople who had not yet taken a stand were being torn between the two groups. Fervent representatives of each camp were out campaigning, plastering posters up around town with the same kind of vigor and zeal as if they were running for president.

When Chelsea arrived home after her morning class she was deluged with phone calls. They ranged from words of support and encouragement in her efforts to establish proof of the battle, to heated arguments about how her actions were destroying the very fiber of the town. By the fifteenth phone call Chelsea knew she had to get out of the house or risk her sanity, which at the moment was already in serious jeopardy.

When she got into her car her only goal was to get out of Corbet for a while. Escape. Find solitude. Take a few hours to think.

She turned on the radio. A singer crooned a love song. She switched it off. She made a right turn off Pratt Lane onto Dummer Road, rolling down her window all the way to let in a breeze. It was a surprisingly hot day for late May. Wriggling out of her sweater, she wished she'd worn a light cotton skirt instead of jeans.

Absently taking a sharp left at the four-crossings juncture, thinking only that she meant to wander aimlessly through the back roads, Chelsea realized she'd unconsciously chosen her destination. The road she'd taken was the one leading straight to Deer Hollow Creek.

She smiled to herself. It had been years since she'd gone out to the old swimming hole. Not since high school, she realized, struck by how fast time had passed. Deer Hollow Creek had been one of her favorite spots. She and her friends had spent countless days there after school in the late spring and after work in the summer. Soon after she'd gone off to college, Corbet had decided to build a town swimming pool, which quickly supplanted Deer Hollow Creek as the favored hangout among the teens.

Chelsea was banking on finding the spot deserted. After all, the creek was no longer in vogue and it was too early in the season, anyway, for people to be thinking about swimming. It would be lovely to sit on the sun-baked rocks, listen to the chirping birds, even, if it stayed this hot, take a refreshing dip. As a girl she almost always won the dare to be the first one into the icy water at the start of the season.

As she wound her way up the twisting dirt road to the creek, she felt an almost giddy sensation when she saw no other cars parked. It was almost as if she were playing hooky from school. As a student, she'd always been too responsible, too diligent and too scared to cut school.

She parked her car under a shady tree and dug a blanket out of her trunk. The air was still and smelled rich and piny. She took in a deep, cleansing breath. It was good to get out of Corbet, good to escape the controversy that had mushroomed into a full-fledged battle. And it was especially good to get away from the repellent Dr. Scheurer who had forced her to see history, or at least one noted historian, in a new and altogether unpleasant light.

As she made her way to the creek, Chelsea threw back her head, letting the warm air caress her face. A soaring blue jay winged across her path, a path that followed a narrow stream that she knew would widen into the clear blue-green creek just ahead.

Scrambling with ease onto a wide flat boulder on the south bank of the creek, Chelsea spread her blanket and stretched out. She closed her eyes, relishing the warmth of the sun, the gentle breeze, the tranquillity, just letting herself drift, her mind wander back through time.

"Hey, Chel, dare you to dive in off bear rock."

"Oh yeah, Mike. Double dare you to follow me."

"Are you crazy?"

"Nah, Chelsea's not crazy. She's in love."

"Oh cut it out, Kenny. Quit teasing her. You're just jealous."

"Julie baby, me jealous? Of a flatlander? No way."

"Hey, speak of the devil . . ."

"Hi, Chelsea."

"Oh . . . hi, Walker. I thought you were going back to the city this weekend."

"I told the folks to go without me."

"Uh-oh, Chel. Watch it. A flatlander with his own pad."

"Shut up, Kenny."

"Just joshing, Walker. Hey, I wish my folks would go off for a weekend."

"Wanna take a swim, Chelsea?"

"Sure, Walker. Off bear rock?"

"First one in gets his wish granted."

"Or her wish."

"I hope we have the same wish. . . ."

Chelsea's eyes blinked open. Tears spilled. *Oh Walker, we never did admit our wishes to each other. My wish then was that you'd never leave. What's my wish now?*

She sat up, hugged herself tight. Two days ago, in Walker's arms, her wish had been clear. She'd wanted him. She remembered how she'd clung to him, almost as if fearing they'd be flung apart if she didn't hold fast. As they'd made love, his touch had swept through her, he was everywhere a part of her, enveloping her. And she had melted, opened, become a part of him. It had been the most wondrous and frightening experience of her life, awakening so many of her needs and terrors at the same time.

She was so confused. She felt as if she were coming unglued. And the whole town seemed to be coming unglued along with her. She'd never imagined the troubling ramifications and repercussions of what she'd always viewed as the pure pursuit of knowledge, the possibility of making a significant historical discovery, the chance to advance her own career as an historian. She'd made light of Walker's concerns about what such a discovery could do to the community, but now it seemed he was right on the mark.

Troubled, too weary to sort through her feelings, Chelsea decided that a swim in the icy creek was just what she needed to revitalize her. Checking around to make sure she was alone, she slipped out of her shirt and jeans, hesitated for a moment and then, feeling risqué, removed her bra and panties, too. She'd only gone skinny-dipping once before. Sixteen years ago. On a dare. With Walker.

Poised on the rock ready to dive into the creek, Chelsea felt a rush of excitement and anticipation. Then, taking in a quick breath, she made a shallow dive into the sun-sparkled blue-green pool.

The moment she landed, all of her muscles constricted against the shock of the frigid water. She gasped aloud, for an instant ruing her impetuosity. But then, catching her second wind, she kicked out in a strong crawl, welcoming the bracing sensation, feeling almost light-headed and free of constraint.

She was floating serenely on her back, her eyes half-closed against the bright sun, reveling in the simple joy of the water's embrace when she caught a flash of movement on the rocks.

A deer she thought at first. Still floating, she cupped one hand over her brow to block out the sun and get a better look.

What she saw wasn't a deer but a man. Walker Jordan, to be precise. He waved right at her as she dove for cover.

"Hey, how's the water?" he called out cheerily, when she resurfaced. Stripped down to the skin, he dove in before she could make any response.

He hit the water in a smooth, clean dive less than ten feet from her.

Treading water, she glared at him. "What are you doing here? Of all the places you might have gone..."

"I followed you," he confessed unabashedly.

She sputtered. ''You followed me? You ... you hid in the bushes and ... watched me get ... undressed?''

He grinned. "I wasn't hiding. And unfortunately I missed seeing you get undressed."

Chelsea regarded him with a puzzled expression as she trod water. "You just said you followed me."

"I should have said I followed your car. I was pulling into your street when you pulled out. I've been sitting parked behind your car for about a half hour trying to decide whether to continue on foot or not."

He swam closer to her. "Hey, your lips are turning blue. We should swim or get out."

"Swim." Brushing her dripping hair from her eyes, she broke out in a powerful sidestroke through the water.

Walker easily kept pace with her as they cut through the mirror images of trees and rocks reflected in the water. They swam vigorously, silently, their strokes in sync.

Finally, too cold and tired to swim anymore, Chelsea headed for the edge of the creek and grasped a low-hanging tree branch. Her teeth were chattering and she was exhausted. She was also naked, and at the moment it didn't seem to matter that only two days ago Walker had not only seen but caressed just about every inch of her body.

Walker's hand moved over hers as she clung to the branch. Her gaze met his and locked. He smiled at her and then let his eyelids fall closed deliberately.

She pulled herself out of the water and scrambled back to the rock where she'd left her clothes. Having no towel to use to dry off, she wrapped the blanket around her. She was still clutching it to her chilled, shivering body when Walker, clad only in his trousers, approached.

Without saying a word, he wrapped his arms around her and rubbed her back and shoulders.

"Better?" he murmured.

Awkwardly she drew away. "Why did you follow me, Walker?"

Instead of answering, he sat down on the rock, legs bent, his arms hugging his knees. He looked around at the picturesque setting and smiled. "I have fond memories of this place." He stared out at the water as Chelsea slipped her clothes back on under the blanket. Then she sat down beside him.

"It hasn't changed a whit," he said, glancing over at her.

"No, it hasn't."

"You know, I always wondered why they called this Deer Hollow. In all the times I came here, I never saw a deer."

A smile played on her lips. "That's because you were never here at the right time."

Walker cocked an eyebrow. "And what's the right time?"

"When thar here, of course," she answered in a thick Vermont twang, breaking out in laughter.

Walker laughed, too. "Now, that's got to be an old joke."

"Old as the hills, Walker. Only a flatlander would fall for it." But his laugh thrilled her.

He took her hand. "Cold hands, warm heart," he murmured.

"Don't be nice to me, Walker," she said guiltily. "You were afraid I'd turn your patch of paradise into a three-ring circus and instead I've triggered an invasion."

He pressed her hand, palm up to his lips. "It's nothing compared to the chaos going on inside of me."

She lifted her eyes to search his face. "Walker..."

"I'm in love with you, Chelsea."

She closed her eyes, held her breath.

He placed a moist, feather-light kiss on her palm. "Together we can bring sanity back to the town. And you can soothe the chaos inside of me at the same time."

Chelsea could feel her insides tightening. She slipped her hand from his. "You mean... just give it up? Pretend the battle never happened?"

"What about the battle going on now? Neighbors have become adversaries. Friends are now rivals. Instead of a warm, friendly, peace-loving town, the community is divided into factions, poised for battle. Isn't this battle more important than one that might or might not have taken place over two hundred years ago, Chelsea?"

She shook her head. "I keep asking myself the same question, Walker. Maybe you don't believe this, but it's not just an issue of my own ambition. Something happened here of vast historical significance..."

"Something *may* have happened here," he corrected. "Something *is* happening here right now. Between you and me. And I don't think our real struggle has anything to do with history. Not Revolutionary War history, anyway."

She drew further away from him. "If you're going to tell me I'm only involved in verifying the Battle of Fremont to avoid getting involved with you, you can save your breath, Walker."

"You're going to tell me you're not scared?"

Her eyes widened as she met his gaze. "Oh Walker, I'm scared to death of loving you."

"Chelsea." He tried to pull her to him, but she held him off.

"But that's beside the point. I also happen to believe I have an obligation...a...responsibility to my profession, to my conscience."

"Come on, Chelsea. You didn't take a Hippocratic oath. Besides, look what your responsibility to your conscience and your profession is doing to our town, to us."

"I hate what's happening as much as you do. But I think it's all the more reason to settle the issue once and for all. If there was an important battle here in Corbet, then we can appeal to the town to act on the knowledge in a calm, responsible fashion. Maybe, having experienced this chaos, they'll realize how much wiser it would be not to let things get out of control."

Walker didn't respond. His expression was unreadable. He stared out at the water for what felt to Chelsea like an interminable time.

"It's a reasonable proposal, Walker. You could at least consider it. It might work."

Still silence.

"I know what you're thinking," she kept on in frustration. "That I'm just trying to con you into letting me do exactly what I've been wanting to do all along. You...you probably think I'm merely taking advantage of the situation to get my way, and that I don't care what happens to this town. Well, it's not true, Walker." She gnawed on her upper lip. "I'm surprised at how much I...care."

Finally he broke his silence. "A special meeting's been set up in town tomorrow night." He paused. "Your good friend's moderating."

Chelsea's brow creased. "Ned Hunt?" She knew that out of deference to her, Ned had removed himself from the controversy as much as possible.

Walker smiled darkly. "Jack Scheurer. Noted historian, champion of true and just causes. The Sons and Daughters of the Green Mountain Boys will, no doubt, carry him in on their shoulders. The Preservationalists, on the other hand, are raiding the general store for nice, ripe tomatoes. It should be quite a meeting."

Chelsea groaned, her suspicions about Scheurer muscling in on her territory now confirmed. "He's only going to stir things up more," she muttered harshly.

Walker's eyes followed the golden streak of sunlight on the creek. "Why don't we discuss your proposition after the meeting."

Chelsea gave him a sardonic look. "Okay. I know what you're thinking. That after the meeting I'll be convinced you're right, but—"

He pressed his finger against her lips to silence her. "Now, I have a proposal for you."

Chelsea swallowed hard. "What . . . is it?"

He placed his hands on her cheeks and brought her face close to his. "Let's go skinny dipping again." He twined his fingers into her hair and touched his lips to hers. "First one in gets his wish granted."

Chelsea's whole body trembled. "Or hers." *Oh Walker, if only we could have the same wish. . . .*

Chapter Thirteen

Chelsea and Walker both ignored their discarded clothes as they staggered out of the creek.

"I'm...freezing," Chelsea gasped. And Walker did exactly what she wanted. He drew her against him. She could feel his muscles quivering from the cold.

He sought her lips. They kissed lightly. "My teeth are chattering," she murmured.

"I thought mine were chattering," he said with a low laugh. "Wait," he said, breaking away.

A moment later he returned with the blanket, and then led her to a secluded grassy bank above the rocks. He wrapped the blanket around both of them and sank with her onto the fragrant grass.

Chelsea had visions of public shame. Indecent exposure. Lewd and lascivious behavior...

"Can you imagine! The two of them, stark naked, carrying on right there in the open. Disgusting, I tell you. We should run them out of town...."

"Walker...wait. Somebody might...come by..." Her words came in tiny bursts, broken by little moans of pleasure as Walker's hands explored her body, slowly, with a delicious wantonness.

He caressed her breasts, murmuring, "No one will find us. It's just you and me and nature, Chelsea."

She knew he was right. Even if someone wandered down to the creek, they wouldn't be spotted here in the shelter above the rocks. She pressed closer to him, their bodies fitting as snugly as a child's puzzle.

Connected to Walker, Chelsea felt a wondrous integration with the world around her—the creek, the birds, the grass dotted with ferns and wildflowers, the warm, rich rays of the sun. The connection felt so intimate, so absolute.

"Wait," he whispered as he moved on top of her, his thrusts strong and confident. Soon, Chelsea's whole body drew together to one blazing point, too intense to be contained.

"Now," he murmured and together they slipped over the edge.

Afterward they stayed wrapped in each other's arms in the blanket, embracing lightly, their hair still damp, their bodies as warm as the sun.

"Walker, look," she whispered.

He followed her gaze. Then his face lit up with delight. "A deer."

"NED," CHELSEA SAID with a sharp intake of breath, surprised to spot her old friend rocking on her porch.

Ned's eyes traveled past her. "Isn't that Walker's car just went by?"

She shot a look around even though she knew perfectly well it was Walker's car. He'd followed close behind her on the drive back from Deer Hollow Creek.

"Uh . . . yes," she said, turning back to face Ned's amused smile. "What?" she asked sharply, absently wiping her cheek with the back of her hand, feeling the heat of her skin.

"Nothin'," Ned replied laconically, attempting a straight face. "Just that you've got a blade or two of grass in your hair."

"We were . . . swimming," she said lamely. Not that swimming explained the grass. But then Chelsea had no intention of explaining the grass. Besides, from the look in Ned's eye it didn't need explaining.

She sank down into a chair beside him. The sun had gone down and there was a brisk breeze picking up. That was something she really loved about Vermont. The deliciously cool mountain evenings each spring.

They didn't speak for a time. Chelsea closed her eyes, rocking back and forth. Tears began to slide down her cheeks. She struggled to control herself. She could hardly explain that she was crying because she'd just had a rapturous sexual encounter.

She turned her face from Ned, surreptitiously wiping her damp cheeks. Then she tipped her head back and took a deep breath.

"I suppose you heard Walker put in a bid on the Currier Building over on Maple."

Chelsea looked back at Ned. "No. Why does he want to buy the Currier Building? The place is a wreck."

"He wants to fix it up, open his law practice there, rent out the rest of the space for offices. He made a good offer, but . . ." Ned let the sentence hang.

"But what?" Chelsea demanded.

Ned shrugged. "I don't think Hopkins will accept it, the way things stands."

Chelsea's eyes narrowed. "What are you saying, Ned? That Hopkins is going to turn down a perfectly reasonable offer for a building he's been trying to unload for years because of Walker's refusal to let us dig for muskets?''

"Hopkins did make a counteroffer," Ned said slowly. "To buy the Fremont place. Not that Hopkins could do it on his own. He's part of a group headed by Jed Howell over at the First National Bank. It was a generous offer, I'll grant 'em that.''

"But since Walker refuses to sell, he gets a turndown on the Currier property?''

"That's about it.''

"But that's so unfair, Ned. Walker wants to turn a wreck of a property into a functional, useful building. There's hardly any office space in town. Walker would be doing Corbet a service. Not to mention that we could certainly use a brilliant young lawyer in this town.''

"Question at this point is, who'd use his services if he did set up practice? Seems like most of the business community would boycott him, the way I hear tell. And I heard this morning that Hal Opheimer pulled his construction crew off the Fremont house restoration. Told Walker his schedule was too tight and his men wouldn't be able to get back to it until sometime next spring. It's not gonna be easy finding another contractor this late in the spring. Not to mention that Walker'll probably have to get someone in who isn't local.''

Chelsea gave Ned an incredulous look. "Has everyone gone completely crazy?''

Ned smiled humorlessly. "Y'hup. Sure looks that way." He rubbed his jaw. "Oh, that professor friend of yours dropped by before.''

Chelsea's mouth set. "He's no friend of mine.''

"Well, he's making plenty of other friends in this town."

"I know. Walker told me he's speaking at the town meeting tomorrow night. I just can't believe the way he's waltzed into this town and taken over."

"He asked me if I'd show him some properties. Thinks he might like to buy a little summer place in town."

"Oh no," Chelsea groaned.

"Told him I was on an extended vacation," Ned said with a crooked smile.

"I love you, Ned."

Ned usually quipped "Love ya back," but this time he didn't say anything. Without the reassuring words, Chelsea felt a loneliness well up in her. If she wasn't careful she'd start crying in earnest.

"Do you blame me for all of this?" she asked finally, not courageous enough to look Ned in the eye while she waited for his answer. He might not tell her the truth, because she knew, whether he said it or not, that he truly did love her. But he was a man whose eyes always spoke the truth, whether he wanted them to or not.

"Blame's a waste of time, Chelsea."

She looked at him then. His eyes mirrored his words.

"Walker says he loves me." She hadn't meant to say that. The words came of their own volition.

"Y'hup."

Chelsea's eyes narrowed. "Is that all you're going to say on the topic?"

He lowered his chin and gave her a no-nonsense look. "Is that all you're gonna say on the topic?"

Chelsea had to laugh. "It's not a topic I'm well versed on, Ned. I couldn't even tell Walker…I love him back."

"It's a scary thing to say, even when you are well versed."

"You were in love once, weren't you, Ned? With that teacher who took over the Fremont estate with her sister and opened the finishing school. Did you ever tell her?"

"That was close on forty years ago. Why is it, girl, you always revert to talking history when you get close to your feelings?" Ned asked softly. But he answered her anyway. "I told her, in a roundabout way. And in a roundabout way, she let me know she felt the same way about me. But she felt she had a responsibility to stick by her sister. When the school folded here, the sister thought to relocate closer to a city. Picked Chicago, and off they went. I heard from her once. The sister had made a good choice. They had themselves a fine school and were doing very nicely."

Chelsea studied him quietly for a minute. "Do you think she ever regretted her decision?"

"I'm the wrong one to ask. All I can say, to be absolutely truthful, is that I hope she did. Male ego, you know." He winked at her.

"Seriously, Ned. Would you have married her if she'd stayed?"

He turned abruptly sober. "Would you marry Walker if you stay?"

Chelsea flushed. "He hasn't asked me."

"What would your answer be?"

"I don't know," she admitted. "I've never seen myself…married. I've seen myself famous, respected, admired, sought after in my field, but married...never."

"It's no wonder, given your own folks' marriage."

Chelsea was about to agree, but then, slowly, she shook her head. "Do I use my parents' unhappy marriage as an excuse my whole life, Ned? I mean...lots of people have parents who had terrible, even tragic relationships. Does that destine us all to the same fate, or to avoid relationships all our lives?"

She felt Ned's hand fold over hers and when she looked up into his eyes she was startled to see tears there.

She tenderly touched his cheek. "I do love Walker. Even though it scares the dickens out of me. But it isn't so easy, even if I could overcome my fears."

Ned sighed. "You still want to prove that battle took place and Walker still stands in your way."

"He wants me to forget about it. But does loving him mean having to turn my back on my dreams?" Her own eyes glistened with tears now, too. "I know that battle happened, Ned. It's not just the musket. I've felt it in my blood for a long time. Oh, I can't deny I want the recognition for the discovery. But I refuse to believe I'd ever let my success make me lose sight of my obligations or my principles."

Ned smiled. "No, I don't think you would be easily corrupted." The smile faded. "But then, I don't know that you'd be all that happy with fame, either."

"I guess I just want the chance to find out. And Walker's the only one who could give me the chance."

"If he gives you the chance, he stands the chance of losing you," Ned said softly. "And no man wants to lose the woman he loves. Take it from one who knows."

THE TOWN MEETING had barely gotten underway before it got out of hand. Owen Fowler, the town manager, kept striking the gavel for order, but emotions were running too high for parliamentary procedure to hold sway.

Jack Scheurer's appearance on the stage only added fuel to the already fiery debate. Chelsea's sole satisfaction was in seeing him throw up his hands in frustration after a couple of minutes and return to his seat.

Owen Fowler was threatening to dismiss the meeting if folks didn't calm down. But it wasn't until Walker Jordan made his way up the aisle to the podium that a hush fell over the room.

Chelsea caught sight of Jed Howell giving the nod to Bob Hopkins. Could they really believe Walker would cave in under pressure? Certainly Isabelle Alpert didn't think so. She was smiling confidently in a seat two down from Chelsea's.

Silently Walker looked out at the audience. When he did speak, his voice was so low that people had to strain to listen. Which was just what Walker wanted them to do.

"It seems to me the friends and foes of the American Revolution probably battled back and forth this way. Before they took to the actual battleground to settle their differences." His eyes lit on Chelsea. "History is repeating itself. Emotions are replacing logic and communication."

He paused, stepping around to stand in front of the podium. "Whether or not there was a battle fought here in Corbet during the Revolutionary War, I, for one, don't want another battle fought here now."

He folded his hands together in front of him. "Only this morning I had hoped to persuade Chelsea to give up her quest. I'm ashamed to admit that I even hoped to persuade her to convince everyone in town that her theory had been wrong, after all.''

Chelsea paled. Had their lovemaking been part of some persuasion plan?

His eyes swept the room. "I guess that's what comes of fourteen years of stepping on toes, doing whatever it takes to get what you want. Or what you think you want.''

"We know what we want," Bill Laird spoke out from the back of the room. "We want to see Corbet in the black for a change instead of in the red. You walk down Main Street and see quaint little shops. We see shops that are empty too much of the time.''

"And what would you rather have, Billy Laird?" Graham Sawyer called out from the front of the auditorium. "Hordes of outsiders overrunning our shops? How long before some of them will be opening their own shops—big, fancier shops..."

"Boutiques, they'll be calling them. With fancy prices to match the fancy names," someone else shouted out sarcastically.

"More shops aren't necessarily bad," Norma Lund protested. "They'll provide a substantial boost to our tax base. Which means more money for town improvements—"

"And teachers' salaries," a fellow in the front row added snidely.

Walker raised his hands to the audience. "Nothing wrong with giving teachers a raise. I'm sure they deserve it. And nothing wrong with a few more businesses or boutiques opening up in town, providing they don't put local shopkeepers out of business.''

"Walker Jordan, you just said you wanted to keep the town the way it was," Isabelle Alpert argued. "I thought you were a firm supporter of the ecology..."

"I most certainly do not want to see the precious fauna and flora of Corbet disturbed. Why, only this morning I saw a deer." Walker's eyes sparkled as they fixed on Chelsea's face. "It was a wondrous sight."

"You can't have it both ways, Walker," a middle-aged man just behind Chelsea yelled.

Chelsea stood up. Immediately all eyes turned to her. She swallowed uncomfortably. "I'd just like to... go on record... that all this feuding is based on the mistaken presumption that the Battle of Fremont is a given." She felt a bead of sweat trickle down the front of her blouse.

Scheurer, finally seeing his opportunity to be heard, leapt up from his seat. "Granted, the current evidence is meager, but it's extremely encouraging. If we can convince you, Mr. Jordan, to let us pursue this further, I feel confident we will be able to establish that this battle did occur and that it was, indeed, a turning point of the war." He cleared his throat. "Given that this period of history has been my lifelong work, I would feel privileged, and if I might be so bold as to say most qualified, to supervise the further investigation—"

"I'm sure you would, Jack," Walker said with a sly grin. "But first of all, I'm not ready to give my permission for further investigation. And second of all, if I do give my permission, it'll be granted to only one person, and that's Chelsea Clark. Whatever grief it may have caused me, I have always admired a woman who was determined to finish what she started." Walker's eyes were teasing as they found Chelsea's, but there was tender affection there as well. "Besides," he added, with an openly seductive grin, "Chelsea was the one who turned me on to history in the first place."

Chelsea smiled back openly, for the first time unconcerned by the curious, wondering glances of those around her. Let them think whatever they want. Let them gossip. Suddenly it just didn't seem to matter to her anymore.

"So what's your point, Jordan?" someone shouted, pulling both Walker and Chelsea back to the heated debate at hand.

Walker looked straight at the audience. "I'm saying that we ought to be able to handle this if we calm down and work together. The ecology and simple pleasures of this small, friendly town should certainly be preserved. I doubt even the fine Sons and Daughters of the Green Mountain Boys want to see Corbet turned into a cold, impersonal commercial attraction. What they want is simply to see the town prosper. And not just so they can line their pockets. We all know Corbet could use a more solid financial base. A successful ecology plan takes more than earnest efforts. It takes funds."

There was a surprisingly enthusiastic response to Walker's words from both groups.

Walker smiled. "What I'm saying is we need to consider both sides, so that we can come to realize we're really all on one side. I realize now, even if this battle theory doesn't pan out, we should be thinking about how to improve our economic picture in Corbet."

"You're not gonna improve it by turning Corbet into a tourist trap," one of the local farmers argued.

"That depends," Walker said calmly. "Here's the deal. We set up a committee with members from all diverging groups to develop a town plan—one that guarantees a system of slow and carefully controlled growth and expansion with strict protectionist laws for all wildlife areas, nature preserves and possibly new sanctuaries. We establish clear guidelines, zoning codes and planning standards, so that everything that is done is accomplished evenhandedly.''

Walker's plan was greeted with a hum among the residents of Corbet.

After several minutes a voice rose from the group. "And if we develop this town plan, you're willing to let Chelsea have free rein on your property to pursue her investigation into the battle?'' Jed Howell asked.

Walker grinned. "Within reason.''

Chelsea stared with amazement at Walker while the rest of the people in the auditorium broke into a round of applause, his compelling solution having struck a positive chord in just about everyone. Everyone except Jack Scheurer. Out of the corner of her eye, Chelsea saw the professor beat a hasty exit from the auditorium. She smiled. He was probably wishing right now that he'd never given her the name of his literary agent.

"One question,'' Norma Lund asked. "What if Chelsea does find conclusive evidence on your property? Would you open the field to the public as a historic landmark? Or would you agree to sell it to the town?''

Walker grinned. "That's two questions, Mrs. Lund. And I'm willing to work out a satisfactory solution...if Chelsea's instinct for history is as good as folks here have finally come around to believe it is.''

After the meeting broke, crowds of high-spirited people gathered around both Chelsea and Walker outside. The respective villains had turned into heroes, and people couldn't say enough words of support.

Bob Hopkins told Walker he'd be reconsidering his bid on the Currier Building, and Hal Opheimer even commented as to how he'd straightened out his scheduling mix-up, and he saw no reason why his crew couldn't be back out at the Fremont place come morning. The biggest boost came from several leaders of the opposition groups who enthusiastically praised Walker for his suggestion of a comprehensive town plan. "A new plan is long overdue," Jed Howell reflected, shaking Walker's hand. Isabelle Alpert kissed Walker on the cheek and thanked him dramatically for speaking in defense of the environment. Alice Wilson, resigned to having lost out to Chelsea, merely smiled winsomely at Walker as she murmured her praise.

As for the group gathered around Chelsea, Walker was certainly right about people coming round as far as her battle theory was concerned. Oh yes, they were telling her, they had known she was onto something all along. After all, she was a first-class historian, and they certainly admired her dedication. Not that they ever doubted she'd triumph in the end.

When the crowds finally dispersed, Chelsea and Walker, left standing alone in front of the town hall, both looked a bit dazed by the roller coaster events of the evening.

"Well," she murmured.

"Well," he murmured back.

They stood facing each other awkwardly.

Finally Walker said, "Can I drive you home?"

"I've got my bike."

They smiled at each other.

Walker secured Chelsea's bike on the bike rack on the trunk of his car. Then he slid in behind the wheel, Chelsea beside him.

The air inside the car seemed weighty. Chelsea glanced over at Walker as he turned the key in the ignition. He'd always been a man of angles and edges, but in the short time he'd been in Corbet the edges had smoothed out, softened. *He really has found his home,* she thought with mixed emotions. Whatever he would decide about his property, she knew he was here to stay. This was his town. His concern for its well-being was self-evident. As was his concern for her.

"Walker," she whispered, "I don't know what to say to you." Her voice was heavy with emotion.

He glanced at her, his expression tender and gentle. "You don't have to say it. It's in your eyes."

"You are a brilliant lawyer, Walker. I really couldn't imagine any way to resolve the chaos. You not only resolved it, but thanks to you, the whole town is going to be better off. They're lucky you picked Corbet as the place to plant your roots, Walker."

They're lucky, she'd said. Walker swallowed hard. He couldn't be angry about it. Not when he'd as good as handed her her ticket out. He started to shift the car into gear, but Chelsea placed her hand over his.

"Wait," she said softly.

He took his hand from the gearshift and stared out the window while she studied his profile.

"There was something important I wanted to tell you up in Burlington. And then again ... this afternoon." She hesitated, wondering if, even now, she'd be able to get the words out. Then Walker looked over at her, and she was torn between the desire to open her heart to him and the desire to flee from the car clutching her emotions to her heart in desperation.

In the end her heart spoke. "I love you, Walker."

His eyes bore into hers, but his expression was unreadable. Then he moved closer, smiled wistfully and draped his arms around her shoulders. "I know," he murmured.

WITH TWO WEEKS of day-and-night work, the newly formed Corbet planning board had put together a remarkably comprehensive and carefully considered proposal for their little town which garnered unanimous approval from both the business and environmental groups. All agreed it was quite amazing what could be accomplished when all sides pulled together. It was a lesson they hoped to apply when other town controversies came up, which, of course, they were bound to do.

The plan was put into Walker's hands on the morning of June 12. That afternoon at three o'clock, he phoned Chelsea and told her to bring over her shovel.

She was at his place by three-thirty. Walker was waiting for her out by the barn, leaning against his own shovel. He'd been off the crutches for ten days and his ankle was no longer even taped.

Chelsea looked up at the barn and saw that the workmen had finished shoring it up.

"Is it safe to poke around inside?" she asked.

"As long as we're careful," Walker answered in a casual voice that sounded manufactured.

A smile quirked on Chelsea's lips. "Are you okay?"

He smiled back at her. A sad smile. No, he wasn't okay. His smoky gray eyes rested on her, admiring this lovely country creature with her scrubbed clean face, tumble of chestnut hair, dressed as she'd been that first day, in jeans and an oversize, overwashed pale blue work shirt. He thought of that first day he'd stumbled and landed on top of her in her trench. He thought of the sight of her long, shapely legs as she'd stood there that afternoon, jeans cast aside, tugging on her shirt-tails, her cheeks flushed with embarrassment. He thought of the morning he'd gotten caught without his pants in her office and the look on her face when her student walked in. He thought of her standing in his bathroom, clutching a towel to her beautiful naked body, pleading for his help. And he thought of the two incredible times they'd made love.

She'd filled him with such a wild, giddy joy, such fulfillment. Out of the chaotic events of these past weeks, he'd come to know what love was truly about for the first time.

Chelsea watched a mix of emotions play on Walker's face. She wasn't sure if her own features showed it, but inside she was a jumble of feelings as well.

He came closer to her, lightly clinked the handle of his shovel against hers. "Yeah, I'm okay," he murmured, an elusive smile on his lips. "As long as I remember that history repeats itself."

Chapter Fourteen

MAJOR REVOLUTIONARY WAR BATTLE UNEARTHED IN VERMONT

Corbet, Vermont—In a field in the sleepy little town of Corbet, Vermont, just ninety miles south of Burlington, significant findings have been unearthed to establish a crucial and heretofore unrecorded Revolutionary War battle between local Green Mountain Boys and British Loyalists. Local historian and lecturer at Corbet Community College, Chelsea Clark, was instrumental...

"Stanford University," Julie exclaimed as Chelsea sat curled up on her wing chair absently munching a doughnut. "Stanford University wants you for a summer lecture series in little more than a week and you just sit there chomping? You're going to accept, aren't you?"

Chelsea draped her blue-jean clad legs over the arm of the chair. "In the past three days I've gotten inquiries from six publishers, a slew of literary agents, a dozen universities..."

Julie grabbed one of the two remaining doughnuts from the box on the coffee table. "Wow. That's fantastic. You can write your own ticket."

Chelsea slipped her finger through the doughnut hole and absently studied her hand. "I know. It's a little overwhelming. My brain feels like a bag of marshmallows. Roasted marshmallows."

Julie flopped onto the sofa. "It's Walker, isn't it? How's he handling all this?"

"I haven't seen him since the day after I hit paydirt. He's gone incommunicado." Chelsea sighed. "Not that I can blame him. He's been besieged by reporters, sightseers, assorted interest groups. So, he cordoned off the field, reposted his No Trespassing signs, hired security guards, put the relics on display at the high school and took off for parts unknown."

"Without a word?"

Chelsea flicked a doughnut crumb from her shirt. "Oh, we had some words before he took off."

"A fight?"

"I wish it were a fight. I could have handled a fight. It would have made all this..." She made a gesture toward the pile of mail on her coffee table, "a lot easier. I could have gotten all indignant about his trying to dissuade me from fame and fortune. I could have accused him of being jealous, selfish, opinionated. If I could have felt angry, it would have been...easier to say goodbye."

"But I thought you said the two of you had words," Julie said, puzzled.

Chelsea laughed dryly. "Walker had words. Words of support, congratulations, best wishes. He...he wants me to live out my dreams, accept all the accolades, go off to places like Stanford and Columbia to lecture, negotiate for a teaching position at a prestigious college."

Julie looked at her with confusion. "But, isn't that what you wanted? I think it's great that Walker understands and can be so supportive. I don't honestly think Zach would ever be able to be so generous, magnanimous, unselfish..."

"Uncaring," Chelsea added sharply, finishing off the doughnut in a single bite.

"How can you say that? Walker's putting aside his personal feelings and encouraging you to do what you've always dreamed of doing. Chelsea, you've worked for years to get to this point. You developed a brilliant theory, pursued it even when you didn't get an iota of support from anyone—including me I'm ashamed to admit. But, you never gave up and now it's paying off in spades."

"You're right. I know you're right." She sat up to inspect the remaining doughnut in the box. "It's just...I keep thinking about something Ned said to me a while ago."

"What did he say?"

Chelsea pushed aside the doughnut box, swung her legs back onto the floor and stared morosely down at her knees. "He said no man wants to lose the woman he loves." Slowly, she looked up at Julie. "I thought Walker loved me. Loved me enough to put up a fight. Ever since he moved here he's been giving me lectures about the downside of success, the cutthroat competition, the loneliness, the emptiness. Now he seems to have changed his tune completely."

Julie confronted Chelsea straight on. "Look kiddo, you can't put this on Walker. This is your struggle, not his."

Chelsea looked about to argue, but then she grabbed up the last doughnut and muttered, "I know."

A BANK OF DARK CLOUDS with a skirt of rain was moving toward the secluded cabin in the woods. Walker used the palm of his hand to wipe away a circle of dust from the window and peered out.

"Looks like another nor'easter."

Ned Hunt came up behind him and peered over Walker's shoulder out the window. "Nope. It's comin' in from the west. Just a summer storm. We could use the rain. Almanac says this is gonna be a particularly dry summer."

Walker stepped away from the window. He gave the cabin he'd been staying in all week a casual survey. It was really only one moderate-sized room, lined with knotty pine walls and a couple of seven-foot-high partitions for the bathroom and the bedroom area. In one corner of the main room was a kitchenette and directly across the room were a few serviceable unholstered chairs and a Franklin stove. In short, it was small, compact, secluded and just what he'd needed.

"Thanks again, Ned, for letting me use this place. And for coming out to see that I'm surviving." He gave the older man an appreciative pat on the shoulder.

Ned shrugged. "No problem. Like I already told ya, I've only got a renter for it after July fourth. Until then it's all yours. A little rustic, but it's got running water, electricity and a phone. In case you do want to let anyone know where you are."

Walker smiled. "I appreciate your getting the phone hooked up for me, but I haven't really felt like...using it yet." He paused. "I do appreciate your not mentioning where I am to...anyone. I just need a little while to get a handle on things."

"Sure. I understand."

Walker was quiet for a minute. "I still keep seeing the look on her face when she struck gold," he mused. "It was really something. She was incandescent with excitement. I don't think she ever looked more beautiful. I guess that was when I realized... Well, she's on her way now."

"Leaves for Palo Alto on the twenty-eighth," Ned said offhandedly, but he was watching Walker's reaction out of the corner of his eyes. "Stanford University wants her for a two-week lecture series. Then there's Columbia wanting her to come to New York in the fall to lecture. And there've been some publishers who'd like to see her write a book. Chelsea's been toying with the idea of doing one on the fateful love affair between Abigail Fremont and Henry Cotton set against the backdrop of the Revolution, and the Battle of Fremont in particular. She's got some theories..."

But Walker was only half listening, his mind like a record needle stuck in a groove. "The twenty-eighth? Of this month?" Walker's voice sounded strained.

"What? Oh, you're referring to Stanford. Yeah, the twenty-eighth of June. That's when their summer term starts. Not much notice for her. Ten days. But," he shrugged with feigned nonchalance, "I suppose if that's what she wants..."

Walker was deep in his own thoughts. "That means she won't be here for the Fourth of July," he muttered. Then realizing Ned was watching him closely, he gave the older man a rueful smile. "Well, I guess it's only fitting that she proclaim her independence with Independence Day right around the corner."

Ned pretended interest in the storm brewing outside. "Seems a shame for her to miss spending the

Fourth in Corbet. Now that the Battle of Fremont has been established, folks in town are feeling especially patriotic and fervent about the vital role their forefathers played in the American Revolution. Word's buzzing around town that we ought to do something special to celebrate the event. And I know there are several groups who'd like to do something in particular to honor Chelsea, since all of this is her doing. And yours, too. You've both done a lot for this town. Enriched our heritage and helped us plan constructively for our future at the same time.''

Walker's features hardened a little. "Thanks, Ned, but don't forget that we each had something to gain by it as well. I wanted to see Corbet remain unspoiled and tranquil. And Chelsea had a lot invested professionally in proving her thesis. She may miss the local honors for her accomplishment, but she'll be getting plenty of plaudits from her colleagues and distinguished historians. That's what she's been dreaming about.''

Walker looked away from Ned's sympathetic gaze. He'd vowed to handle Chelsea's impending departure with a little class. After all, hadn't being classy always been one of his fortes. Never let 'em see you sweat. Never lose your cool. That last day with Chelsea he'd been Mr. Cool, Calm and Collected himself. *Great going, sweetheart! You've earned it. I wish you the best. You're on your way.*

So, he'd chalk up what they'd had to a summer romance. That seemed to be what fate had in store for them. A summer of love, albeit separated from the last one by sixteen years. Heck, they wrote all kinds of love songs on the theme. And didn't all the songs end with one or the other or both going off, going their separate ways?

A branch of a tree whipped against one of the cabin windows, the sound pulling Walker from his ruminations. He gave Ned a determinedly cheery look and rubbed his hands together. "So, what do you say, Ned? How about a cup of tea? Or a beer?"

Ned considered. If he left now he might beat the storm. Even in good weather it was a forty-minute drive down winding roads to Corbet. When there were heavy rains, those roads got treacherous, sometimes flooded. But he knew perfectly well, despite all of Walker's attempts at affability, that he was hurting and in need of some company. Ned remembered, even though it was all of forty years ago, having been in a similar boat himself. And he knew that if he'd had it to do over again, he would have done it different.

"A cup of tea sounds pretty good."

Walker's pleasure was obvious. "Great. Great. Sounds good to me, too." He hurried over to the stove and turned on the kettle. "Anyway, I wanted to... uh...talk to you. About an idea that I've been tossing around in my mind. I thought I'd kind of fling it out, see what you think." He grabbed a couple of mugs from a shelf, opened the box of tea bags he'd brought along to the cabin. "The thing is, there may not be enough time. I mean it might be too hard to organize on such short notice. And, of course there's the cost. But I think there are ways to keep the cost under control."

Ned had no idea what Walker had in mind, but he let the man ramble on.

"Then again, maybe people in town won't go along with it. Or they might feel it's hokey. And I do have some concern that it could get unwieldy, but I've got some ideas on that score...."

The kettle started to whistle, but Walker didn't even hear it. He felt if he could just keep on talking he wouldn't have to deal with his despair.

While Walker paced and talked, Ned went over and took the kettle off the stove, preparing the tea that he knew neither he nor Walker really wanted.

CHELSEA HELD THE PHONE, unaware that she was clutching it as if it was her lifeline. "A reenactment of the Battle of Fremont right on the very spot where it took place? On July fourth? It's a great idea, Walker. Really. A great idea."

"Ned thinks so, too, although we both agree we don't want it to turn into a vaudeville show. I'd like to keep it as authentic as possible. Ned wouldn't say anything, but I know he'd love to play the part of Harmon Fremont. I think he'd be perfect," Walker said enthusiastically, in truth, far more charged up by hearing Chelsea's voice than by her reaction to his idea.

"Oh? So you and Ned have discussed all this on the phone already?" A note of disappointment. So she hadn't been the first one he'd thought of.

"No, I just saw him. Well, he left about twenty minutes ago. It looks like a storm's brewing, but it's not raining too hard yet. I urged him to get on his way before he had problems making the drive back to Corbet. I imagine the roads out here could flood in a downpour."

Chelsea hesitated. "Out where, Walker? Where are you?" And then, before he could answer, she felt compelled to add, "Not that you have to tell me. I mean . . . obviously you've chosen to keep your whereabouts to yourself. Well, of course, not entirely, if Ned knows where you are. But, you certainly have the right to decide—"

"Chelsea."

She took in a breath. "Yes?"

"I'm in a cabin over in Marion. It's one of Ned's rental properties."

"Marion?"

"It's not a bad little cabin. It's got electricity, running water . . . telephone. And it's real private."

Neither of them spoke for a couple of moments.

Chelsea wound some of the phone's coiled wire around her finger. "You disappeared so fast, Walker. I was still trying to catch my breath from all the excitement, and you were gone."

"I know. I just needed some time to myself. Besides, you know me. I'm just not keen on being in the limelight these days."

"Oh Walker, you really have gone country. *Keen on.* No one's used that phrase in decades."

"I know, sweetheart."

Chelsea smiled wistfully. "The *sweetheart* just doesn't come off anymore. You're no longer that glib, hotshot L.A. lawyer who fell on top of me that April day."

"No. No, I'm not," he agreed in a low voice.

"Did Ned tell you I'm going out to Stanford in about a week?"

"Ten days," he said. Somehow ten days sounded less imminent than a week. "Yeah. Yeah, a two-week lecture series. That's great, Chelsea. Really great."

There was an awkward silence.

Walker broke it. "So, anyway . . . You really think I can pull this off?" he asked.

"It's quite an undertaking. Choreography, costumes, weapons, music. You'll need a lot of help."

"Right. Right, I'll need plenty of help. Ned's already offered to pitch in. And he's going to bring it up tomorrow at the Historical Society."

"Oh...well, I'm sure Isabelle and Alice will jump at the opportunity to...pitch in, too. And the others."

Walker laughed.

"What's so funny?"

"Oh...I was just thinking of that day at my place, trying to get rid of Isabelle and Alice so you could come out of the bathroom."

"It will definitely go on record as one of my most embarrassing moments," Chelsea said, grinning.

"Chelsea..."

"Yes, Walker?" She was at once sober and serious.

"I was just wondering..."

"Yes, Walker?" She switched the receiver to her other hand, rubbing her sweaty palm on the leg of her jeans.

He hesitated. "No, never mind. You're probably working round the clock on your lecture series for Stanford."

"Not around the clock. No...not really."

"Well, that's good. You need your beauty sleep. And you've got such a busy schedule ahead. Stanford, then Columbia, isn't it?"

"I mean...I've got the lecture series pretty well organized. It won't really take that much more time. Actually...I've got...time on my hands, you might say."

"Really?"

"Really."

"I guess that leaves you some time to...to follow up on all the other offers you've received this week. Ned said you're even being wooed by several publishers. I suppose the smart thing for you to do would be to head for New York after you finish at Stanford, meet with the different houses, get a feel for..."

"Walker."

"Yes, Chelsea?"

"I'd love to help you."

"You would?"

"I would."

"I wasn't going to ask..."

"I know."

"So...we'll get together and...go over all the diaries and papers you've got. And we could use some of the weapons that have been dug up."

"And, of course, we can even do something with the Abigail Fremont, Henry Cotton angle." She hesitated. "You'd be a perfect Henry."

Walker shut his eyes, knowing there was no one else but Chelsea who could play Abigail to his Henry. "Nah. I'll orchestrate from the sidelines. Maybe Julie and her fiancé..."

"Yeah, they'd be...great," Chelsea said in a flat voice.

"We should get on this right away. Say...tomorrow. I'll drive in first thing in the morning."

"Well...it's going to be hard to...concentrate here. Everyone in town is likely to jump on the bandwagon. I just thought...maybe we should sketch things out first...where it's quiet...."

"It's quiet here."

"In Marion?"

"We wouldn't be disturbed. We could put in a couple of days sketching things out, making phone calls..."

"I know for a fact that the Sheldron Museum has some authentic old weaponry that we might be able to use. Once we get the ball rolling we can drive back into Corbet and form some committees. We'd only have about a week, but if we keep it relatively simple..."

"Oh, definitely simple. And I'd want it to be strictly a celebration for the people of Corbet."

"We could sell tickets as a fund-raiser for charity."

"For the new wildlife sanctuary over by Bartlett Road that the town voted in."

"Walker...it sounds like fun."

Neither of them said it was too bad she wouldn't be there for the actual celebration, but they were both thinking it.

"I guess it's about an hour to Marion," Chelsea reflected. "How hard is it raining out there?"

"It's starting to come down. You'd probably be wiser to come in the morning."

"It isn't raining here yet. If I drove out now, it'll give us more time. We shouldn't waste any time...."

"No, we shouldn't." He quickly gave her the directions, afraid she might change her mind.

"Simple enough," she said. "So, I guess I'll be seeing you soon."

"I'll be here."

A RUSH OF WIND buffeted the cabin. For the hundredth time in the past few minutes, Walker checked his watch. Where was she? It was close to two hours since they'd hung up. It had certainly sounded as though she meant to leave right away. Okay, she'd have to gather up all her papers, pack an overnight case....

Overnight. They hadn't really discussed the fact that they'd be spending the night, maybe a few nights, under the same roof. He felt aroused and uneasy about the prospect at the same time.

Maybe she took it as a given that they wouldn't be sleeping together under the circumstances. Or maybe... she took it as a given that they would. A last fling.

The words *last fling* grated on his mind. He scowled. Weren't men supposed to be the ones open for that sort of deal? Take it when it was offered. Live for the moment. Grab it while you could.

His jaw dropped in a cartoonish way as it really hit him how much he'd changed in the past few months. He didn't want momentary gratification. He didn't want to separate sex—okay, great sex, the best he'd ever had—from his emotions. He didn't want to live for the moment. He wanted permanence, commitment, love everlasting, roots, family, a chance to grow old with the woman he loved.

He started pacing up and down the room, getting worked up over the thought that Chelsea might have no qualms at all about a last fling; that she could put achievement and success over love without a second thought; that she had no desire for the kind of intimate relationship that lasted into a new season. And then endured through all the seasons of the year. All the seasons of a lifetime.

The more agitated he got, the faster he paced. *Well,* he thought with a feverish intensity, *I'm not going to be a...a sexual object. I've got my self-respect, my integrity to consider here. No way are we sleeping to-*

gether. I don't care how tempted I might be. She'll just have to accept the fact that . . .

He came to a dead stop and laughed out loud as he finished the thought. *I'm not that kind of guy.* He stood there in the center of the room wondering if all men in love went through such trials and tribulations.

The laughter faded as he checked his watch again. Another ten minutes had passed. He crossed the room and opened the cabin door. The rain was coming down in sheets now. Maybe the roads had flooded and she'd had to turn back. But she would have called, he reasoned. Maybe she'd gotten stuck. An accident . . .

He grabbed his slicker and raced out to his car. He'd go crazy sitting here waiting and worrying. Best to drive down the road and see if he could spot her.

CHELSEA'S MIND was rattling through options as she came to an abrupt stop at a badly flooded section of road. Should she turn around and head back to Corbet, keep trying to make it through, or take the side road off to the right and hope that it would connect back up to the main road? She'd already lost a lot of time because of flooded patches back up the road. A couple of times her car had even stalled out. She worried that Walker might be thinking she'd had second thoughts about coming. She decided on the side road.

Fortunately it was a gently hilly road providing a good water runoff and Chelsea had no worries about flooding. Unfortunately the road wasn't paved and several times her compact bottomed out. But she kept going, reaching another road a couple of miles up that paralleled the main road. Heartened to find it paved, Chelsea hooked a left and prayed that she'd make it to Walker's cabin without any further delays.

Her overnight bag clunked to the floor as she made her turn. The thud reminded her of the fact that she was planning on spending the night, maybe a few nights, alone with Walker in his cabin.

Neither of them had discussed sleeping arrangements on the phone. At the time, Chelsea had been just so relieved at the prospect of seeing Walker again, the logistics hadn't even crossed her mind.

Had the logistics crossed Walker's mind? Had he taken it for granted that they would sleep together?

She felt a giddy, nervous rush of arousal, followed by a cold dose of common sense. No, she thought, she couldn't sleep with him again...knowing that in ten days she'd be gone. Not that she'd be in Stanford for that long, but then she was considering New York. There was Columbia, a potential book deal, other prestigious colleges in the region that were eager for her to come speak. She'd even broached the subject with Ned of putting her house on the market this summer. If ever there was a time to sell...hopefully to a year-rounder, someone who would get invested in the community, take pride in its unique heritage. Someone like Walker.

She silently resolved that she was not going out to Walker's cabin for sex. Okay, great sex. The best sex she'd ever had. Not that she was very experienced, but she was nonetheless convinced there would never be anyone to take Walker's place in that department. Who was she kidding? In any department. If she were in the market...

She wasn't in the market, she reminded herself sharply, recalling Walker's almost effusive sendoff. Maybe, for all his talk about planting roots, finding himself a wife, having a family, Walker Jordan wasn't any more ready to make a serious commitment than she was. She even considered that this was one of the reasons he'd finally given her permission to dig again. Maybe he wanted her to prove that battle happened so she'd go off to make her mark and he'd be free to explore before he did any planting!

IT WAS NOW the kind of rain that forced drivers with any common sense to pull over to the side of the road and wait it out. But Walker kept going, panicking about the possibility of Chelsea having gotten into an accident. If anything had happened to her . . .

WHERE IN THE WORLD IS HE? Chelsea fretted when she stepped into the cabin and found it was empty. Had he gotten tired of waiting for her? His car wasn't parked outside. Maybe he'd driven back to Corbet.

She saw the phone. She peeled off her raincoat which had almost soaked through. Her ever untrustworthy car had stalled two cabins down and she'd had to abandon it there and go the rest of the way on foot. Sticking her coat over the shower rod in the bathroom, she went back into the main room and dialed Walker's house. No answer.

She did a quick check of the cabin, not missing the fact that there was only one bedroom, one bed. She sat down on it, feeling angry, abandoned and distraught.

WALKER WAS FINALLY forced to turn back because the state troopers had closed off the main road. He asked one of the cops if there'd been any accidents, but none had been reported. Not that that proved anything.

A half hour later he was turning into the narrow dirt road leading to his cabin. About two thirds of the way down, the road washed out. Muttering under his breath he got out of the car to make the rest of the trip on foot. His slicker offered some protection from the rain, but he hadn't thought to wear boots, and he was sloshing through puddles more than knee-deep in spots.

As he rounded the bend to the cabin he put aside his discomfort, hoping somehow he'd merely missed spotting Chelsea's car along the way and he'd see her Chevy parked out front.

But there was no car. He entered the cabin sickened by visions of Chelsea lying bleeding on the road next to her wrecked car.

THE RAIN AND WIND masked the sound of the front door opening. Chelsea was still sitting on the bed when Walker came into the bedroom to change his soaked trousers.

It was a toss-up who looked more stunned. Or more relieved.

"Chelsea."

"Walker."

"I thought something had happened to you. Your car? Your car wasn't parked out front..."

"I was afraid you'd taken off. You said you'd be here and then you weren't and I thought..."

The rest of the words were swallowed up by Walker's kiss as he joined her on the bed. They clung to each other, giddy with relief, kissing greedily.

Finally catching her breath, Chelsea said, "Walker, your trousers are totally soaked."

His gray eyes sparkled. "I guess there's only one thing for me to do...."

CHELSEA'S HEAD was on Walker's shoulders, his leg draped over hers.

"Walker, I've been thinking..."

"Yes?" He was nibbling on her earlobe.

"About the Fourth."

"Yes?" His lips had progressed nicely to her neck.

"I just don't think Julie and Zach are right," Chelsea said firmly.

Walker's lips were at the soft, sensitive hollow of her throat. Her pulse raced. "They're not right about what?"

"No. No, not *about what*. I mean they're just not right for Abigail and Henry."

"You don't think so." He was caressing the curve where her neck and shoulder joined.

Chelsea was succumbing to a heavy languor. "Henry and Abigail are...a part of us. No one else could do those parts justice."

Walker looked up at her, searching her face. "You want to be Abigail?"

"Yes," she whispered. "It seems...right somehow. If you'll be Henry? Stanford will have the Fourth off anyway. I could fly back, even if I can't reschedule."

Walker almost swallowed the next question, but he had to know. "What about Columbia? And all the rest."

Chelsea's eyes skidded off Walker's face. "I...don't know. I can't think that far ahead at the moment."

Gently, tenderly, he grazed her lips with his. "Okay, let's get to Independence Day, Chelsea...." He smiled down at her. A knockout smile. "Or should I call you my dearest, bravest, loveliest Abigail?"

Chelsea's eyes sparkled. "I pray you, sir. Do not make me blush."

Chapter Fifteen

On the morning of July fourth the clouds that had been threatening rain all week broke away, and the Green Mountain Boys prepared to battle the Redcoat Loyalists. In the barn on the Fremont Estate, Colonel Harmon Fremont gathered his Green Mountain Boys around him. With a stick, he began scratching his battle plan into the dirt floor.

"Now men, the Loyalists are operating at a tremendous disadvantage."

"Right," Arthur Newcomb, the pharmacist piped up. "We know about them but they don't know about us."

"Exactly." The colonel made a wavy line in the dirt. "Now this here stands for the creek just to the east of the barn. I figure the Redcoats will cross just about here—" he made an *X* "—because this is the shallowest point."

"But, Ned, do we really know that it was the shallowest point over two hundred years ago?"

Hal Opheimer swatted Jerry, a young carpenter, on the back of the head. "Hey, don't call him Ned. It's Colonel Fremont. Show some respect."

Jerry gave Hal a friendly shove. "Hey, you struck me. That's cause for a duel."

Hal chuckled. "Cool down, kiddo. You don't even know which end of that sword you've got is which."

Jerry was about to toss a snide retort, but he held back, reminding himself that Opheimer, in real life, was his boss.

"Settle down, boys. We agreed we wanted to do this as close to the real thing as possible. Now, for the next couple of hours, you'll all address me as Colonel or, for those who happen to be close friends, Harmon."

The two dozen Green Mountain Boys, outfitted with muskets, powder horns and swords, settled down.

"Okay now, let's run through the drill," Ned began again.

"When does the local militia band play?" another rebel interrupted. "Before the battle or after the battle?"

Arthur Newcomb gave the teenager a wry smile. "If they blast music before the battle don't you think that just might give our position away to the enemy?"

"Could we please focus on our battle plan, gentlemen?" Ned said, his patience wearing thin. "Or shall we simply let the British overtake us so history can be rewritten?"

Once again, the excited group calmed down.

"Now, the Loyalists are going to be making their way due south of Old Wicker road..."

"Say, when does Washington show up?" Bill Laird asked.

Everyone had agreed, even though Chelsea had yet to verify the fact, that George Washington should play a role in the battle. This reenactment was going to take a little dramatic license with authenticity.

"He's gettin' his britches sewed up," Hal said grinning.

"All right men," Ned said, "let's not worry about Washington. He'll be along. Now, our plan is simple enough. We stay put in the barn until we see..."

"The whites of their eyes," Bill Laird said with a chuckle.

Ned grinned. "Something like that.'

"CHELSEA, YOU LOOK just beautiful in that outfit," Nan Prescott Green exclaimed, setting down her quilting needle. The rest of the sewing circle looked up and seconded Nan's opinion.

To mark the occasion and Chelsea's success, the Sheldron Museum had loaned Chelsea an exquisite red silk brocade gown with a low necklines whose deep V was outlined in white ribbon to the pointed waist. The three quarter length bouffant sleeves, ruffled at the edges, were finished off with delicate lace.

"Don't call her Chelsea. It's Miss Abigail," Dot corrected her sister. "If we're going to do this, we must do it right."

Norma Lund agreed. "Yes, we should focus on playing our roles to the hilt. After all, our committee has striven for as much authenticity as possible. We've got this quilting group set up here in the parlor, a bunch of women baking original eighteenth-century New England recipes in the kitchen, another group out back weaving. We should all get into our characters so that when the doors open to the townsfolk, people will really feel as if they're stepping back in time."

Isabelle Alpert, dressed in a starched gray gown, came in from the garden, her perky white ruffled cap askew. She'd been doing some last-minute pruning. "It looks lovely out there."

Dot sighed. "I still think we should have tried to squeeze in the annual garden tour."

"This is so much more exciting," Nan argued in typical fashion.

Dot narrowed her eyes at her sister. "Bull."

Everyone's mouth dropped open until Dot broke into a surprisingly girlish laugh. The rest of the group joined in.

Alice popped her head out of the kitchen. "We're running out of flour."

"There's an unopened sack on the second shelf in the pantry," Chelsea called out to her, "behind the sugar," she finished, only to find the whole group observing her with faint smiles. She knew they were all thinking about how it was that she knew her way around Walker's pantry so well. Chelsea merely smiled guilelessly back at them and curtsied.

Isabelle set her bonnet straight. "So where is Captain Cotton, if I may be so bold to ask?"

"He's convening with his Loyalist band about a mile down Old Wicker Road," Julie announced with a thick Irish brogue, having just stepped into the parlor from one of the guest rooms. She was dressed as an eighteenth-century seamstress in a creamy beige homespun linen gown, white apron and brown kerchief draped around her shoulders and knotted at her breast.

"How's General Washington faring?" Chelsea asked her friend.

Julie held up a long, thin sewing needle triumphantly. "He's fine now, as long as he doesn't sit down."

Norma rubbed her hands excitedly. "Oh, I just can't wait for it all to begin. I think most of the town is coming for the festivities."

Chelsea smiled. It really was going to be fun. The women would be demonstrating eighteenth-century handicrafts in the house, the battle would be recreated out in the field, the victorious militia band would play afterward, and then they'd all share a big picnic. She and Walker had worked day and night to get things rolling, and practically the whole town had taken some part in organizing the festivities which would be open only to locals—no outsiders or press invited. It was a celebration strictly for Corbet's own. Chelsea had found it all exhausting, exhilarating; the most fun she'd ever had. And today was the payoff. A sudden wave of anxiety overtook her. It was also the day she'd have to tell Walker where they stood.

"So, Miss Abigail," Isabelle said, "I understand you leave by carriage for California anon."

Chelsea gave Isabelle a sharp look. "How did you know?"

Isabelle shrugged. "You booked your *carriage* reservation with Marilyn Reed. Marilyn and I play doubles."

Chelsea did have a plane reservation booked for July seventh. Shortly after she'd offered to help Walker plan the reenactment, Chelsea had contacted the chairman of the history department at Stanford and they'd agreed to rearrange her lecture series.

Julie came up behind Chelsea and tugged on her sleeve. "Mistress Abigail, may I have a word in private with you in the drawing room?"

Chelsea was happy for the distraction.

Once they were cloistered together in the room, Julie gave Chelsea a conspiratorial smile. "I've got a message for you from the enemy," she whispered, digging into the pocket of her apron for an envelope with a waxed seal.

Chelsea took it gingerly. "Walker?"

"Captain Henry Cotton," Julie said with a mock curtsy.

She stared down at it.

"His exact words were, 'Be certain that Miss Abigail opens it with expedience.'"

Chelsea grinned. "I believe Captain Cotton is a born ham, Mistress Julie."

Julie's eyes sparkled. "There's a little ham in all of us. You should see Zach dressed in regimental gear. He and a dozen other men are the cavalry backup. Poor Zach hasn't ridden a horse since he was a boy. I just hope he doesn't break his neck before I get him down the aisle."

"We'll get him down that aisle if we have to carry him on a stretcher," Chelsea teased.

"You're still going to be my maid of honor...?"

"What a question, Julie. Of course I am."

"I know it's smack in the middle of the new dates for your lecture series at Stanford. It'll mean flying back and forth—"

"I wouldn't miss your wedding for the world," Chelsea said emphatically.

Julie grinned slyly. "And I wouldn't miss yours, Mistress Abigail."

Chelsea stiffened. "You know perfectly well, Mistress Julie, that Captain Cotton and I could never be wed. We're on opposing sides." Brusquely, she tore open the seal and pulled out the letter.

Julie stepped back discreetly while Chelsea read the brief note.

My darling Abigail
I pray you receive this letter in time. We have ransacked the fort at East Hoseck and will be moving swiftly due east, coming in south of your field instead of due north across the creek as had originally been planned. You must get word to your father so that he and his men will not be surprised by the enemy instead of being the ones to surprise.

And may I beg one more favor, my sweetest Abigail. I know we solemnly agreed to postpone all talk of personal desires until such time as you felt ready to declare yourself, but I must see you once more before I sojourn to Saratoga. So, my sweet, if I survive this battle, I pray you meet me one last time in our own private paradise...

> With my most ardent love and respect,
> I remain yours,
> Henry

SWORDS WAVING, muskets at the ready, the Green Mountain Boys charged the Redcoats as they stealthily crossed the Fremont property south of the field just as Henry Cotton had written. A cannon borrowed from the fort at East Hoseck blasted and there were the rattles of drums to simulate gunshot from the firearms. Out of the woods rode the cavalry, all of them managing with varying degrees of adeptness, to stay astride their horses. The British dispersed into the pine woods, running like rabbits. The Green Mountain Boys whopped with glee, lifted General Washington, alias

Graham Sawyer, up on their shoulders, and the crowd ringing the field went wild cheering.

Flamboyantly the rebel winners formed into a column behind the militia band who'd been so excited they'd begun to play before their signal. In the rear came the valiant cavalry, all of them sitting tall in the saddle.

Children, and some townsfolk who had slipped into their second childhood, joined the victory parade. The Redcoats, hands raised in surrender, finally surfaced from the woods and joined in the celebration by stripping off their red military jackets and tossing them in the air.

Soon, everybody was joining in the festivities, dancing, cheering, setting up for the picnic, examining the costumes and weaponry close up.

Two people slipped away from the revelry.

The light was dim inside the barn and it took a few minutes for their eyes to adjust.

"Over here, Abigail," Walker called out softly.

She crossed the barn to see that he had propped a new, sturdy ladder against the hayloft. They climbed up. Fresh hay had been spread out.

He took her hand. "May I say, my sweet Abigail, that you have never looked lovelier?"

"Alas, you are too kind, Colonel Cotton. And far too reckless." She slipped the missive from her pocket. "I suppose you realize, my dearest Henry, that if this letter fell into the hands of the British you would be tried and no doubt hung for treason."

"Ah, and do you desire such a fate for me, my sweet?"

Chelsea stared at him. "You would commit treason for me?"

"I would do anything for you, my love."

"Even . . . let me go?"

He took a deep, heavy breath, his expression as intense as a physical touch. "Is that what you want?" His lips curved in a smile that said her answer couldn't be *yes*. His smile was as poignant as a soft caress.

Chelsea felt tears gathering in her eyes. "Oh Walker, what am I going to do? I love you . . ."

She stopped. The band, which had been playing a raucous folk tune had suddenly begun playing an altogether surprising piece. "The Wedding March."

Chelsea shot Walker a look. Then she peeked out the newly restored door of the hayloft.

A gasp escaped her lips. Two rows of Green Mountain Boys stood at attention, their muskets raised to form an arch. At the head of the group stood Owen Fowler, dressed up like a minister.

Chelsea spun around. "Was this your doing, Walker?"

Now his smile was familiarly provocative. "This is my theory, Miss Abigail," he murmured, drawing her into his arms. "I believe that Henry Cotton, your ardent lover, did not, despite the evidence, engage in treason."

"What . . ."

His lips brushed hers to silence her. "You've given me some lessons in history, my love. Now let me advance my theory."

Chelsea was distracted by the strains of the wedding march. "Walker . . ."

"Now, as I was saying, it is my theory that Henry Cotton was not a traitor but a plant."

"Rhododendrum or hydrangea?" Chelsea teased.

But Walker remained serious. "It is my thesis that Henry was never on the side of the British. I believe he was a spy for the Green Mountain Boys all along. Think about it. How did our boys know the arsenal at East Hoseck was going to be looted? How did our boys know the Loyalists would be coming right past the Fremont property?"

"Walker, really..."

"If my theory is true, then Abigail and Henry weren't ever on opposite sides. They met not only as lovers, but as conspirators."

All of a sudden Chelsea was paying attention. She stared hard at Walker, her mind racing.

But Walker's mind was on only one thing. "So this is what I think happened. After the British were defeated out in the field, Henry returned to the barn for a celebratory reunion with his true love, they got married and lived happily ever after."

"Walker, it's not such a dumb theory," she muttered.

Walker grinned. "You mean I may have a future in this?"

"Seriously. I never really looked at it from that angle."

The band raised the volume of their rendition of "The Wedding March."

Walker took her hand and pressed it to his heart. "Our fellows await our taking of the vows, my sweet. Will you marry me, dear... Chelsea?"

Chelsea gently touched his cheek. "Yes," she whispered huskily. "Yes, Walker. I'll marry you." She circled her arms around his neck. "It was meant to be."

He held her off for a moment. "What about fame and fortune?"

She smiled. "I'll keep my Stanford date. And I can schedule some guest lecture spots later, but now I've got this whole new theory about Henry and Abigail to research here in Corbet. It could take a long time. A lifetime."

Walker hugged her to him.

When the two lovers finally emerged from the barn, the whole town cheered. It was obvious from the looks on their faces that this wedding ceremony wasn't merely a historical reenactment but a rehearsal for the real thing.

Back by Popular Demand

Janet Dailey
Americana

A romantic tour of America through fifty favorite Harlequin Presents, each set in a different state researched by Janet and her husband, Bill. A journey of a lifetime in one cherished collection.

In August, don't miss the exciting states featured in:

Title #13 — ILLINOIS
        The Lyon's Share

   #14 — INDIANA
        The Indy Man

Available wherever
Harlequin books are sold.

JD-AUG

Harlequin Superromance®

**This August, don't miss Superromance
#462—STARLIT PROMISE**

STARLIT PROMISE is a deeply moving story of a
woman coming to terms with her grief and gradually
opening her heart to life and love.

Author Petra Holland sets the scene beautifully, never
allowing her heroine to become mired in self-pity. It
is a story that will touch your heart and leave you
celebrating the strength of the human spirit.

**Available wherever Harlequin books
are sold.**

STARLIT

Harlequin Superromance®

CHILDREN OF THE HEART
by Sally Garrett

Available this August

Romance readers the world over have wept and
rejoiced over Sally Garrett's heartwarming stories of
love, caring and commitment. In her new novel,
Children of the Heart, Sally once again weaves a story
that will touch your most tender emotions.

You'll be moved to tears of joy

Nearly two hundred children have passed through
Trenance McKay's foster home. But after her husband
leaves her, Trenance knows she'll always have to
struggle alone. No man could have enough room in his
heart both for Trenance and for so many needy
children. Max Tulley, news anchor for KSPO TV is
willing to try, but how long can his love last?

"Sally Garrett does some of the best character studies
in the genre and will not disappoint her fans."
Romantic Times

**Look for *Children of the Heart* wherever
Harlequin Romance novels are sold.** SCH-1

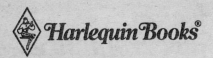

Harlequin Books®

GREAT NEWS...
HARLEQUIN UNVEILS NEW SHIPPING PLANS

For the convenience of customers, Harlequin has announced that Harlequin romances will now be available in stores at these convenient times each month*:

Harlequin Presents, American Romance, Historical, Intrigue:

> May titles: April 10
> June titles: May 8
> July titles: June 5
> August titles: July 10

Harlequin Romance, Superromance, Temptation, Regency Romance:

> May titles: April 24
> June titles: May 22
> July titles: June 19
> August titles: July 24

We hope this new schedule is convenient for you.

With only two trips each month to your local bookseller, you'll never miss any of your favorite authors!

*Please note: There may be slight variations in on-sale dates in your area due to differences in shipping and handling.

HDATES-RR

*Applicable to U.S. only.

**THIS JULY, HARLEQUIN OFFERS YOU
THE PERFECT SUMMER READ!**

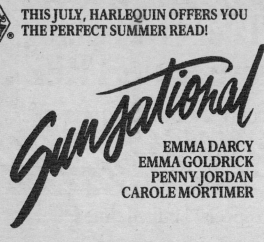

**EMMA DARCY
EMMA GOLDRICK
PENNY JORDAN
CAROLE MORTIMER**

From top authors of Harlequin Presents comes
HARLEQUIN SUNSATIONAL, a four-stories-in-one
book with 768 pages of romantic reading.

Written by such prolific Harlequin authors as Emma Darcy,
Emma Goldrick, Penny Jordan and Carole Mortimer,
HARLEQUIN SUNSATIONAL is the perfect summer
companion to take along to the beach, cottage, on your
dream destination or just for reading at home in the warm
sunshine!

Don't miss this unique reading opportunity.

Available wherever Harlequin books are sold.